Co

Imogen Winn
London. Since
has had various jobs, but she now works in
publishing and is also a freelance journalist.
Coming to Terms is her first novel.

IMOGEN WINN

Coming to Terms

FONTANA/COLLINS

First published in the U.K. in 1985
by Fontana Paperbacks
8 Grafton Street, London W1X 3LA

Copyright © Imogen Winn 1985

Made and printed for
William Collins Sons & Co. Ltd, Glasgow

TO BECKY AND SIMON, WITH LOVE

THE WRITING ON THE WALL

NICARAGUA

SPRING 1980

It was a time she had come to know so well. Those few hours before the rain when there was no respite from the blanket humidity and slumberous heat. It was a waiting time. The villagers had deserted the streets, taking their children and animals safely inside. An unnatural night had fallen and no flicker of a breeze disturbed her candle flame. Only the insects moved in frenetic circles around the lamp and her hands jerked, instinctively swatting at them.

She longed for Cesar to return and share the silence with her; to soothe the red welts the mosquitoes still left on her pale arms. There were some things she would never get used to: the mosquitoes, and the solitude before a storm. Why had he chosen today to leave for supplies? When she would now worry about him finding shelter, and when she needed him most. She half expected him to sense her anxiety, turn the jeep round and hurry back to her. She took a bottle out on to the porch and sat, with her long grey skirt smoothed around her ankles, watching down the dusty track for the glare of headlights and the sound of the rusty jeep grinding its way home.

She took the note once again from her pocket. It was crumpled now. At first she had thought she was dreaming. '¡*Hay un gringo*!' the child had squealed. A white man has come. He is looking for you.

It had been crisply folded. Four hard creases formed a cross on its creamy surface. The boy said he had been told to give it to her.

Dear Elizabeth Carleton,
I am writing a series of articles about life out here and

would very much like to include your story. Could I tempt you to the hotel for dinner? I'll be here until tomorrow.

Sincerely, Paul Ritz.

Her heart had started to pound and her hands seemed to belong to someone else as she stared down at the paper, her palms moist with perspiration. She had read it again and again. How clean and white the notepaper was. It looked so new and out of place.

The boy had retreated down the steps and was squatting on his haunches staring blankly at the pigs snuffling around in the mud. She called down from the veranda. 'Who gave you this? A white man at the hotel? Who is he?'

The boy shook his head. The *gringo* told him to give it to the nurse in the village. He could tell her no more. She waved him away and began to pace up and down. She still had her overall on. She had just finished the afternoon clinic.

Paul Ritz. The signature was as neat and controlled as the message. Paul Ritz. The name stirred some vague memory. Who was he? No one came out here, no one. The hotel was like some ghostly outpost, standing almost always empty up there on the hillside. The proprietor was mad to keep it open, hoping the troubles would one day be over and tourists would return to these parts. The occasional student, usually an American, found his way there, but this man was a journalist. Why did that thought terrify her? Nicaragua practically crawled with them.

By evening her panic had subsided. It was out of the question. She resolved not to see him. She could ignore the note. It was obvious a journalist would try to make contact if he learnt an English woman was in the neighbourhood. It would make a good read for a glossy magazine – the lone white woman, living with the natives, thousands of miles from home – besides here, on the edge of the rain forests, he would be glad of some company, even that of a stranger.

10

But still she wouldn't go. If he was lonely that was part and parcel of his job. He would be used to it. She wandered back inside, relieved to have made a definite decision. It was the only one she could make. It was dark, but there were still some glowing embers in the kitchen fire. She watched as the note blackened and burst into flames.

She had always dreamt they would find her. Faceless men in suits and bowler hats would storm the clinic in Magritte-like realism and formally order her to leave, to come back to her senses, go back to the world, pay the price for her misdemeanours. She would awake clinging to Cesar's familiar flesh and feel his springy hair against her chest and know that she was safe for a while longer. Now she wasn't dreaming, and she was alone. The roar of the rain on the roof was some comfort, but her mind was alert and racing, her thoughts disjointed. At times she was not even sure whether she was dreaming. Her eyes longed to close but her eyelids prickled. She was tormented and felt lost in the enveloping darkness. Just as she had in prison, waking up in the night in that bottom bunk and stretching out her hand to feel only the rough cell wall. There too she had lain trapped in darkness, shut in with only herself to reason with, unable to sleep. There too she had felt the tears but she had never let herself cry. That would have been defeat. She had vowed night after weary night that she would never have any regrets, never. If she had done any wrong it was not that she was in prison for. That was the irony. There too she had cried out silently for her love. Think of me, think of me.

When she awoke, the thundering river of water had ceased and the accustomed sounds of the village rattled on again. The hum of the jungle and the random shrieks of the howler monkeys signalled all was as usual. Outside, children squelched around in thick mud and one of the women came to tell her that a hut had been washed away in

11

the night. In the hours she spent helping the men to retrieve the damage, she forgot herself.

Just before noon, when the family had been resettled, she returned to the clinic carrying Maria Elizabeta, the child they had named after her, the first child she had delivered in this village ten years ago, and whom she had watched growing into a chubby little girl with long black braids and a beaming smile. The little girl clung to her, chattering and pointing proudly at her leg which was badly cut and bruised from being washed along in the debris of a collapsing home. '¡*Hay un gringo!*' The child noticed him first, standing on the porch.

'*Si, si.*' Her arm gripped the child's shoulder. 'Don't be afraid.' She wasn't sure who the words were for. She walked past him up the steps. 'This child is hurt.' How odd the English words sounded. 'You'll have to excuse me.'

'Can I help?'

'I doubt it.' But he followed her into the whitewashed clinic.

'It's not exactly modern, but we manage.' She was already defensive as she saw for the first time what the shabby examining table and inadequate medicine cabinet must look like to a stranger.

Paul Ritz watched her as she bathed the child's leg and dabbed on antiseptic, quietening the little girl's screams with what he imagined were jokes and impressions and stories. But when she had bandaged the wounds, kissed the bruises better and sent the child hopping back out into the mud, her face that had looked so animated and childlike itself, set into a frown. Faint wrinkles spreading from the sides of her mouth and eyes suddenly made her look old as she tossed back long strands of greying hair defiantly. She was slight, almost frail, but she held herself with dignity. Her large grey eyes looked straight into his. She made him feel like an intruder on the intimacy of her world and her expression asked him to explain himself.

'I'm sorry.' His words came out involuntarily. Sorry for

what? Sorry for making a pretty face become old and hostile. Sorry for sharing a precious moment of healing with a child? He struggled to regain his composure. 'Let me introduce myself at least. My name is Paul Ritz. I sent you a note. I don't know whether you received it? But I thought I'd come down and find you.'

She turned away. Her hands were shaking.

'I'm a journalist . . . '

'I know you're a journalist, but you must have lost your way. You should be talking to the soldiers, asking them what they are doing to this country. Not me. I'm not involved.'

'Look, I'd better explain. I'm not interested in the political situation . . . '

'Well, go away then. Whatever your reasons. We don't need people who are not interested. Do something. Go to the city, look, see what is happening. Telex your paper and tell them what the graffiti says . . . tell them the writing on the wall.'

'As I was trying to say, I'm doing a series of articles on Central America. Obviously I've interviewed politicians and the military, but what I'm trying to get right now are profiles of individuals and how their existence has been affected.'

She turned to face him, her eyes questioning him. Ritz shivered with a sense of *déjà vu*. He was thrown off balance.

'May I sit down?'

She watched him pull a wooden chair from the table. His linen shirt was as pristine as the note he had sent. Who was this well-dressed man? The arrogance of his manner angered her. A faint smell of aftershave wafted on the air. It was subtle and expensive. He had the looks of a rich playboy but his expression was intelligent and determined. It struck her that he was a man used to getting what he wanted. But what did he want from her?

'Well, Mr Ritz, I still don't understand what you could

possibly want from me.'

'Look, Ms Carleton, I appreciate how rude it must seem, my just turning up like this, but I had a couple of days to spare before my flight out, and I heard about you in Managua from the Red Cross people.' He was surprised to see a look of fear on her face. 'I was hoping to do a short piece about you, your life out here as a white woman. The problems the villagers have, how the revolution has affected their everyday lives, that kind of thing. What I want to do is to give people at home an understanding of the situation here, if you like.'

'I see.' Her face relaxed.

'We could just talk and I'd ask you some questions – all very painless.' He smiled.

'No doubt it would be for you, Mr Ritz, but I have better things to do with my time than answer your questions. I think you would be disappointed. There's nothing in the least interesting about my life "as a white woman" here, no little story for you to unearth.'

'If you're very busy perhaps you could take up my invitation and come up for dinner this evening?'

'A meal in exchange for a story. It's all about stories, isn't it, your line of business? I'd forgotten all about civilization, if that's what you can call it . . . I mean, really, Mr Ritz, to be crude, what's in it for me?'

'What do you get?' Her question threw him. 'If you want to talk about payment we could do that.'

'Payment, money . . . it must be so easy for you.'

'Then perhaps you mean something else. Look, we can sit down and do this in a civilized way.' He threw back her words with mocking emphasis. 'I'm not quite the scurrilous hack you seem to think. I am a serious and not unknown journalist and I'm also the author of a book that's about to be published. What I'm trying to say is that you can trust me. I'm not going to write racy little titbits, but something that might be positively beneficial . . . Well, could you think of it this way, it's your chance to say what you want

14

about Nicaragua to the world?' He smiled encouragingly.

'I have nothing I want to say to the world.' She thought how rude she must sound to him. She shouldn't be so defensive. He was not the threat she had thought. Perhaps after all he was just a journalist who had stumbled on her. She decided to be placatory. She pulled up a stool opposite him.

'I'm sorry, Mr Ritz, but I'm afraid I'm going to have to say no. I can quite see your aims in this series of articles, but I do not want to appear in the British newspapers, for reasons I'm not prepared to explain. But I don't want to seem inhospitable. Would you like a drink?'

'Thank you, yes. It is a pity. Your story would have been interesting. Would you have any objections to just talking off the record?'

'Well, if you can really promise not to quote me, I'll tell you all about my life . . . ' She was amused to see him sit forward as if about to share a confidence. 'Let me see, where to begin . . . Well, at six o'clock in the morning, I get up. The electricity may or may not be working. I usually have a cup of coffee, after I've had a pee, of course, then sometimes I have another cup of coffee. Then I brush my teeth. Often we have to use salt because, as you no doubt appreciate, the supply of toothpaste has been severely affected by the revolution . . . '

Paul Ritz frowned.

'Fascinating, isn't it?' Her eyes were mildly triumphant and suddenly she smiled. A smile so open and disarming that she looked like a young girl. Before he knew it he had thrown his head back and they were both laughing loudly.

'Now, Mr Ritz, I've given you all this privileged information, do tell me a little about yourself. This book you mentioned, is it your first? You must be very excited.'

'Yes, I suppose I am. What would you like to know? Its title is *Embassy* . . . Like most of my work I expect it will annoy quite a few people. It is my contribution to revealing the sordid secrets of East-West diplomacy.'

'Oh,' she said, and he noticed that she shifted uncomfortably on her stool. 'That would seem to be very different from what you're doing now?'

'I don't think so. I believe my work should do two things – investigate human motivation and make public what goes on behind the facade of political propaganda.'

'Fine sentiments, Mr Ritz.' She filled his earthenware mug with more *chicha*. 'Tell me more.'

He found himself telling her about his work and how he had come to write *Embassy*. He talked about his rise in journalism and his travels. She was a sympathetic and intelligent listener and seemed to be genuinely interested. It was a long time since he had had to step back from his life and talk about himself objectively to someone who had never heard of him. He surprised himself at some of the feelings he expressed that he had not consciously known were there. He felt a sense of freedom telling her some of the private thoughts of Paul Ritz, those he kept well-hidden from the rest of the prying world. From time to time he smiled at the irony that he had for many years refused to give personal interviews and here he was being interviewed by a complete stranger.

'But enough of me,' he said finally. 'Tell me how much you are able to keep in touch with the world.'

'It must sound strange to someone like you,' she replied, 'but I have lost my enthusiasm for knowing what goes on in the world as much as I have for participating in the whole caboodle. But sometimes the world out there comes to me – like you! And Cesar brings the odd newspaper back from Managua. He is the doctor who runs this clinic.' She cupped her hands around her mug and laughed. 'How jaded I sound! When I think of my Oxford days when I used to read everything.'

'Oxford! Were you at Oxford? I felt we must have something in common. It can't be possible, do I vaguely recognize you?' He put down his mug and leaned across the table.

She looked at him. 'No, we can't have been contemporaries, unless life has been kinder to you . . . ' She fingered a strand of her hair. 'Paul Ritz, Paul Ritz, no, I don't think so.'

He looked embarrassed. 'Well, I have to confess that on the advice of my literary agent I did change my name some time ago. He thought it too "ethnic". My real name is Rizzoli.'

Elizabeth threw her hands in the air. 'I don't believe it! Paul Rizzoli! How could a girl forget Paul Rizzoli? Well, well, well. You were known as Ravioli – spicy with a lot of sauce!' She burst out laughing. 'But we didn't know each other, did we?'

He was struggling to remember. 'Just a minute, weren't you tutored by Susan Howitz? Moral Philosophy?'

'I don't believe it! I mean it's ridiculous. Yes, I was. How small the world turns out to be. Do I recall that you were tutored by her too – not to put too fine a point on it?'

Ritz looked abashed.

' . . . My God, you've changed. I do remember you. You were a pretty boy with flowing locks and the killer smile. You looked so charming until you smiled. It's all coming back to me now. But did we ever meet?'

'Yes, I think we did. Just before prelims. You were waiting outside Susan's room to go into a tutorial and I came along to give her a message. I asked you to give Susan a note.'

'Yes, you're rather fond of notes.' Elizabeth smiled again.

'And you refused. You were incredibly superior and said you weren't going to play the go-between. That was your exact phrase. I was absolutely furious. Women never said no to me.'

'Which was exactly why I did. You were an absolute rogue! Weren't you even having an affair with her? There was speculation all over the gossip columns.' Elizabeth clapped her hands together with glee. She expected him to join in, but he sat with a stony, distant face. 'Oh, come on, Mr Ritz, I mean Paul, you must see the funny side of it.'

But his face had frozen. She was amazed to see the effect of her needling, but was rather enjoying seeing him uneasy and at a loss for words. 'Well, here I am putting you on the spot. What fun! I see you have no ready reply. Surely you can do better than this?'

He picked up his drink and the evening sunlight reflected on the small silver ring he wore on his little finger.

'Do you know what became of Susan?' she continued. 'She was one of my favourite tutors. She was the only one I really liked and admired. Yes, I really admired Susan. She was such a character. Those amazing clothes she wore and her hair. It went all the way down her back. Her room was always filled with the smoke of those wonderful Turkish cigarettes. I think she was the only tutor in that whole damned place who could see beyond the dreaming spires. Well, do you know what happened to her? Is she still at Oxford? She must be quite old by now.'

'She's dead.'

'What? Recently?'

'No, no, she died then. She committed suicide.'

'Paul, how awful. Why? She was so together. So composed.'

'Apparently not.' He reached for the bottle. His face was like a mask. Then, in an instant, it changed and he adopted an animated smile. 'Weren't you called Lefty Lizzie – the toast of Balliol?'

'Was I really? But we were all so full of *joie de vivre*. I wonder if it is still like that? The world was our oyster then. Just some of us never found the pearl.'

'Said with much feeling. You ought to write, Elizabeth.'

'I don't think so. But it was true. We were all so young, so naive. Who could have predicted that we would turn out like this? Or perhaps I should speak for myself. You seem to have done very well.'

'Materially, yes. But I have joined the rat race. Some

people would envy your existence for its simplicity. I don't pretend to understand why you've chosen this life, but you obviously think it's the right thing for you.'

'I never consciously chose this way of life.' She looked down at the table. 'But it happened, and here I am. It's certainly a different world to yours. But I have enjoyed our talk, even though I didn't help you much with your articles. I wish you all the best for them, and of course for your book . . . Have you lots of ideas for another one?'

'I think I'll wait until I happen upon another subject I really think I can do justice to. That may take some time.' He laughed. 'But one is always looking for new perspectives. Tell me, what would you think an interesting subject, Elizabeth?'

She seemed to be giving his question serious thought.

'You said your interest was in human motivation and public revelations . . . I suppose the obvious choice is treachery. We have too narrow a perspective on traitors. We think that only a few are capable of betraying their country, because only a few are discovered. Who knows? There may be many who have not been revealed. Perhaps it is closer to us all than we think . . . ' She looked as though she had forgotten he was there. 'But it's getting late, and I'm rambling. Shall we finish this bottle with a toast? It's not often I have visitors. To the future and whatever it may hold?'

'That's rather unspecific. What else do we share?'

'A part of the past. Oxford. Let's drink to Oxford,' she said. 'To that most valuable quality it inspired. Optimism.'

THE DREAMING SPIRES

OXFORD

AUTUMN 1978

October that year was a cold month, and as Kay walked through the draughty passages of New College she felt excited but slightly disappointed. Everything was new to her, but the dull mist, the faint smell of gravy and the echo of a Stones LP playing loudly on the other side of the quad were lifeless and miserable and not at all the things she had heard and read stories about. At last, she had arrived in Oxford, but the whole day had been unpredictable. She was the only student to have travelled, suitcase in hand, on the train. Everyone else seemed to have brought their entire wardrobe with them, posters, hi-fi, kettles and even irons. Many arrived with their parents and Kay had been surprised at their effusive goodbyes. She wanted to make an absolute break from home. But looking at the others she had suddenly felt lonely. Lonely for what, she didn't know. It wasn't Sevenoaks and her parents. When she had left them at the station she had resolved never again to think of Sevenoaks as home. She was moving on, stepping out into the world. But now that it was really all up to her it was somewhat daunting. In the taxi she had stared out of the window at the colleges which stood on either side of St Giles like unwelcoming mediaeval fortresses. History was everywhere, centuries of academic brilliance. Men and women had walked these streets and gone out into the world to do great things. What did it hold for her? There had been a challenge in the fading afternoon light.

Meeting her tutors and fellow students hadn't inspired her: the tutors were dry, had talked about exams and proffered small glasses of cheap sherry; the students looked dull and unfriendly but there was a whiff of competition in

23

the air. They were all now bicycling to Schools where the Freshers' Fair was held, dying to join as many societies as time would allow. She was feeling apprehensive about seeing Will again. It was a year now, the longest time they had been separated since childhood. She had missed him. But that was what he had wanted. That's what he had said to her but she had never really understood it. She climbed staircase six to the second floor and knocked.

'Kay! We've been waiting ages for you.' Will opened the door, beamed and bent to plant a chaste kiss on her forehead. As he did he whispered something about Bob having put on his best suit in her honour and giggled. He was acting as if he had seen her only yesterday.

'Well, hello!' She stepped beneath his arm into the room.

'Bob, may I introduce my aunt, Miss Kay Trevelyan,' Will said, grinning.

A tall, slim, wistful-looking man wearing a grey suit and narrow tie turned round from the fireplace and held out his hand. 'How do you do?' He shot an angry glance at Will, who had collapsed with laughter on to the sofa. 'I hardly expected your aunt to be quite so young. Or indeed quite so pretty.'

Kay blushed. That perennial joke of Will's. It had become boring long ago and now it was completely inappropriate. When they were younger they had enjoyed watching people's reactions. Technically she was his aunt even though she was a year younger than he. But it was childish to bring it up now. She took off her duffle coat.

'Now I know you're not some old fogey, can I offer you some of this?' Bob handed her a loosely rolled cigarette. 'It's Moroccan.'

She was bewildered. She had never dared try dope when it had been offered to her at parties. She certainly didn't know that Will smoked it. Perhaps that was why he was giggling so much. He was stoned. She accepted the joint and inhaled deeply. It was pleasant smelling and warming.

'Are you staying long?' Bob had a rather loud voice.

24

'Oh, about half an hour I should think.'

'No, I meant in Oxford. I mean, are you up for the weekend, or just the day?'

'Didn't Will tell you? I'm going to be here three years. It's my first day.'

'Oh, what fun!' said Bob. 'What do you think of it so far?'

'Well . . . ' Kay started on a full-length description of her room, how it was like a broom cupboard, with one wardrobe, one chair and a creaking desk. How the walls were paper thin and she had already heard her next-door neighbour practising the cello. How the college was more like a girls' boarding school than the esteemed seat of learning she had expected, how the lunch they had provided was the most nondescript food it had ever been her misfortune to taste.

' . . . and you should see my bed!' she finished. 'It's absolutely tiny. I think they imagine we're all going to stay virgins!'

'I'm sure you'll be a great success.' His appraising look brought her to an abrupt halt. She wasn't sure why he was being so attentive. Perhaps she was talking too much, possibly boring him. Why wasn't Will joining in? She turned to look at him. He had fallen asleep on the sofa. She felt let down. Bob got up to change the record.

'I really must be going,' she lied. 'I'm supposed to go to Freshers' Fair and join lots of things, and I've still got some unpacking to do.' She hesitated over the sofa, wondering whether to wake Will up. He stirred in his sleep and motioned a kiss with his lips. It was a reflex action that had remained from childhood. Then he opened his eyes as though he had sensed her staring down at him.

'Don't go yet,' he said sleepily. 'I haven't asked you how you're getting on, how you've been keeping.'

'No, I must go. I'll see you soon, won't I?'

'It was awfully nice meeting you.' Bob showed her to the door and held out his hand formally. 'Cheerio!'

She was quite relieved to get away. There was something

about Bob's superior manner that was a little overpowering. He was such a typical product of public school. Rich, suave, well spoken and probably arrogant. 'What fun!' indeed! But why did she feel threatened? It must have something to do with seeing Will again. She headed up Parks Road towards her college and as she walked past the museum, a bicycle sped by, its rider pedalling furiously against the wind, the trousers of his dinner suit rolled up to his knees and his gown billowing around him. Kay smiled to herself. Perhaps Oxford just might be fun.

That evening she and a few of the other first years at college traipsed to the nearest pub. Kay found the conversation artificial. What school did you go to? What A levels did you take? Have you had a year off? What does your father do? It was a time for estimating worth, for assessing the competition and for selecting friends. An unusual girl with hair dyed bright orange and wearing an outsize boiler suit sat in the corner non-committally. Kay caught her eye once or twice when the conversation veered too much towards school, exam results and the trivia they both thought they had left behind.

'I remember you from the interviews.' The girl pointed at Kay.

'Really?' Kay had been too nervous to remember anything. She wondered what impression she had made.

'Yeah, you were the only other one who wasn't doing that damn knitting they had left for us while we waited to be called. To keep our minds off the impending terror, and of course to add to the Oxfam blanket.'

Her sarcasm was refreshing amid the piety of the others. 'Smoke?' She produced a packet of untipped Gitanes.

'Thanks.' Kay didn't want a cigarette, but she felt it would be unfriendly to say no.

By closing time only she and Zoe remained.

'Eleven o'clock and the good girls have gone to bed,' said

Zoe. 'What shall we do next? I can't bear the thought of going back yet. Let's start as we mean to go on.'

'Well, there's a Freshers' Disco, I believe,' said Kay. 'But my mother told me to beware of the wolves,' she added with mock innocence.

'I can't believe it! So did mine!' laughed Zoe.

They finished off their drinks and walked slowly down the street to St John's College.

'Watch out, wolves, you've met your match!' Zoe whispered as they stumbled into the darkened hall.

Kay wished she had Zoe's confidence. Her heart sank. It would be like those dreadful parties they'd all gone to in the sixth form. You were supposed to latch on to a male and succumb to wet, tonguey kisses, even enjoy them. But surely it would be different in Oxford. One hour later Zoe grabbed Kay's arm.

'If I get asked one more time what A levels I did and what grades I got, I'm going to throw up.'

'And if I get incompetently touched up by one more acned youth, I'll join you.'

They left, drunk and depressed. 'Where are you, wolves?' shouted Zoe into the rain. But Kay was more despondent.

'Do you think it's going to be like this for three whole years?'

'Don't kid yourself, love, these are the good times.'

Zoe had been put in a house on the college campus, but Kay's new home was in a college house in a residential road a few hundred yards away. They parted at the college gates. As Kay walked along Bradmore Road, she noticed the leaves were beginning to fall from the horse chestnuts, helped on their way by the drizzle that had persisted all day. In the wind she kept catching the sounds of a distant party. Someone was having fun. As she walked up the driveway to the large Victorian house, she thought she heard the leaves stir. It was very dark and in the distance one of Oxford's many clocks struck one. She fumbled for her keys and a

27

match was lit behind her. Kay froze for a second, then turned round.

'Will! What the hell are you doing here?'

'Did I frighten you?'

'Yes, you did. That would really have been the end to a great day. I thought I was going to be attacked.'

'Keep your voice down,' someone whispered from the shadows. 'We've been waiting here for an hour. The other inmates of this locked castle have been giving us a pretty rough time. Mind you, we have rung the doorbell several times.' The unmistakable public school tones of Bob. 'We've come to whisk you away, young damsel. If that's OK, of course.'

The men took an arm each and frogmarched Kay to the decrepit *deux chevaux* parked in the road that turned out to be Bob's. As they drove northwards, away from the city, Kay was anxious to know whether they had really upset the other students in the house. She hadn't met most of them yet and she didn't think it was a good idea to start off on the wrong footing.

'It's OK,' Bob reassured her, 'there's only one you need be afraid of. She is called Delia. She was wearing a rather unbecoming bath cap and towel. What an Amazon she is too. "If you don't go away I shall call the authorities!" ' he mocked in shrill tones.

Kay couldn't help being amused. She would have a reputation from the first day.

They drove through the suburbs and into the countryside with Bob's tinny radio tuned to Luxembourg, then turned off the main road into a neon-fronted transport café.

'It's the only place open for breakfast at this time of night,' Bob explained, 'and both of us have a terrible attack of the munchies.'

They queued amongst lorry drivers and purchased bacon and eggs and toast and sat on orange plastic seats around a marble-look table.

'Decidedly kitsch,' said Kay.

28

The boys asked for a description of her evening and she chattered breathlessly, her glossy black hair swinging.

'Zoe sounds awfully nice,' said Bob.

Kay looked at him closely. What did he think of her? Beside the tall, punky Zoe she would seem very small and young. Perhaps he did find her boring, perhaps his encouraging conversation and smiles were merely public school good manners. He really was very good looking. His hair, about the same corn colour as Will's, was short at the back but hung in a long wave across one of his slate-coloured eyes. His skin was soft, almost effeminate, and his face quite gaunt. There was something vulnerable about him, as if he hadn't eaten properly. In repose, his expression was like that of some long-forgotten poet, caught in a faded photograph: sensitive, remote, truly Romantic. But when he spoke he became confident and disappointingly human. For a moment they both realized that they were staring at each other.

It was a magnificent autumnal day and Kay awoke with the sun streaming into her room. She lay under her blankets for a while, suddenly disorientated. She realized that she hadn't given her mother a thought and she had promised, albeit reluctantly, to call her. Perhaps she would ring today. There was a knock at the door.

'I've sought you out.' In came Zoe with two mugs of coffee. 'Friendly neighbours you have, I must say. The coffee is black because not one of them would lend me any milk. There's a real cow called Delia.'

'Oh dear,' said Kay, somewhat ashamed.

'What have you been up to?'

Kay began to explain the night before.

'Sounds fantastic, this cousin of yours . . . '

'Nephew.'

'So, tell me all about him. Are you very close?'

'Well, we are, at least we were, very. Will changed my life. He was my best friend.'

29

'Sounds dramatic.'

'Oh no, not really. It's just that I led rather a secluded life until Will came along. I was alone with my parents and then suddenly along came this golden-haired youth and life got to be much more enjoyable. I was nine at the time, so you see he had a very formative influence.'

'Lucky you! I was a pretty lonely kid too, but I didn't have a knight in shining armour . . .'

'Oh, I hated him at first. He was such a prep school prig. And his accent! It still grates sometimes. But after I showed him who was boss, we got on very well!'

'Why is he your nephew? You must have a sibling somewhere.'

'Oh yes, my sister Dorothy is his mother. She is much older than me. I think I was very much an afterthought or a mistake for my parents. They're quite old.'

'Mine are too. They'd been trying for years to have a kid and when mum hit forty she produced me. Poor cow. Anyway, when do I get to meet Will and Bob?'

'I'm meant to be seeing them tonight. Why don't you come along? We arranged to meet in this pub, the Turf Tavern, near New College.'

He changed my life. A dramatic cliché that had sprung from her lips in a conversation with a near stranger, but as Kay sat down in her dusty armchair to read *David Copperfield* for her first essay, she realized how true it was.

He had come to spend the summer when she was nine. Will was the only son of Dorothy and her husband Wilfred. Although Kay had been told she had a nephew, she couldn't remember meeting him. His family was often abroad and when Dorothy came to visit, Will was usually in the middle of school term. He was a quiet child with a round face and big blue eyes. His most striking feature was his curly blond hair. When she was told by her mother that Will would be spending the summer with them, she felt resentful that a stranger would impose on her world and had asked her mother why he couldn't stay with Dorothy and Wilfred. Her mother had explained patiently that they had been posted to the embassy in Djakarta and everyone felt it would be best for Will to stay in England in the summer holidays, and besides it would be nice for Kay to have someone to play with. Kay wasn't sure.

One evening her father arrived home from work with Will beside him in the car. Kay was summoned downstairs and told to show Will to his room. She ran upstairs, not waiting for Will, who struggled up with a suitcase. Neither spoke to the other. Will stared bleakly out of the bedroom window.

'Do you go riding at all?' His voice was rather high and his accent smart. Kay shook her head. 'Pity. Perhaps I'll ask grandfather if I can go to the local stables. There must be one near here. I can see horses over there.'

'Can you ride then?'

'You bet. Can you?'

'Sort of.'

'Well, I'm going to ask grandfather now if I can go riding. It's better than doing nothing while I'm here.' He walked out of the bedroom with a sad look on his face and down the stairs. Before he got to the bottom, Kay slid down the bannister beside him.

'Are you really older than me?' she shouted at him.

'Yes, I'm ten. It was my birthday last month.'

'I'm nine but I bet I can learn to ride as well as you can.'

He started riding regularly and made friends with several children who went to the stables. He became quite a different person – always smiling and full of energy. Kay refused to go to the stables. She spent her days lying on the nursery floor or sitting on the swing, reading. That was how she had spent her holidays until then. Her parents lived in a large rambling house with a vast garden. Her father worked in the City. He commuted back and forth and wasn't there most of Kay's day. Her regular meeting with him took place

31

at dinner. They would eat at the large dining room table, sometimes with candles if father was in a good mood. He was a severe man. Even as a young child she was aware of the strain he found it to make conversation with her. It was her mother who chatted to Kay and took her on shopping trips or to a park. Father was always busy, working in London, or in his study. If Kay made too much noise playing around the house, her mother used to shake her head and say, 'Now, now, darling, not so much noise. Father is working.'

Her mother organized her life around her husband. They led a sedate life, rarely going out, and when they did it was always a duty, something they felt they had to do, for appearances, or for father's work. Kay grew up with few friends, and those she made she was not encouraged to take home. Now and then her mother would drive her to a friend's house to play for an afternoon, but like everything else her mother did it was without great enthusiasm.

As Kay had grown older she had realized with a shock that her parents were very old in comparison to her contemporaries' parents. It had hurt her when a girl in her class had pointed this out one day. But in her mind it became a reason for their lack of energy, and even for their lack of interest in her. She grew to treat them as she would two elderly, boring strangers. She learned to entertain herself.

One day she was sitting in the nursery curled up in a chair reading *What Katy Did*, when Will wandered in with his hands in his pockets, whistling. Kay looked up, annoyed at the intrusion.

'Have you ever thought of building a treehouse in the oak tree?' He was staring idly out of the window.

'No . . . well, yes. But father said I couldn't. I don't know why. Perhaps he thought I'd fall out or something.'

'It really would be a wheeze to have a treehouse up there.'

'You speak very poshly, don't you? My friends would

32

think you're really funny. I even heard you say "old chap" the other day.' Kay sniggered.

'No, I didn't. Anyway, what if I did? It's got nothing to do with you. You haven't got any friends anyway.'

'Yes I have, lots.'

'I don't believe you. I've never seen them.'

'They wouldn't want to come if you were here. We don't like boys much. They're all silly and wet like you.'

'If you were a boy I'd hit you hard, but you're only a stupid girl.' Will walked behind her chair and pulled her hair in one sharp tweak. 'Besides, your hair is awfully silly.' He sauntered out of the room. Kay rubbed her head. It hurt. She hated him. She began to cry silently until he came back.

'I'm sorry, Kay. Can't we be friends? Let's shake on it.' He held out his hand with great solemnity.

Kay glowered at him. 'I suppose you think that it's really grown up to shake hands and all that. Well, I won't. And you're not having a den in my tree, so there.'

'Oh, very well then, stupid girl.'

'I'm not stupid. You are. Really, really stupid. Riding horses and calling people "old chap". You're really stupid.' She hoped that he would cry, but he just walked away. She got up and ran after him.

'Listen, Will Younger, you pulled my hair and it hurt and I'm going to hit you very hard.'

She slapped him across his right cheek. The noise reverberated. Will stared at her astonished.

'Go on, fight, stupid boy. I dare you. Go on!'

Without further thought, Will hit her. She leapt at him and they began to struggle. He pushed her to the floor and sat on top of her, staring triumphantly into her eyes. She glared back. Suddenly he began to tickle her.

'You look really funny when you're being tickled. Your face is like a squashed tomato.' He dug his fingers into her ribs. Suddenly she began laughing too. He held out his hand to help her up.

'I'm sorry I hit you.'

33

'That's OK, stupid boy. It didn't hurt. I'm going to do some drawing now. You can borrow my crayons if you like.'

After that they had become inseparable and would spend happy hours playing around the pond and planning a den in the oak tree. When the holiday came to an end, Kay was secretly sorry that Will had to go back to school, but all the same, she refused to drive with her father to the station to see him off.

When she thought about it now, she realized that Will had been her one distraction for many years. She had felt isolated at school, where her intelligence and bookishness branded her a snob, and at home she was lonely. Will had been everything to her, friend, family and ally. As she grew older she used to have more and more bitter arguments with her father. Every time they spoke it seemed to turn into an argument. He wouldn't even allow her the dignity of acknowledging that they were arguing. 'We're simply having a heated discussion,' he would insist. Will understood her humiliation.

'Fathers are like that. Hard luck. Mine's a bore too.'

Around the time she took her O levels and passed them with top grades, she noticed something changing in their friendship. At school she was surrounded by nothing but conversations about who could now wear a bra, who had started to use tampons, and who had gone out with most boys. Kay hated these confidences but the changes she could see distorting and reshaping her body drew her closer to her school friends. She needed them to understand what was happening to herself. You weren't supposed to talk to boys about things like that, and her mother just didn't seem to be able to cope with such intimacies. Kay was teased at school because she didn't have a boyfriend. Once again, Will came to her rescue when he came to meet her one day from school. The next day several of her classmates asked who 'that gorgeous hunk' was. They assumed he was her

34

boyfriend and she did not bother to disabuse them. But she was disturbed by this. Will could not be her boyfriend. He was her nephew.

One afternoon Kay, her mother and Will went into London on a shopping trip. Will needed a new suit. Kay had gone off on her own to wander down Oxford Street and arranged to meet the others at a tailor in Savile Row. When she arrived, Will was trying on a suit, closely supervised by her mother.

'Now doesn't he look smart. It's such a lovely fit. You look very dashing, Will, very dashing indeed.' Her mother chattered away, pleased with her choice. 'I simply can't believe how you've grown up, Will, dear. It only seems like yesterday that you and Kay were climbing trees! Well, doesn't time fly. You look very handsome.'

God, wasn't she embarrassing, Kay thought, and turned to exchange a despairing glance with Will, but she found herself in the grips of the strangest of feelings. He really did look gorgeous in that suit. She was aware for the first time how much taller he was and how his body had changed. Her mother was right. He was a man. Kay felt herself turning bright pink from her chin to the roots of her hair.

That summer had been a particularly uncomfortable one for Kay. She was all of a sudden excruciatingly aware of her own body and Will's.

One day they were lying on the lawn in the sun. She was reading D. H. Lawrence and getting bored. She began to tell Will about the novel and why she thought it poor, how the characters were inadequately developed, the structure flawed, and the writing self-indulgent.

'But it's all about sex, Kay.'

'Don't be so stupid, Will. It's about other things too. Anyway, what do you know about it?'

'I might not have studied literature in the great depth you have,' he replied, 'but that doesn't mean I don't know about sex. In fact, I probably know all there is to know.' He rolled on to his back. 'Well, do you think old D.H. knows what he's talking about, or, Aunty Kay, could you teach him a thing or two?'

Kay shrieked and threw the book at Will. It hit him in the groin and he let out an agonized groan.

'Will, I'm sorry.'

'Don't ever do that again. It bloody well hurts.'

'What do you mean?'

She still winced remembering the episode.

The next day, she was in the kitchen with her mother, helping to prepare the Sunday lunch. Her mother was fussing over the Yorkshire pudding, when she stopped and wiped the flour from her hands.

'Kay, darling, there's something I must say to you.' Kay looked up as her mother continued with obvious effort. 'Well, darling, I'm not much good at talking about these things, as you know, but I must say it. It's just that I was talking to Mrs Reid after church and she mentioned . . . now, you mustn't think I'm interfering, I know what you're like, Kay . . . Well, she told me that a few people had commented on how close you and Will seem to be. Of course, darling, they all like him very much. What I'm trying to say is that you must be careful . . . '

'Mother, what are you talking about?' Kay bristled.

'What I'm talking about, darling, is this. People know you're related to Will and it's just not nice for you to go around, well, with your arms around each other. You're not children any longer.'

Kay was furious. Her mother never talked about things like that. How dare she mention her closeness with Will and how dare she gossip about it with people at church. It was as if she and Will were being threatened from every direction. With great effort she quelled the desire to shout at her mother.

'Mummy, how silly. Will is my best friend. Anyway, he's back to school tomorrow.'

36

Her mother sighed. 'Sometimes I think I'm naive, Kay, but really . . . '

But her mother's words had marked a turning point in her relationship with Will. She did not see him again until that Easter and after that things had just never been the same. Perhaps she had been naive. Perhaps her old mother was not so stupid after all. But what did it matter if they could be friends again now.

Zoe referred to that evening as the meeting of the highly strung quartet: Bob and Will and Kay and Zoe. They got drunk together on the aromatic mulled wine in the Turf Tavern and burnt their throats on vindaloos at the Taj Mahal restaurant. For the rest of the year all four social lives revolved around each other. While each retained an individuality, none cared to see other people much. There was a harmony among them untroubled by jealousy or rivalry.

Although they were a group of four, they seemed from the start to divide naturally into two couples. Zoe and Will had an instant joking rapport. He treated her as he might treat a male friend and wasn't protective as he was with Kay. Kay believed she had regained her own special closeness with Will. They saw each other always as part of the happy quartet, rarely on their own. Sometimes Kay would reflect on this. At one time they had spent so much time alone, but now she thought she might be uncomfortable to be on her own with Will. But she pushed these thoughts from her mind. Will didn't seem to notice anything was different and, besides, they were happy. At times she almost felt ecstatic with happiness. When the four of them were together it was such fun. They laughed and giggled or had earnest, intimate conversations. For the first time in her life Kay had made friends for herself. She and Bob got on well together too. They were the serious couple. They were always talking about politics and literature, anything and everything.

'Stop being so deep and meaningful!' Zoe would shout at them from time to time, and they would be embarrassed as if they had been overstepping the lines of friendship and becoming too involved in each other's thoughts.

Kay was dreamily content for weeks on end. She felt, perhaps for the first time in her life, comfortable and secure. Of the four, she was probably the most intelligent and yet the most naive. These aspects of her character had always distanced her from the crowd, but in the quartet her innocence was cherished. The others were genuinely admiring of her talents. Kay's work was always good and she spent long hours by herself writing stories and articles which began to appear regularly in *Isis*, the literary magazine. Sometimes Will accused her of being a blue-stocking, but Kay felt that the world of academia might turn out to be her forte.

The quartet had its limitations though. It was wonderful to have close and loving friends, but sometimes she found it claustrophobic. Within an evening of moving into her room she had created a Them and Us situation in the college house. The primary antagonist was Delia, a neurotic biochemist, who had the room next door to Kay's and spent her spare time grinding at her cello. Will had once made a facetious remark about an advanced case of 'penis envy' next door, and Kay was sure that Delia had overheard, for since then she had taken every opportunity to complain to the warden about the noise from Kay's room and the fact that men were in there until all hours. She even accused Kay of stealing some of her shampoo. Luckily, the warden, a postgraduate student, had found the scenario amusing, but she had warned Kay not to entertain guests later than ten o'clock at night.

At college, too, Kay and Zoe were the odd ones out. Zoe's flamboyant clothes, their habit of smoking at break-fast, and the two very attractive blond men who accompanied them everywhere, were cause for remark. And although Zoe claimed that their tutors were too dull to notice the notes she passed Kay and their stifled giggles, Kay was sure that she detected reprimanding looks from time to time. She wanted to do well and she didn't know how to tell Zoe without offending her, or seeming like a prude.

At the start of the Hilary term Kay resolved to work harder and socialize less. She had been alarmed at the amount of reading she had had to catch up on in the vacation. But within a week of being back her resolution vanished. There was just too much to distract her, too many new experiences to savour. Zoe refused adamantly to join any societies or clubs, but Kay decided she would at least join the Literary Society in spite of Zoe's disparaging remarks about 'arty-farty literati'.

One evening, Kay had just come out of a meeting and was bending over her bicycle, which was chained to a lamppost, when she felt a hand on her shoulder.

'Will, you made me jump,' she said, relieved it was him. 'What are you doing lurking in the shadows?'

'Been in the library working. We medics, you know – all work and no play.'

'I got the impression it was the other way round. Do you call accosting young damsels in dark streets work or play?'

'Depends on who they are. How about a quick drink before closing time?'

'Why not? Only I refuse to try any of your real ale. I hate it.'

'Your education isn't exactly broadening your horizons, is it?' He threw an arm across her shoulder. 'I feel you're becoming a little sophisticat, my dear young lady. I think you could almost manage a plausible pout if you tried. It can't be Zoe who is leading you into such evil ways. She's about as sophisticated as an incontinent lab rat. Must be the Hon Bob. You've fallen for his public school ways. Well, don't say I didn't warn you.' Will started to whistle noisily.

'What on earth are you talking about? Sometimes you

talk nonsense.'

'There you are, you see, "nonsense". Before you would have said shit, crap or some other enchanting expletive.'

Kay struggled back from the crowded bar. The King's Arms was always so full, especially at this time when everyone came out of the Bodleian. The air was full of smoke and people lounged against the walls, bags of books and scraps of paper propped against their ankles. She could see Will staring at her across the room.

'Why are you looking at me like that? Have you been smoking dope again?'

Will raised his glass. 'Cheers!'

'Isn't it funny drinking without the other two? It's weird how we all get on, don't you think? We're quite different. I mean I'm not at all like Zoe and you're not at all like Bob. Whatever did you two young beaux do to entertain yourselves before we arrived?'

'Oh, we managed.' Will's voice became prickly.

Kay felt nervous. She began to talk quickly. 'I went to Lit. Soc. this evening. It was really exciting. Nigel Nicolson was talking about his parents and *Portrait of a Marriage*. Have you read it? I wonder if I could ever write as interestingly as that about father and mother. Not that there's much to write about. They're too ordinary. Actually, ordinary doesn't really describe father, does it? He is *so* ordinary it's extraordinary . . . '

'You look quite daunting when you're being all earnest. Quite the Aunty Kay,' Will interrupted her. She was irritated by him calling her Aunty Kay again. There was something disapproving in his voice. She felt he was trying to put a damper on her excitement.

'What's the matter with you?' she snapped. 'Oh, don't be so sober, Will. You must get excited about things. I just don't want it to end, that's all.'

'Why should it? You're here for another two years for God's sake.'

'Oh, all I mean is that I hated home so much. You know I

40

never felt I belonged there. Now things are so good I can't believe they'll go on being good. The only thing I miss is the way we used to be . . . you and I. You know it was like you were my brother.'

'What do you mean, the way we used to be? Which way?' A hard edge crept into his voice.

'All I meant was the way we were so close. I wasn't trying to be profound or anything. Why are you being so difficult?'

'Oh, Kay, you want so bloody much.'

'Why not? Why shouldn't I? Anyway, I don't understand what you're on about.'

He was silent. She tried again.

'Look, I didn't mean to be heavy or anything. I was simply saying I wish we were like we used to be. It would be nice. I sometimes think you don't like me as much as you used to. That's all.'

'On the contrary, I like you fine. I think you're very nice.' He mimicked her. She blushed and felt angry and humiliated.

'I must go. It's late. Come on, don't be such a grouch. Walk me to my bike.'

'If you like.' He shrugged his shoulders.

After that evening Will carried on as though nothing had happened, but Kay felt uneasy when she was with him. She felt he had put up a barrier between them. She found herself confiding more in Bob. The quartet had become less harmonious as each part had found friends outside. Will often went drinking with his rugby friends, Zoe began to act in alternative theatre and was often rehearsing, and although Bob spent several evenings a week at political meetings she saw him most often. At the beginning of the Trinity term they all decided to go to a fancy-dress ball. Kay had decided that she would make a special effort to talk to other people. As they walked down the High Street she turned to Bob and said, 'Why don't we have a competition tonight to see who can meet the most new and interesting people?'

He withdrew his arm which was resting lightly over her shoulder and said, 'Oh, you think you've grown out of us now, do you?'

She was hurt. She hadn't meant to sound dissatisfied and he hadn't got any right to be so possessive. After all, they were just friends. 'All right,' she said. 'Just wait and see. I'll have all the men on their knees for me. They call me the next Zuleika Dobson!'

Bob looked down at her with a look that she interpreted as contempt.

Kay had thought for days about what to wear and in the end had blown a full week's allowance on a beaded twenties flapper dress from a second-hand shop in Walton Street. It was midnight blue, with silver glass fringes of beads, and her headband, hastily improvised from Baco Foil, looked surprisingly authentic. Bob had hired a tuxedo and looked divinely decadent with his long eyelashes mascaraed by Zoe and his lips a mulberry pout. Zoe and Will had bought a packet of bin liners and, having Sellotaped them together and cut two holes for their heads, announced that they were an oil slick. They were having trouble in flowing down the Broad, Oxford's main street, and Kay could hear squeals of laughter as they tripped over each other.

The sixteenth-century hall was brimming with people: schoolgirls, punks and the occasional gorilla dancing and drinking and looked down on by the disapproving faces in the portraits of dons of yesteryear. Kay left Bob at the door and headed straight for the bar.

'I can see you mean business,' said a voice behind her as she poured a large glass of wine.

She turned and smiled at a tall, bearded man who looked utterly ridiculous in a bunny-girl suit.

'You do English, don't you?' he continued.

'Yes.' How did he know?

'I've seen you at Professor Matthews' lectures on Spenser.'

'Oh, I'm thinking of giving them up. They're so boring, aren't they?' she replied archly. She didn't like the way 'boring' was creeping into her conversation the whole time, but everyone said it.

'Actually I think he's rather good. Nigel, by the way.'

'Kay Trevelyan.'

'Oh, you're the girl who writes for *Isis*. Wonderful stuff.'

They shook hands formally, knowing that they had now exhausted what they had in common. Kay looked around for someone to move on to. Bob was deep in conversation with a ballet dancer and the oil slick was swaying about on the dance floor.

'Cheer up!' said Nigel.

'I'm perfectly happy, thank you.' Kay swished away, her beads clinking angrily.

'I've just been dared to come and talk to the prettiest girl at the ball.'

It was Simon Leach. He had been pointed out to Kay in the King's Arms a couple of weeks before. Oxford's leading wit, greatest actor and most camp homosexual.

'And what, pray, do you know about pretty girls?'

'Oh, my dear, you've been hearing ugly rumours about me, I can tell. But none of them is true, I can assure you. Come and have a dance, to show you mean no offence and to help me win my wager.'

They moved into the centre of the hall and swung around, posturing vaguely. Kay wished that Bob would turn and see her. Then *Rock around the Clock* came on and Simon grabbed her and whispered, 'Relax, follow me and we'll show these clodhoppers how to jive.' They were both natural dancers and by the end of the record they had cleared the floor. He threw her round, twisting her under his arm and pulling her through his legs.

'Thanks!' she said breathlessly, when they had finished in a final, intricate swirl.

'My pleasure.' He smiled. 'I've been dying to meet Kay Trevelyan and get you into my column. I can't think why we haven't met before. I've always thought you so aloof and serious, sitting in the Bodleian. But I've admired your bookish beauty over the library desks. And now it turns out that you're sweet. Come and see me for tea.'

'I'd love to.'

She knew that Bob and Will had only bad things to say about Simon Leach. That he thought himself an updated version of Anthony Blanche in *Brideshead Revisited*. Well, what was wrong with that? Certainly he led an extravagant lifestyle. Kay had heard that he had resurrected the Hysteron Proteron Club which existed in T. E. Lawrence's day. A club that worked on the premise that everything should be done the wrong way round. So they would start the day with a seven-course meal: a soup, fish course, followed by champagne sorbet, two sorts of meat, a sweet and cheese. All washed down with expensive wines and followed by vintage port. In the evenings they would sit down in their pyjamas and eat platefuls of eggs and bacon, devilled kidneys and toast and drink coffee and orange juice. A couple of weeks ago it had been reported that the club dressed in full subfusc and went down to the lecture halls at two in the morning demanding loudly to be educated.

Simon lived for the University paper gossip column, most of which he wrote himself, about himself. Bob strongly disapproved of this, saying that he perpetuated the myth that Oxford was full of privileged ne'er-do-wells. But Kay was intrigued by him and he was the only person who had told her that her dress looked perfect. Simon kissed her hand and minced off to his gaggle of friends. Several men approached her for dances and she found herself locked in an embrace with an *Isis* colleague called Matthew. The disc jockey was playing *Je t'aime,* and Matthew was caressing her back through her beads, but Kay was thinking about Bob. She was relieved when he approached, tapped

Matthew on the shoulder and took her to one side.

'I see you *have* made an impression,' he said condescendingly.

'And I see you've finally managed to extricate yourself from the limbs of Margot Fonteyn,' she snapped back. 'Where are the other two and why are you looking at me like that?'

'They've gone back to Will's room to get stoned. Are you coming?'

'Where?'

'Wherever you want.'

'But . . . but we haven't even danced yet.'

Bob took her hand, almost surreptitiously, and they looked around the room. The music was winding up and there were just a few couples smooching to the slow numbers. She looked at him through a blur of alcohol and knew that she had a choice. There were several men skulking around who had asked her back for coffee, but she wanted only Bob. The feelings that had nagged between them all this time had been resolved as he had taken her hand. She ran her thumb around his dry palm.

They walked back to New College in silence, running the last few hundred yards to get in before the porter locked the gates at midnight.

'Coffee?' Bob offered when they had reached his room.

'Yes, please.'

She was suddenly nervous again. There was a barrier that neither of them dared cross. Or perhaps she had imagined it all. 'Pounce!' Zoe's advice on how to get off with men rang in her ears, but Kay didn't know how to. Instead she smiled at him and started nonchalantly discussing the people at the party.

'I told you at the beginning of the year that you would be a success,' he said. 'But now I wish I had locked you up and kept you for myself.'

Could he mean . . . ? She pretended to be deeply interested in her coffee and dared not say a word.

hands and kissed her. Then they were both laughing and hugging each other and kissing each other's faces.

'Bob. What are we doing?'

'We're falling in love.' And as he kissed her again and again she wondered why it hadn't happened before. It was all so easy.

They didn't emerge from his room until late the next afternoon. She was wearing Bob's stripey school blazer over her beaded dress. They walked arm in arm through Magdalen deer park as the warm sun disappeared behind the luscious green trees and a faint breeze rustled their foliage. They talked about everything and nothing, as though they had to make up for lost time.

'It was good, wasn't it?' Bob had said. She had nodded her head. It had been wonderful, better than she had ever imagined it could be. As they wandered back down Holywell Road they stopped for a moment and kissed again.

'Control yourselves! Not in public.' Zoe's voice screeched and a few steps behind her walked Will. Her boisterousness could not cover everyone's embarrassment. Will eyed Kay's dress knowingly.

'Well, we all know what you've been doing at last,' said Zoe.

'We're in love,' Kay said, trying to avoid Will's glance. Bob squeezed her hand.

'How sweet!' said Zoe. 'I hope you've gone on the pill.'

'Knowing Kay, I doubt if they've got that far.' Will pushed past Bob. 'I suppose I ought to say congratulations, you bastard.'

For the rest of the term they spent long hours together. Kay came to know what the expression 'walking on air' meant. At first she couldn't believe that Bob could reciprocate the all-enveloping emotions she felt for him. But he did. They would sit by the river under great shady trees, pretending to

'Kay.' He knelt in front of her and took her face in both

46

read, but fingering each other.

'I'm crazy about you,' he would murmur.

'I adore you.'

'*Je t'aime.*'

The quartet dissolved. Kay and Bob became a rhapsodic duet. For the rest of the term they were absorbed in each other. Kay learnt from Bob that Will had taken it very badly and for a few weeks his friendship with Bob cooled.

'Funny chap, Will. I really can't understand what all the angst is about. He obviously thinks the world of you, and I even thought he quite liked me. Perhaps he thinks I'm a bad influence . . .'

Kay did not make any attempt to see Will. She was annoyed at his reaction and she didn't want anything to spoil her happiness. When Zoe asked her what was going on she shrugged her shoulders and said, 'I just don't understand Will any more.'

'But this is weird. You're both being so silly. Will is such a sweetie. I hate seeing him all grizzly and bad-tempered. Can't you do something about it, whatever it is? I miss the old Will. Honestly, Kay, anyone would think you were lovers, not cousins.'

'He's not my cousin, he's my nephew. How many times do I have to tell you?'

'Keep your hair on. You're being so cold and superior about him. What is going on? I thought you two were best mates.'

'We were. Well, we still are. For God's sake, can't you give it a rest? It's not bloody *Hamlet*, you know.'

Bob and Kay talked about their future. Kay already bemoaned the fact that Bob would have to spend the next year in France as he was reading Modern Languages. He assured her they would spend every weekend together in Paris or Oxford. 'I won't be able to live for five days without you.'

'But we've only really known each other a few weeks.

How can you say that?' She was teasing for assurance, not wanting the bubble to burst.

'I love you. I want you forever. I want you to have our children.'

'Oh Bob, don't be silly. We're here and now. I'd be a terrible mother, anyway.'

He told her he wanted eight children and three dogs and a huge rambling house on the Norfolk coast.

'Sounds like a romantic novel!' she laughed.

It had all been so clear in those halcyon days in that fairytale summer. It wouldn't be so long before Kay would look back on their naiveté and remember their words with amused irony, and burning tears.

They spent most of the summer holiday at Sevenoaks together. Kay loved the old house when Bob was there to appreciate it too. Her mother pampered him, and he seemed to know exactly how to charm her father. Kay was irritated that her father listened to Bob when he talked about socialism. He acted as if he and he alone had discovered it. She had had so many rows with her father when she had gone through her revolutionary phase. He had caught her reading Marx when she was sixteen and had thrown the book into the fire, telling her she was a silly and dangerous dreamer. But Bob, with his suave voice, got away with murder.

'Your parents are very nice,' Bob said as she sat on his lap in a rocking chair on the terrace, drinking Campari, 'but I'm rather glad they've finally gone on hols. I want to sleep with you, without worrying that one of them is going to walk in on us *in flagrante delicto*. You're not really like either of them, are you?'

'How not?'

'Well, your father is a fascist, but that's beside the point. No, it's just that they don't treat you like a person, more like a stereotype. You do quite a good act of playing the loving daughter. It's like some game you're all playing.

Were you ever close to them?'

'No. Not at all, really. They're quite old. I suppose it's just a generation gap.'

'I bet you had an easy childhood. All this garden and two indulgent parents . . .'

'It didn't seem easy at the time.'

'Didn't it? Mine was . . .' Bob rambled into a long anecdote about the matron in his prep school and how he had been her favourite. Kay laughed at his reminiscences. She could just see him dressed in school uniform, everybody's darling. She loved him so much then as he talked and parodied, mimicking his teachers and remembering every detail.

Later, as he slept lightly beside her in her chintzy bedroom, she thought how different her childhood had been from Bob's. She had never felt wanted and she had always been plagued by that dream. It had occurred again and again throughout her young life. The details were always the same and as it went on it became menacing. She knew as soon as it began that she would experience the same disturbance and upheaval. She was frightened now that in conjuring it up in her mind, she would have it again.

'What's up?' Bob was half awake.

'I was just thinking about this dream I used to have. Nightmare really . . .'

'Tell me all about it and you'll never have it again.'

'Well, if you want to know, I am a toddler playing on the lawn. I'm wearing my best dress. It's a warm summer afternoon but the sky is slightly misty. I can hear quite clearly the birds singing in the trees. I sort of walk towards the fence – you know, the one which divides the front lawn from the rest of the garden. As I reach it, I stumble and fall on my hands and knees, but I pull myself up and look through the bars. I can hear mother's voice calling me and she is walking down the path. I can see her skirt between the bushes on the verge. She picks me up and tosses me in the air. But then I know that there is someone watching us,

49

standing in the shadow of the tree. I point my finger towards the tree, but mother doesn't notice. I start to cry, then scream, but mother still doesn't notice . . . then I know that something dreadful is going to happen, and I become someone watching me and my mother, and then I wake up . . . Oh, Bob, it's horrible!'

'Kay, darling, it's OK, it's OK.' She was shivering. 'It's a weird dream. You don't feel secure with your mother, somebody is watching you . . . Maybe you're adopted or something.'

'Hmmm. That's what Will used to say. But we decided I couldn't be. It's not as if my parents couldn't have children. They had Dorothy, although I don't look like her . . . '

'Oh, come on, Kay, I was only joking. Dreams don't have any significance anyway.'

'So says Sigmund Bob.' But he was already asleep.

'You didn't sleep much last night. You look drawn.' Bob looked down at her, worried. 'Let me make you tea and then you should sleep the rest of the morning.'

'OK, I will.'

'You look so vulnerable and cuddly tucked up in your bed. When you wake up, you're just like a sleepy child.'

'What do I normally look like then?' Kay giggled.

'Very together. A little bit cool and intimidating, I think.'

'Oh, Bob, you don't find me intimidating, do you?'

'Well, perhaps that's the wrong word. Mysterious, unattainable. I'm sort of proud to be seen with you. All of New College is jealous of me, you know.' He was looking down at her and she thought she saw his whole person gazing through his eyes.

She reached up her arms. 'Well, I don't find you at all intimidating any more.' He looked dismayed. 'But I love you. Where's that cup of tea you promised?' But the tea grew cold as she fell into a blissful doze.

'Kay, Kay,' Bob whispered. 'I've got a surprise for you.

Will's here. He's just got back from Chile. He came straight from Heathrow to see us. We'll have a house party.'

'Where is he?'

'Here,' Will poked his head round the door. 'Hello, Aunty. How are you?'

'Will, you look so brown! Did you have a good time?'

'I had a great time. Look, is it OK if I stay here a while? I don't want to get in your way.'

'Of course it's OK. It's your home too.'

The last time she had seen Will was when he had sent her a note at the end of the summer term inviting her over for tea. She had decided to go, but had made up her mind not to mention Bob. She didn't want to go through all that. If Will wanted to explain his behaviour then that was up to him. But he had said nothing about it. He had invited a crowd of his rowing friends and they had had quite a jolly time. When Kay left he kissed her on the cheek and she had taken this to mean that he had got over whatever it was that had angered him so much.

She was pleased to see him now. He had arrived from Chile where he had been visiting his parents, Wilfred and Dorothy. He was laden with raw alcohol and boasting how easy it was as a diplomat's son to smuggle. They made exotic cocktails. Kay put on her twenties dress and Bob and Will wore boaters and baggy old white shorts that they found in Kay's father's wardrobe. They sat on the veranda pretending to be old colonials as the sun went down. Kay felt a flood of affection for them both.

'Well, what did you do in Chile? How is Dorothy?' she asked.

'Mum? She's in her element out there. Queening it in diplomatic circles, giving wonderfully English parties. She wears her county clothes and claims she's keeping up "some sort of standard".'

'And Wilfred?' Kay had never liked her stuffy brother-in-law.

'Oh, he's a bit out of his depth. I think he thinks he's

being bugged. Keeps saying, "William, do remember your position. Don't tell me about your riotous activities. I prefer not to know that your friends are all drug-taking hooligans!" He's not really got Mum's class, you know. I think he's working very hard. They both asked after you.'

'And what did you tell them?'

'Oh, that you've taken up with a drug-taking socialist and deserted me . . . '

'Oh, Will!' Kay laughed and moved closer to Bob on the white wicker garden seat.

'I say, it's terribly hot. Shall we take a dip in the lake?' said Bob.

'*No*!' Kay and Will spoke at once.

'I mean, it's dangerous, we couldn't.' Kay looked away.

'A funny thing happened, actually.' Will fidgeted in his chair. 'I was looking through an old photograph album and there was this picture of mother when she was about eighteen, sitting right where you are now.'

Kay turned to him. 'How fascinating, what was she like? Bob, stop it! Will's telling a story.'

'Oh, she looked pretty much the same, but sitting next to her was someone who looked exactly like you, but with long hair. I asked Mum what you were doing in such an old photo and she snatched the picture away and said, 'Don't be silly, Will, that's not Kay. Kay's hair is short, isn't it?' I didn't really think about it at the time, but now that I see you sitting there, I wonder why I didn't ask her who it was. Strange, isn't it?'

'Oh, it was probably some cousin, wasn't it?' said Bob.

'Well, that's just it. We don't really have any relations, do we, Kay? So who could the mystery woman be?'

'Well, you said it was an old photo. I don't see how you can be so sure it looked like Kay.'

'What does it matter? I'm going in. These mosquitoes are biting my legs.' Kay stood up.

'I'm having some more of that punch,' said Bob.

She decided to sit in the study and read. She had

52

promised to write a book review for *Isis* and if she didn't get down to it soon, she would never do it. As she sat rocking backwards and forwards in the rocking chair, the voices of Bob and Will drifted in from the garden. Sometimes loud laughter interrupted their sentences. She couldn't hear what they were saying and she felt excluded, shut out of their male camaraderie. She remembered Bob's hand wandering across her neck and cheekily stroking her breast under her thin frock. She had seen the expression on Will's face. He had looked hurt. She frowned. They were both her friends, her closest friends, her only friends apart from Zoe. She had once been their friend too. But now she was Bob's lover, and as for Will . . . She could hear Zoe's screech: 'Mates, that's what we are, bessie mates!' but Kay felt she wasn't any longer. Not with Bob and Will. And part of the reason was there, she fully realized now, through the dusk that would soon turn to night, at the bottom of the garden. The pond . . . the lake Bob had referred to. She had tried not to think about it for two years. Now she could think of nothing else.

The pond was always there. It always would be. The water was so clear that she could see the pebbles which lined the basin. They were brown and black but a few white ones gleamed like forgotten pearls. The surface was still, perfectly still.

She could remember it so clearly. That fateful Easter Monday, over two years ago, when she and Will had been alone in the house, one of those freak spells of weather arrived. The sun and clear sky promised a warm, almost summery day. She was lying on her back on the grass above the pond when she felt a shadow fall across her face. She opened her eyes, struggling against the warm drowsiness that had overtaken her.

'Hey, you, get out of my sunshine. You're spoiling my tan.'

Will's face seemed miles away looking down into hers.

He flopped down on to the grass beside her.

'Mmm, quite warm isn't it?'

Kay's limbs seemed to sink heavily into the earth beneath her. Will lit a cigarette and the smoke curled up above them.

'I could just do with a glass of wine right now. In fact, if you're lucky I might even go and help myself to one of Grandpa's cellar? Would madame like that?'

'Mmm.' She turned on to her stomach and rested her head on her arms. The smell of grass and earth penetrated her nostrils and she took a very deep breath. She could feel the sun on her back. She turned and watched him opening the bottle and pouring the wine into two glasses. She drank quickly. She could feel the wine running down into her stomach.

'Christ, Kay, it's not orange juice, you know.' She reached out for more and giggled. It was already having an effect.

'Why is there a pond here?' he asked.

'I think some farmer was once going to build a huge grain silo or something and they dug it out for the foundations. The bottom is full of pebbles. It's quite deep in the middle.'

'Can you swim in it?'

'Oh yes. Do you mean that in all the time you've been coming here you've never been in the pond?' He shook his head. 'Well, fuck me pink and knock me down with a blue feather!'

'Kay, that's rather vulgar, if I may say so. You swear like a trooper at times.'

'Wonder where I get that from.'

'Ha, ha. I think you're pissed.'

'I am and it's pretty damn wonderful too. Will, even old Wilfred, your venerable papa, used to throw decorum to the wind and take a jolly summer's dip in the pond on occasion, and you never have?'

'Nothing like the first time, is there?' Will stood up and began unbuttoning his shirt.

'Will, it'll be freezing cold. You're absolutely mad. Why don't you wait until the summer. We could have a midnight party down here.'

'Oh no, I'm going in right now.' His hands reached for his jeans zip and then he hesitated, embarrassed. Kay burst into giggles. He stood in his underpants looking down at the water. 'Shit, it looks freezing. Pass me the vino. Cheers, Kay, here's to life!' When he had drained the bottle he threw it into the pond, right out into the middle.

'Will! Not in the pond. The glass.'

He stared at her as she sat up. 'Well, Aunty Kay, you'll just have to go in and retrieve it, won't you?'

'Don't be stupid. It's freezing. Besides, I haven't got my costume.'

'No, neither have I.' He indicated his near bare body with a wave of his hand.

'But I couldn't, I mean . . .'

'Yes, what do you mean? Tell me all and I will explain unto you the meaning of life.'

'And I thought it was me that was meant to be pissed.'

'Oh, come on, Kay, be a devil. Let's go in. Just think, a spring dip. The thrill of the water caressing your body.'

'No, you go in, I'll watch.'

He looked vulnerable in his nakedness. Kay looked away. 'Will, wait, wait!' she shouted suddenly. 'I'll come in, only don't get in before I do.' She struggled out of her jeans, finding it hard to keep her balance. When she was behind him, without turning round, he said, 'OK?', then he was in the water, swimming as though his life depended on it. Her feet were numb with cold, she sank down into the water until it reached her shoulders. The shock that ran through her body was as if liquid ice had been poured into her bone marrow. She gasped. Will was beside her shouting, 'Swim! Swim!'

They were lying on the pebble bank which sloped down into the pond, and the water which covered them was only a few inches deep. Will was looking at her. She put out her hand and could feel the water dripping down her arms.

'Hello there,' she fingered a strand of wet hair which hung over his eyebrow. His mouth closed on her wrist.

'Grrr, I'm a sea lion.' He chewed her arm. The water was moving around them with little gurgles. Her arm flopped back gently into the water and Will was still making growling noises with his empty mouth. Everything seemed distant. Will's hand moved from her elbow to her shoulder and he smiled at her.

Suddenly she was there. With every ounce of energy and consciousness, she was looking at him. It was as if a warm current had suddenly melted the freezing numbness away from her limbs. He slid his long leg across her body and put his elbows behind her head. His face looked down directly into hers and she could feel the weight of his body pressing her down into the pebbled bank. Her heart was thumping under her breasts. She opened her mouth but he bent his head and kissed her. She could feel his lips pressing against hers, nudging them apart. Her arms went round his neck and she began to kiss him. Her tongue moved gently in and out of his mouth. She felt ecstatic. Her head moved and their noses touched. Her hands were pulling down on the back of his neck.

'Kay, Kay.'

He covered her face in kisses and then their mouths were together again, searching. She could hear their breathing but she wasn't sure who was making what noise. His hands were running slowly round the form of her breasts, her nipples were painfully erect and then his penis hardened. For a moment she was panic-stricken. They were alone in the land of the unknown and racing on.

'Will, no, no, no.' She was pushing him away from her. Then she was out of the water on the bank. For a moment she thought she was going to be sick. Then she looked at him, still naked and prone in the shallow water. The look of anguish on his face made her want to hold him. But she didn't dare move.

He got to his feet and walked quickly up on to the grass verge. He stopped, gathered his clothes and walked away. She heard him starting to run. She put her arms around her breasts and began to cry. Her teeth chattered. It was the only noise in the grove. The pond was silent with only a few ripples dying away on its surface.

It was now dark outside and she could hear their voices. They were lower and earnest. The rocking chair creaked gently as she moved backwards and forwards. Tears slid down her face. Was it all because of that? It had just happened. But nothing had happened. They had been drunk. He had written her a letter a few days later. He had written that he was sorry but he thought it best that they shouldn't meet for a while. He had signed it 'Will', without any love or kisses. She hadn't seen him again until her first day at Oxford.

The day that Bob was to leave for Paris grew nearer, and Will left to go back to Oxford early. Kay hated herself for being glad to see him go.

'I'm sorry if I've ruined your love nest, Kay.'

'Of course you haven't,' she lied as she waved him goodbye.

Kay found herself beginning the autumn term with a certain reluctance. She was cheered by the thought of sharing the top floor of the house with Zoe, but as she struggled with her suitcase from the station to the waiting cab and they crawled through the traffic towards North Oxford in the pouring rain, all the glamour and romance she had taken for granted that summer term before seemed to have quietly died, never to return. She felt almost guilty that she couldn't share Zoe's optimism and excitement as they sat in her bare attic room huddled round the gas fire. They were eating Pot Noodle and drinking instant coffee with powdered milk when Zoe said, 'You're just missing Bob. Don't worry. But guess what? I've got myself a man.'

'What?' Kay gasped. 'We've been sitting here for a good hour and you haven't told me. That must be the longest time in your life you've ever kept a secret.'

'Give me a chance. It hasn't been going on for very long, but it's really nice. He's exactly my type, lots of curly hair, boyish face, terrific in bed and seems totally besotted with me. He's also American but you can't have everything. You know I was working in Harrods over the summer? Well, I was sort of floating staff and I soon found the cushiest job was working on the lifts. If you got on the right side of Stan, the chief lift operator, he gave you about three short shifts and didn't care what you did for the rest of the day. So I used to shoot off to the V and A, or window shop in Beauchamp Place or wander in Hyde Park. One day I was eating my lunch on a park bench when this American guy came up and asked me the time. As I was reading *Time Out* we struck up a conversation about things to do in London. He seemed to have a lot of money and I had a great time describing all the most expensive nightclubs in vivid detail, which of course I've never been to, and impressing him like mad. We got on so well I thought he was going to invite me along to the Zanzibar. I was a bit peeved when he didn't. But that afternoon he just walked into my lift and we both did a double take. I didn't exactly look like one of London's jetsetters in my green uniform, shouting "Going Up". Anyway, he stayed on the lift for about four journeys up and down and I told him my life story and explained why I was doing one of the least glamorous jobs in England. He offered me dinner that night and since then we haven't looked back. The best thing is that he turns out to be a Rhodes scholar at Wolfson and he's living just round the corner.' Zoe was gleeful.

'When do I get to meet him?'

'Give me a chance, Kay. I want to get really established before I introduce him to Oxford's fucking beauty queen.'

'Aw, don't be ridiculous.'

Kay had never understood why she had achieved the

femme fatale image since that fancy-dress ball and she cursed Simon Leach for his gossip column. But secretly she was flattered to be known as 'Miss Trevelyan, Oxford's most sought-after nymph'.

She had tried to talk him into leaving her out of his column altogether, but had only succeeded in exacerbating the problem. 'As, in my view,' he had said, 'you are the only truly feminine and beautiful woman living in the confines of this bluestockinged hell, I feel it is my duty to let all the poor heterosexual men, few as their numbers be, know what you are doing.'

'But Simon,' she had protested as they supped vintage port in his art-deco furnished rooms one evening, 'I'm so uninteresting. I lead a very domesticated life here and hardly show my face outside the Bodleian and New College . . .'

'It is your charming modesty that makes you so irresistible.' He refilled her glass. The next issue of *Cherwell* had held a mock competition: 'Miss Trevelyan says she is bored – a prize for anyone who can think of the most original way to relieve her ennui'. Sixty-seven replies had been written. Kay shuddered when she remembered some of the suggestions. Bob had been incensed.

A new year brought a fresh batch of trendy young freshers, and Zoe and Kay had to agree that they felt part of an older generation when they saw 'all the young ones', as Zoe put it, vying for social and academic success.

'Do you think that we've grown up at all?' Kay would ask, seeing people make the same mistakes she had done in her first term. Like wearing a gown in the lecture halls because it said so in the statute books, whereas the tradition had long expired. Or bicycling the wrong way down Turl Street. Or making loud conversation in the King's Arms with the regular use of the word 'boring'. She wouldn't do any of those things now, but she didn't feel she had become any wiser. She could use all the adult words and could name-drop philosophers. She could argue logic-ally, make the odd witty remark. She knew how to behave at a drinks party. It had taken long practice and Bob's tuition to learn how to balance a wine glass in one hand and light a cigarette with the other. But when it came to the really grown-up things like applying for the dole in the holidays and paying the bills, Kay let others cope. Going to the family-planning clinic to pick up supplies of the pill was always nerve-wracking, and even finding a dentist to replace a lost filling seemed like an incredibly complicated business.

'Grown up? We've become positively senile,' said Zoe. But Zoe had always taken life in her stride. When Kay had spent so much of her time with Bob that previous term, Zoe had been envious, but she had understood. It had seemed the most natural thing that she should move into Kay's college house in the second year. Bob had been against it. He had claimed that Zoe would dominate Kay, although he refused to say what he meant by this. Kay had voiced his fears to Zoe, but she had squashed any doubts.

'Poor old Bob. Can't you see he's just jealous? He knows that I won't let you sit around missing him.'

It was true. In those first few weeks Zoe had made sure that Kay continued as usual. Kay was a little surprised herself at how little she actively missed Bob. She thought of him often, but filled her life with other things. She found herself often alone in the evenings when Zoe was staying with Chuck and she began to write more. She sent copies of *Isis* to Bob to show him how she filled her time, and he replied with amusing jokey letters, chronicling his exploits and *faux pas* in Paris and urging her to come and stay at the apartment his father had bought him in Montmartre.

Kay did go to Paris once, for a week, but felt out of place. Bob was possessive about his friends and 'comrades' and unwilling for her to join in. They spent long hours furiously making love, as if to spend all the physical energy they had stored from the weeks before. Something about the urgency of it all made Kay feel cheap. She found herself dawdling over meals and spending hours gazing at pictures in the Louvre with Bob standing next to her impatiently stamping his feet, making hints and planting wet kisses on her when she least expected it. Coaxing, almost demanding her as his right. Once she thought she exchanged a sympathetic look with a prostitute who stood in the square Bob's apartment overlooked.

She began to feel owned and she didn't like it. He persistently told her that he loved her, but she was unable to keep up the passionate intensity when he was in Paris and she in Oxford.

'You're making me feel as if I have to live up to an image,' she said to him one evening when he had insisted on cooking a candlelit supper for them. 'Please don't idolize me. I can't cope with it.'

'I'm sorry.'

'And *don't* keep saying you're sorry.'

'What's the matter, Kay darling, why can't we be like we were?'

'It's so difficult when we're so far apart. That's why. I can't think about you the whole time, if you're not there. It doesn't mean I don't feel as strongly about you. It's just different.'

'Is there someone else? You're always on edge.'

'No, of course there isn't. I'm just tired.' She felt awful making excuses. She felt as if she had in some way failed to live up to what she had promised. But she also felt he was being unreasonable in expecting her to. He had his own life in Paris that she couldn't share, but he seemed to want her life to revolve around him. He never offered to come and see her in Oxford as he had promised, because, he said, they would be together there for a year when he came home. But Oxford was where her life was. She didn't go to Paris again and saw Bob only when he came home in the holidays.

Increasingly the delights of the Oxford literary world

61

drew Kay closer into their circle. At first she had written about the things she wanted to write about, opinion pieces on contemporary fiction that were acclaimed, amongst the other students, for their intelligence and clarity. But she had grown to realize that a witty turn of phrase or a pithy observation wore thin after a while and what she really needed was an interview with a star. Editorial meetings in the dingy *Isis* offices on Winchester Street became increasingly fractious as she drew herself into the competition between the rival would-be journalists. The woman she saw as her most promising rival had managed to get, through parental connections, an interview with the year's Booker Prize winner, and whilst Kay was openly half-hearted about such nepotism, she longed for a chance to make her own impact on the magazine.

She grew to realize, much to her chagrin, and after long conversations with Zoe, that she really wanted to be editor. Power had never entered her mind concretely as an objective, but when Zoe had said, 'God, you're so ambitious!' Kay had a sudden awareness that she was, and that she would not be satisfied until she had become editor of Oxford's most prestigious rung in the ladder to success. Zoe had, with her uncanny finger on the public pulse, suggested as a joke that Kay go for big. 'Get an interview with Paul Ritz, you megalomaniac. That book *Embassy* is splashed all over the place. If you could tell the world what the man was really like, you'd be made.'

Paul Ritz had managed to get himself employed in the American Embassy in Bonn as a cleaner, and with his peculiar ability to investigate undercover, had revealed to the world the secrets of diplomatic immunity and the co-operation between America and the Soviet Union, at a time when détente was denied by both sides. In his resulting book, *Embassy*, he exposed the trade links between the two superpowers, the unemployment created in the West by the use of cheap labour in the Communist bloc, and many other facts that shocked the world and had led to the resignation of many senior American diplomats in Europe. It had been said that his revelations caused severe embarrassment to the White House. Paul Ritz was news. Not only because of the implications of his book, but also because of his good looks and the rumours that went round about his love life. He had always been a field day for the gossip columns with his penchant for film star escorts, and his globe-trotting, jet-set journalist image. Paul Ritz surrounded himself with secrecy and never allowed personal interviews, so that even when he had written a serious investigative book, the tabloids still concentrated on speculating about his sex life. Headlines like *The Bedroom Secrets of the Ritz* were rife, but Ritz remained silent. In photos snapped of him at airports, his smile revealed only an annoyed amusement at all the attention.

Zoe's idea, therefore, seemed as ridiculous as she had intended it at the time, but when Kay thought about it, it became fixed in her mind as essential to her quest for editorship. An interview with Paul Ritz became for her the path to success and a career. An interview with the uninterviewable. It would mean she was established. But how? She read his book over and over. All the reviewers would say it was well written, exciting and sound stuff, but it gave no impression of the man himself. He gave away so little of his emotions that she couldn't find an edge. What she wanted to write about was the writer himself, and the double-agent mentality of one who claimed to be politically unbiased. For a number of weeks, Paul Ritz became an obsession with Kay. She read everything about him that was accessible. She wrote to him via his publishers and via the BBC. Finally, she managed to get the number of his agent and she rang him from a call box one day. He was a dapper-sounding man who remarked that he was impressed by her persistence, but if Paul Ritz didn't want to be interviewed then that was that.

'Miss Trevelyan, my dear,' he had said wearily. 'If I could persuade my client to reveal himself in the way you want, I could sell it to any paper for a fortune. I could retire on the proceeds. I want to retire but, Miss Trevelyan, he won't have it, not for you, not for the *Observer*, not for anyone. But I admire your courage and wish you luck.' The pips had gone and Kay had no more ten pence pieces left.

In the end she had given up and was annoyed with herself for spending so much time on a hopeless venture. Who cared about Paul Ritz's dark secrets anyway? If they did, then they were fools. He could remain an enigma if he wanted to so desperately. People who were so set on being mysterious couldn't be that fascinating. 'I think you'll find there's less to him than meets the eye.' Kay said confidently to Zoe.

She had turned her mind to other things and assured herself that journalism was a competitive and stupid world of which she wanted no part. She involved herself in essays and, by the end of the spring term, her tutors were openly promising her a first in her finals. But still her failure nagged at her. She was prepared to give up the editorship of *Isis* on her terms only and she could not quite relinquish her grasp.

One late spring morning, when the air in Oxford was particularly fresh and inspiring, Kay was interrupted in her stroll to the Bodleian by the screams of a small contingent of women gathered outside the front of Blackwell's bookshop. Kay crossed the road to see what was going on. A notice in the window made her heart miss a beat, or did it beat twice in one go?

PAUL RITZ WILL BE SIGNING COPIES OF HIS BESTSELLER *EMBASSY* FROM 10.00 TO 11.00 THIS MORNING.

There was already a queue of at least a hundred people. Kay gathered her books about her and waited. She didn't see him arrive, but at ten, doors opened and people started filing past in awe as if mourners at the state funeral of a

Soviet leader. Each proffered a newly bought copy of *Embassy*. Each smiled, not daring to utter. When Kay's turn arrived she panicked. She had no copy of his book and she had no wish for him to think her a groupie who had been standing around for the sake of a glance at him, and yet she could find nothing to say. His handsome features smiled up at her.

'Hello?'

'I haven't got a book to sign,' she muttered. 'At least I have, but it isn't your book, if you see what I mean. I have read your book. We were sent a review copy. It's very good. In fact, I really wanted to meet you face to face to say . . .'

'Yes?' She detected a note of condescension in his voice.

'Well, what I mean to say is that I have been trying to get an interview with you for weeks, and you have surrounded yourself like a fortress. I mean, I would love to offer you tea or something, if you would be prepared to talk to *Isis*.'

'Tea? At ten o'clock in the morning?'

'Well, morning coffee or a drink?' She smiled as winningly as she could.

He said nothing for a few seconds while he looked at her. He vaguely remembered the carefully typed letters he had received from her. On receiving them he had conjured up visions of an earnest bluestocking, a good deal older than the child who stood before him. Was it possible that this was how young Oxford undergraduates looked nowadays? Surely he hadn't looked so unworldly when he had tramped these hallowed streets twenty years ago. Or had the years taken more from him than he cared to remember? He was embarrassed to feel so old and to have thought that he was still in some way part of this city. It was hers. Hers were the dreaming spires now and she personified the future, the optimism he had toasted with Elizabeth Carleton just a few weeks ago. Seeing her standing there so nervously he almost wanted to interview her, to find out what the young intelligentsia had to say. It might make a nice piece for one

65

of the society magazines. And he admired her nerve. He owed that something.

'Well if you'd like to wait around while I finish up here, I'd be happy to take some "morning coffee" with you.'

She couldn't believe what she was hearing, but tried to look professional. 'Fine. I'll wait outside.'

She stood on the Broad wondering whether she had time to go to the bank to get some money, but decided not to risk it. She had only some loose change on her. How much could a cup of coffee cost and where would she take him? Perhaps he would insist on the Randolph. She cursed herself for wearing such sloppy clothes, and her mother's old saying, 'Go out as you wish to be met with' rang in her ears. Kay looked dismally at her cut-off jeans and big green T-shirt. Her bare legs looked white and that was the sort of thing that Mr Paul Ritz, with his year-round tan, would notice. She peered in through the window and could see him shaking the manager's hand and walking towards the back of the shop. He had forgotten her. She was still looking through the window when a car pulled up behind her and slammed on its horn. She looked round. It was a low, space-age, sports car, bright red. In the driver's seat sat Paul Ritz smiling broadly. 'Hop in, love. I didn't mean to make you jump!'

'Where would you like to go?' she asked. She felt vulnerable seated, almost lying down in the car, and her question seemed superfluous. He was in control. 'I thought I'd take you to Woodstock.'

'How nice.'

They were silent as he drove up Parks Road, screaming round the corners, cutting through the hushed calm of the city. Kay gripped the bottom of her seat, trying to make mental notes. 'Life in the fast lane with Paul Ritz' occurred to her as a title as they swerved to avoid a dawdling cyclist. It crossed her mind that he was showing off driving so fast and the thought made her smile and her confidence rise. She wanted to say, 'Why do you have a red sports car and drive like a maniac? What are you compensating for?' But she didn't want to offend him. Eventually it was he who asked the first question.

'I'm afraid I can't remember your name. I get so many letters . . . '

'Of course. I didn't expect you to. Kay Trevelyan. I write for *Isis*.' She had to shout to be heard at this speed.

'And what sort of things do you write?'

'Reviews mostly. Pieces about the current state of literature . . . '

'What do you read?'

'English.'

'Well, I suppose that follows. Do you enjoy it?'

'Yes, yes I do. But there's little scope for modern literature at Oxford, so I enjoy the *Isis* side because I don't lose touch.'

'So why on earth did you want to interview me? I'm a lot of things, but I don't have much to do with literature.'

He was right but she had an answer ready. 'Well, I'm trying to do interviews too. And I thought I'd go for the top . . . ' She turned to watch his reaction. She had thought he would smile at her flattery, but his face was unmoved. It was an extraordinary face. His eyes reminded her of the wall paintings from Pompeii, large and dark. She had always thought looking at those portraits that the people being painted had a premonition of disaster and had stared at posterity with an acceptance of their fate. Their eyes were their being, all that one remembered. But Paul Ritz's face was strong and the soulful eyes almost came as a surprise amid the sculpted lines of his nose and chin. Kay felt herself beginning to shake as he looked at her briefly, then turned his face back to the road ahead.

'Well, Ms Interviewer, fire away. But I suppose you know the ground rules. I don't answer personal questions.'

'Yes, of course. Now, let me see . . . What was the appeal of writing a book rather than concentrating on your very successful articles?'

'I think I ought to say, love, that one doesn't take a cold-blooded decision to write a book. It happens. Rather like falling in love – once you're smitten then you have to see it to its conclusion.'

'That's an odd comparison, if you'll allow me. Surely falling in love is very different in that it involves two people sharing, supporting each other, but writing is a solitary occupation, particularly *Embassy* where you were necessarily having to be as secretive as possible?'

She surprised him with her thoughtful answer. He had just given her an opportunity to become flippant. Most would have leapt at that break and he would have teased them. Kay Trevelyan wasn't going to allow herself to be teased. She pressed on: 'I think there's a theory, isn't there, that writers will do anything to get a book published as it is a kind of immortality? Was that what you were seeking?'

'I think you're right about most writers. But I don't think that was so with *Embassy*. I didn't see it in terms of a book. I saw it initially as an adventure. Quite frankly I was bored with my writing. When you get to a certain stage you can more or less write an article before you have done the research. Well, not quite, but I found that life was getting too easy. I did a few pieces about diplomats, and basically, I just didn't like them. I don't know if you have met any, but they're a ridiculous breed of human being . . .'

Kay laughed. 'Yes, I know exactly what you mean. My brother-in-law is one . . .'

'They have such prestige but they're living a lie. So I had this Woodward and Bernstein idea to blow the lid off their complacency.'

'Did you have any idea what you would discover?'

'I didn't really, although I had my suspicions . . .'

'And how do you rate your achievements besides, say, Watergate?'

'I think what I did was possibly more fundamental because I think I have rocked people's notions about world politics, rather than just exposed the rotten corruption at top level that we always really knew was there . . . '

'Now, you're always being quoted as saying you're apolitical. How can you explain what you've just said if that really is the case?'

'Let's stop here shall we?' He drew up beside a small pub. 'And you can interrogate me further when we've had a drink.' He opened her door and held out his hand to help her up.

'Do you come out to Woodstock often?' he asked when they were seated at a corner table. He smiled over a glass of whisky.

Kay giggled and tried to lift her gin and tonic to her lips without letting her hand tremble. 'You shouldn't say things like that.'

'Like?'

'Do you come here often? I don't think we would want Paul Ritz to be quoted with such clichés falling from his lips, would we?'

'And how are you going to remember what I've said? No notebook or tape recorder – very unprofessional!'

'Oh, I'll remember everything.'

He laughed. She was really rather sweet. So fresh and honest. When she said she would remember, she would. Every detail. She would sweat to extract every possible nuance from his words. He grinned at her. 'Do you want to be a journalist, Kay?'

'I think so. I think that at least I want to be involved with writers.'

'And what else do you get up to at Oxford?'

'Oh, I don't know. I work quite hard. I do the social sort of things. Tea parties, champagne parties, *Isis* parties, exam parties . . . '

'You enjoy it?'

'Yes, it's great fun.'

'Tell me, talking of parties, what's the political scene like now? When I was here, we were all tremendously committed.'

'Not now. Well, there's the Union, which is really right wing, and there are a few public school boys pretending to be Marxists. I keep away from that, although my boyfriend, I mean a friend of mine, is quite involved in it.'

'Aha, the boyfriend. Who is the lucky man and what does he think of you flitting off to "morning coffee" with me?'

'With one of the world's most eligible bachelors? That hadn't occurred to me actually. Isn't your attitude a little old-fashioned? I'm not Bob's property and anyway he's in France.'

'You sound very monogamous. I thought Oxford was a den of promiscuity these days. Do you reserve your favours for just one man? I'm sure you have many admirers.'

'Mr Ritz, I don't want to offend you, but shall we keep the same ground rules for me as for you?'

'No personal questions? Well, well. You obviously know about mystique, for all your youth.'

'If, of course, you want to break the rules, I shall have to feel at liberty to do the same . . .'

'For *Isis*? What would *Isis* want with the intimacies of my life?'

'I could always sell the story elsewhere.'

'Hmm, very shrewd.' He laughed. 'I think not, on this occasion, however tempting the exchange. Shall we have a pax?'

'Another drink?' she asked.

'Well, I am experiencing the new feminist outlook. Yes. A whisky, please.'

'Actually, it's not as feminist as I would like. You see, I didn't bring any money out with me, but if you'll lend me five pounds, I'll write you a cheque.'

He threw back his head and roared with laughter. 'Kay, I'll say this for you. You've got guts. You'll make a good journalist, if that's what you want, but I'll get this round, if you'll allow me my small triumph.'

She found she was beginning to like him. His manner was

slightly patronizing and he obviously viewed the scenario as a bit of a joke, but his sense of humour was benevolent. And he was very beautiful. On television he was handsome, with the international good looks of a wealthy film star, but close up, his face was more human. There were slight wrinkles when he smiled, slight shadows under his eyes. His thick dark brown hair looked tousled, as if it had been hurriedly washed in the shower that morning and just left to dry. Without the touches of a make-up artist and a hairdresser, Paul Ritz was animated and extremely attractive. She noticed it most in the moments when he allowed himself to relax, like the split second before he took a sip of his drink, or when he laughed. It was as if his public personality and physical appearance were carefully imposed and cared for, and acted as a coat of varnish on his true self, restricting it and locking it behind a sheen of charm.

'And what will you do next?' she asked.

'Now that *Embassy* is published? I suppose I'll do another book at some stage. You're right. There is something satisfying about a book. But, before you ask, I don't have a concrete idea.'

'So, you'll continue to do articles until you come up with one, will you? I saw that recent series *Central America: Behind the Scenes*. I admired it greatly. But of course you came in for a lot of political flak for that.'

'Yes. It seems that nobody can cope with reportage these days. The left thinks I should be shouting slogans, the right thinks I'm subversive.'

'Certainly, you disappoint the left . . . ' Kay remembered Bob and his comrades' dislike of Ritz. They had proposed a motion at one of their interminable meetings to condemn him – 'this meeting strongly recommends that Paul Ritz be considered *persona non grata*'. Kay suppressed a giggle.

'Perhaps you'd care to explain why that amuses you?' He leaned towards her.

'No, it's nothing.' Kay smiled. 'I was just recalling a friend of mine who is involved in Nicaragua Libre or some such, proposing to consider you *persona non grata*. You were asking earlier about politics at Oxford. Well, there's a good example. A bunch of Hooray Henrys deciding to condemn a journalist on behalf of a people five thousand miles away, whom they have never seen or communicated with. No doubt there was a petition too. They're good at collecting signatures.' She was surprised at her own venom against Bob and felt momentarily disloyal.

Ritz looked at her with interest. The young ingénue had a barbed tongue. She wasn't a vapid little debutante. She was smart as a whip. An intriguing mixture of untarnished beauty and cutting intelligence. As a combination it was a turn on. She had, for all her eighteen or nineteen years, an inner poise which he liked. For a moment he toyed with the idea of whisking her back to London for a deliciously naughty weekend.

He would never have guessed it, but Kay's thoughts were running wildly in the same direction. She could not believe that she was sitting in an idyllic Woodstock pub sipping aperitifs and flirting with Paul Ritz. If this could happen, anything could . . . She thought he liked her. She could sense it by the way that he looked into her eyes. Vibes, as Zoe would say; there were definitely vibes.

She reminded him of someone. He studied her closely, but couldn't pinpoint it. Lolita, probably, he thought to himself. And that made him a pathetic Humbert Humbert. Ritz decided to call a halt to his fantasy. 'Well, love, charming as your company is, I must get back to London. I hope I haven't wasted your time.' He was mocking her.

She snapped herself back to reality. 'No, not at all. Can you drop me back in Oxford?'

'Of course, but I would like to tell you something, Kay . . .'

'Yes?' She looked at him dreamily.

'It is always advisable for a journalist to have the bus fare

72

home.' She laughed. She deserved that.

As he drove back to London, Ritz wished he had taken her number or her address. He had dropped her on the Broad and watched her run off towards the Bodleian, searching for a friend to tell. She had amused him. No, it was more than that. He felt a sort of warmth towards her. He would have liked to meet her again, take her to dinner at the Sorbonne, perhaps, as a rich uncle would. He had a wide smile on his face as he stopped in London's traffic. It was probably a very good thing he hadn't established contact. That feeling was definitely not avuncular.

But his chuckles turned briefly to frowns when she forwarded him a complimentary copy of the next month's *Isis*.

Who's afraid of the big, bad Ritz? he read. *He's got it all – dark eyes, a flashing smile, a red Ferrari and no doubt plenty of diamonds as big as the . . . I'm sure he'd like us to think he had a shady past, even links with the Mafia (Rizzoli is the name he was born with), but although he is surrounded by mystery and hounded into virtual exile by the world's press, I'm afraid it didn't take me long to discover Mr Ritz's darkest secret. He's a nice guy!*

He had underestimated her. She had been saucy enough to extract from the very little he had given her, a rather good and witty article. She had written up, quite honestly, but snappily, the entire meeting, gently mocking herself and totally destroying his carefully groomed image. It was a coup. He had to admire it. And he hoped that none of the Fleet Street editors lighted on a copy of *Isis*.

At the end of the Hilary term, Kay was unanimously voted editor of *Isis*. Zoe threw a surprise party in the house for her, and Kay was astonished to find that they knew so many people. Simon Leach buttonholed her at the end of the evening and kissed her hand. 'Why, Miss Trevelyan, I see that fame and literary fortune haven't gone to your head.

You're as demure as ever, despite your encounter with the dreaded Ritz. Tell me, was it *really* so innocent?'

'Unfortunately it was, Simon.'

'Aha! So you've fallen for him, niceness and all? But where, may I ask, is the other half of Oxford's prettiest heterosexual couple?'

'Bob? He's in Paris for the year.' Kay was furious with Bob. Zoe had told her that she had rung him to ask him to the party, but he had said he was too busy.

'Poor Bob. But I see you've found another beauty relatively easily.' Simon glanced at Will.

'Relatively, yes. Actually that's my nephew, Will.'

Will came over and put his arm around her shoulder. 'Is this terrible queen bothering you, angel?'

'No, no. I was just explaining our relationship. He thought we were lovers!'

'There's nothing wrong with incest, my dear, it's an outdated taboo.' Simon flounced away.

'Will,' she said, slightly annoyed. 'Why on earth did you call me angel in front of Simon?'

'Because you are my angel.'

'Oh, for God's sake. You're beginning to sound like Bob. Don't be so wet, even if you are drunk.'

'Sometimes, Kay, you can be a spoilt little bitch.' Will walked out of the party.

That remark had stung. There was venom in Will's eyes when he had said it. She hadn't seen much of him after that until the summer term. When he came round, it was obviously to see Zoe.

It was a particularly warm Sunday morning when Kay heard the doorbell ring. She had been up most of the night, writing a review of Anthony Burgess's *Earthly Powers*. She had been so engrossed in the book that it had been dawn when she finished it and she had scrawled three pages of adulation, which she was sure would be criticized when it appeared. It was such a clear, fresh morning that she

74

decided not to sleep, but bathed and put on a lemon-coloured cotton frock she had bought in the Easter holidays, thinking it would be perfect for summer in Oxford. It was. And the pleasure she had had in choosing it was reiterated as she found it hanging in her wardrobe.

There were several notes pinned to the noticeboard in the hall of the house, which Kay hadn't noticed before. Several were from Zoe. 'You haven't been seen alive for days. Where are you?' and 'Why have you got a DO NOT DISTURB notice on your door? Chuck and I want to know all about him.'

Kay smiled. Zoe would be disappointed that it was a book review and not a man that was occupying her time. Still, Bob would be back soon.

There were other notes. One from Simon Leach reading 'I've come miles out of my way to see you, beautiful child. Come immediately and drink champagne with me beneath a bower of roses.' And Delia's usual note: 'If messages are not taken down within twelve hours, they will be removed.' It was addressed 'To whom it may concern'. Poor Delia, thought Kay.

She was about to open the front door when the bell rang again and there was a pitter-patter of feet running down the stairs in answer to it. Delia came into the hall. She was wearing a pretty Laura Ashley dress.

'Oh, hello, you look nice,' said Kay.

Delia glowered at her. 'Can you see who that is, please?'

Kay opened the door. 'Will!' she said, smiling.

Delia looked at Kay. Her eyes were brimming with tears, her lips pursed and she stamped off saying, 'I might have guessed it would be for you.'

'Oh dear,' said Will. 'Have I interrupted a little tête-à-tête?'

'You must be joking.' Kay grinned. 'It's wonderful to see you.'

'I wondered if you'd like to go punting? I've got a punt booked at the Cherwell boathouse.'

75

'Oh, Zoe's not here at the moment.'

'No, actually I came to see you. What do you think?'

Kay didn't need to think. There was nothing she would rather do than go punting.

'You look lovely as always,' said Will as they walked along the shady residential streets towards the north end of the river.

'So do you,' said Kay. He was wearing a rather crumpled white suit, a navy-blue vest and plimsoles. He looked the picture of health, curling fair hair encircling his face, wide-spaced blue eyes and a ruddy complexion. There was something solid about Will. She could just picture him as a doctor in a white coat.

'How's work going, and how is life in general?' he asked. 'I haven't seen you for quite a while.'

'Oh, things are OK,' she said. 'I've been getting really interested in moral philosophy, of all things; there are some brilliant lectures by that American, Nagel. All my interests seem to be extracurricular at the moment. Moral philosophy, *Isis* . . . I've been up all night doing a book review. Have you read *Earthly Powers*? It's very flawed but quite brilliant. What about you?' She couldn't begin to describe the book to Will, who had always claimed that his favourite literature was Ian Fleming and the *Beano*. 'What about your finals? They must be really soon. I haven't seen you for such a long time, I had forgotten . . .'

'Oh, I'm trying to forget about them too.' Will grimaced. 'They're next week, as a matter of fact. I should sail through OK. As for not seeing me for quite a long time – well, that's what I thought too. So this morning I said to myself, no good sitting around and thinking about it. Go and see her. So here I am.'

'I'm glad.' Kay was relieved and surprised. They had reached the boathouse. Kay went to fetch cushions and Will chose a boat and a punting pole.

'Grab hold of this.' Will produced a bottle of white wine

as they swung out into the river. 'And open it.' A corkscrew miraculously appeared from his other pocket.

Kay took a swig of the warm wine and trailed her hand alongside the punt. 'Isn't the water beautiful?'

They were almost alone on the river. It was too early in the day for most students and tourists. Later on, it would be packed with inexpert punters colliding into each other, trying to race, or shouting abuse. Now they passed only a couple of punts that had become stuck in the weeds on the banks, and narrowly avoided a flotilla of canoes manned by children from the local prep school. But soon they were out in the country, gliding silently through lush green fields and the branches of willows that spilled over on to the river and cast shadows on the sunlit water.

When Will looked at Kay's girlish figure lying there in her lemon frock, sipping wine and smiling up at him, he saw her in all her facets. Her impertinently pretty face, with large, enquiring grey eyes and framed by a curtain of smooth black hair, hadn't changed much since she was a girl of ten. There was something gamine about her. Her face was all cheekiness and innocence, her posture balanced and confident. Men sought her admiration but at the same time they wanted to protect her.

Kay watched him and wondered why he was frowning. They had been punting in silence now for a good hour and the Victoria Arms, a well-known resting point for tired and thirsty punting parties, appeared in the distance.

'I'm hungry, let's stop and have something to eat.' Will aimed the boat at the bank and glided to a graceful halt. He held out his hand for Kay and as they jumped on to the bank he gave her a hug. They sat in the garden eating ham and egg pie and pickle with hunks of fresh bread. 'Well, Kay, here's to life!' He wrinkled his nose with pleasure. 'That seems to have become our toast. Here's to life!'

They were getting on so well, as they always had done. She really did like being with Will. Why couldn't it always be like this? He broke into her thoughts. 'You're supposed to raise your glass, or the bottle or something, you know. Chin chin! You're frowning.'

'Sorry.' She put down her glass and stretched lazily back on to the grass. 'It's been a good morning.'

'Yes, hasn't it. There won't be many more days like this for me with finals next week . . . Kay, there's something I wanted to say to you about us . . . but you're frowning again. Bloody hell, I'd almost forgotten what a temper you have. What have I said now?' He raised his hands in mock dismay. He was teasing but there was a note of determination in his voice.

'You look so earnest, Will. I'm sorry, I don't want to spoil it all by getting heavy. It's been such a lovely day, just like old times.'

'Like old times.' His voice was cold. 'Which particular old times are you referring to? Open your eyes, Kay, for God's sake. I'll be finished here in a couple of weeks. It's all gone so quickly. I don't want to leave Oxford feeling like this.'

'Like what?'

'Come on. Stop playing the little innocent, just because it's convenient. You know what I mean.'

'No I don't.'

'OK, if you insist on making things difficult . . . '

'I'm not insisting on anything, Will. I don't understand. What is it about this place that makes everyone so bloody dramatic? All about nothing.'

'Nothing?' His hands jerked upwards and knocked over the wine bottle. It rolled down the grass bank and fell over the edge. The glass shattered. Kay started to pick it up.

'Leave it, for God's sake, leave it,' Will shouted. 'It's only a bottle of fucking wine. Any excuse not to talk. Christ, you're hopeless.' The rage had gone out of his voice. 'Oh, what's the point. Look, I only wanted to tell you I'm sorry we didn't get on so well as we should have done. It was great at first. The four of us. But it hasn't been the same . . . not since you – well, since you and Bob started. You went and fell in love with my best friend right under my nose, and I found it difficult to take. It reminded me of us, you know, when we were at Sevenoaks. I didn't want to behave like I did. I didn't want to be angry with you and Bob, but I couldn't help it. I really couldn't. You know me. It's not like me to be all jealous and possessive like that. But you pissed me off.'

'Me?'

'Yes, you. You just didn't seem to notice me any more or to care. It was like you were happy so everyone else could look after themselves. You left it all up to me. Everything. I tried. I invited you to tea that time. I came to see you at Sevenoaks when Bob was there . . . '

Kay's face burned. She stared down at the lawn. Her hands nervously tore up clumps of grass from their roots.

'It was as if you didn't want to bother with me any more, so you just stopped thinking about me. Don't you see? Don't you understand?'

'No. I don't.' She leapt to her feet, her shoes caught in the hem of her dress and it ripped. Will was on his feet beside her.

'Kay, please. I want to leave here with good memories.'

'Well, what's stopping you?'

'Christ, you selfish bitch!'

'Don't call me that. You've no right. You've no right to me. Just because we once . . . ' She was overcome with rage. 'Christ, Will, just because we once played around in a bloody pond. We didn't even *do* anything. We were children. We didn't know what we were doing. I've forgotten it. Why can't you?'

He turned and began to walk away. People were staring at them. She ran after him.

'Will, look I'm sorry. I didn't mean it like that. I just lost my temper, that's all. Look, I'm sorry.'

'Are you? Well, tough shit. For once you can accept what you've done and said. I don't want to see you again. Not for a very long time. *Never*.'

The last year was flying by. It was the Hilary term already. Kay had buried herself in her work. She saw little of Zoe, even though they still shared rooms together. When he had returned from Paris Bob had tried to persuade her to move into a flat with him. But she had refused. She had felt guilty at first, feeling that she ought to want to live with Bob. After all, she was supposed to be in love with him, but when she had talked about it with Zoe, she had been dismissive. 'Oh, for heaven's sake, he's not worth it. You've got all your life to settle down in so-called romantic bliss. Bob just wants a wet nurse. Let him get on with it on his own.'

Kay had been enormously relieved but at the same time resentful. She didn't like it when Zoe was so disparaging about Bob. She knew she was partly right but it was a different matter actually saying it. She even found herself envying Zoe's relationship with Chuck. They really enjoyed being with each other. They laughed and joked just like the four of them had done in the first term. She, Zoe, Will and Bob. How long ago it all seemed now.

Life seemed to have lost its sparkle. She did nothing with Bob but quarrel. Perhaps she was just working too hard. All the parties seemed tame. Simon Leach and his friends had long since departed the dreaming spires, and Kay felt that she and the rest of those left were gradually relinquishing their hold on Oxford. The golden days were drawing to an end. Outside, the wide world beckoned and it frightened her. There was pressure to find a career, but she didn't know what she wanted to do. When she tried to talk about it with Bob, he pulled a long face and pontificated about how there was no point in worrying. She would be with him. He was going to write a novel, travel and see the world. But she did worry. Especially about the prospect of being with Bob. It occurred to her that she had always thought their relationship would end with Oxford.

Oxford. It had just slipped away. The last few grains of sand lay tantalizingly in her palm, reminding her there was still time, but so little. She found herself brooding more and more about what she had achieved. What had she done with it all? She wouldn't have missed it and yet what was it but petty dramas and disappointments. She found herself making a bargain with fate. If she worked really hard and got the first that she knew she could, she would be granted some sort of enlightenment about what to do next.

She began to miss Will. He might have understood. But would he? He was lucky. He had always known he wanted to be a doctor. She wondered if he missed her too and felt sad.

'Bob. It's funny, but sometimes I miss Will.' They were sitting at his large leather-topped desk, a row of Coca Cola cans and an ashtray full of cigarette stubs between them, trying to read.

'Why?'

'He's so sorted out . . .'

'Well, he doesn't miss you. I don't know what your big tiff was about, but he seems to have forgotten all about you. When I last saw him, he didn't even ask how you were. Anyway. You don't need him. I still love you.'

'So what?' Each time he made one of those remarks it irritated her more. She wanted to stop him, to hurt him for loving her too much. Or in the wrong way. She wouldn't allow him to love her in the way he wanted to. They were drifting apart. But Bob wouldn't let her get away so easily.

'So what?' He started scribbling notes and muttering under his breath. 'So what? The trouble with you is that you've fallen into the Oxford trap. Everyone tells you you're wonderful and you've actually started to believe it. You ought to have come to Paris and seen what life is really like, instead of writing pseudy articles about Paul Ritz for bloody *Isis*.'

'Thanks a lot. I'm glad you've finally told me what you think.' She was shouting. 'What the hell do you know about "real life" anyway? Living in a studio apartment

81

bought by Daddy in chic Montmartre, reading the thoughts of Chairman Mao in your armchair. It may have been Paris but it wasn't exactly May '68 was it? At least Paul Ritz actually knows what he's talking about.'

'You've got a real schoolgirl crush on that chap. It's pathetic,' Bob slammed back. 'Well, at least the women in Montmartre were a bit more sophisticated, if you know what I mean.'

'No I don't. What *do* you mean? Don't tell me you love me then taunt me with your sleazy affairs.'

'I didn't have any affairs. You know I didn't. I'm sorry. I was joking.'

'Bob. This is ridiculous.' Kay sighed. 'Let's go out and get some air. Why don't we go to the Woodstock roundabout café?'

'Why?'

'Nostalgia?'

'What? Gazing at each other over Formica tables in our youth?'

'Something like that.'

The café was deserted, apart from a motorcyclist playing pinball. They took a large table, spread out their books and drank coffee after coffee. Bob's hand crept across the table and touched her free fingers.

'See what I've written. Every time I should have put *Thérèse Raquin*, I've put Kay Trevelyan. You're obsessing me.'

They exchanged looks. Both acknowledged that they were getting into the realm of desperate gestures. Kay knew that they would have to separate. And when she thought about it in bed that night, she recalled the story of Thérèse Raquin. A woman who had married her cousin and then fallen in love with his best friend. The lovers had drowned the husband and been tormented by his ghost. It was gruesome. Kay wondered if Bob had meant something by his confusion of their names, consciously or subconsciously.

But she didn't dare ask. Instead she got up and began to dress. Bob stirred in his sleep and then woke.

'What's up?' he asked.

'I'm leaving.'

'You can't. What do you mean?' He was suddenly nervous.

'I'm leaving for tonight. Maybe for ever. It's got to end, Bob. We're not happy any more. Anyway, I've got work to do. I can't sleep here.'

'You bitch. Don't you think I've had enough of all your bloody irrelevant work. I don't give a fuck if Kay Trevelyan gets a first . . .'

'You bastard. You don't really care about me at all, do you?' she shouted. It was a rhetorical question.

'Not when you're having a tantrum.'

'Well, if that's how you see it. If you think all these rows are just me having tantrums. I'm quite calm. You're the one having a tantrum. I'm not going to waste any more time arguing with you. I've got work to do.'

'But you can't leave. Not now. It's three o'clock in the morning. Let's go back to bed. You'll have got over it in the morning. Anyway, the gates are locked. The porter will see you.'

'I'm going, right now. Goodbye.'

She walked out into the perfect, balmy June night, shaking. She breathed in great draughts of the summer air. 'You can't go now, the porter will see you.' It was typical of Bob to say something like that. In the middle of the most tremendous crisis he would come out with the trivial. He just didn't understand it had all become too much for both of them. They had been clinging to each other, frightened of being apart, but they could not be together.

When she arrived back, Chuck was sitting in her room.

'Hi! What are you doing in my room at this time of night?' Kay said, surprised but pleased to see him. 'How

83

was your ice hockey? Did you win?'

'Sit down.'

'OK. Do you want something to drink? I could do with one. I've just had an enormous row with Bob. I don't know why I feel so calm about it, but I am.'

'Sit down. I've got something to tell you.'

'What? Where's Zoe, anyway? *You* haven't been having a row too, have you?'

'Zoe's had an accident. She went off to a party in Oseney and fell off her bike in to the Cherwell . . . '

'Typical! Oh, she's not hurt is she?'

'She's dead.'

Kay spent the rest of the term in a daze. After a week or two, she found she couldn't cry any more. She felt as if everything inside her had gone. She was filled with a sense of waste. How was it that such a vital person could be extinguished? Zoe had gone to a party on her own, drunk too much and decided to cycle home along the dark towpath. She had veered off, concussed herself and drowned in the murky waters of the Cherwell. Things like that didn't happen. You read about them in the papers but it was inconceivable that it should happen to one of your friends. Kay was furious with fate and furious with herself.

'You couldn't have done anything about it, don't punish yourself,' Bob told her. But Kay wasn't sure he was right. What if she hadn't been with Bob? Would Zoe have been going to that party? And even if she had, Kay would have ordered a taxi, or walked. If Kay had been with her it would not have happened. At least, it wouldn't have happened like that. If Kay had been there it wouldn't have been the same. Zoe couldn't have been predestined to die like that. Anything might have altered it. She had never told Zoe how much she liked her, what their friendship had meant to her. How much she relied on Zoe's ability to cope, even her scathing remarks.

That summer was a particularly hot and sunny one and it

seemed to Kay that the elements were playing a sick joke on her, conspiring to make Oxford attractive. The sun tinted the old sandstone buildings, the skies were blue. Other students were taking out punts, revelling at the Summer Balls. Every garden that the attic room looked down upon seemed to be the venue for champagne parties. Girls in white flouncey dresses flirted with men in boaters. It was the very atmosphere that Kay had found so enchanting in previous years. It was hard to believe that she had wandered arm in arm with Bob, hard to believe that she had worn cottony frocks and straw hats and stood talking about art with Simon Leach. She could see the same scenarios existed for other people and could still exist for her, but a row of printed invitation cards gathered dust on her mantelpiece.

When she tried to work, she would sit staring at the words and realize after about an hour that although she had turned over pages, she had read nothing. She sat finals, but her papers for which she had worked so hard seemed insignificant now. Her body and mind were numb, except for her anger at Bob. He was devastated too, at first. But now he said that she should pull herself together.

'Don't you see that you have more pity for yourself than for Zoe?' he said. 'Life must go on.'

After all, he said, the fate of one individual had no significance in the human struggle for survival. If Kay could only be philosophical about it, she wouldn't be so upset.

She couldn't believe that he could forget so easily. That he could happily turn his mind away from the horror and 'get on with the revolution'. She began to hate him and every moment she spent with him. In the end she told him that the only way she would get over Zoe was to be on her own for a while. He finally seemed to accept that this might be a sensible arrangement. In the end their relationship just fizzled out. She didn't even have the strength to know any more whether that was what she wanted.

She had seen Will at the funeral. He had sent a wreath of white lilies. Kay was choked with tears when she saw it. But they hadn't spoken. Kay had been too occupied with her own emotions, desperately trying not to break down in front of everyone. It was bad enough for Zoe's parents without that. Outside the church she had tried to catch Will's eye, hoping he would come over. But he hadn't noticed and had left soon after to go back to London. Somewhere inside herself, something told Kay she ought to do something, write to him, say how sorry she was because Zoe had been his friend too, but she was so drained, so empty, she almost didn't care.

FORTUNE COOKIES

NEW YORK

SPRING 1982

'Thank you.' Kay gazed forlornly at the hygiene-wrapped tray of food in front of her and thought how different airline meals always looked from the way they were described on the menu. *Tournedos Bourguignon avec Pommes de Terre Anna* followed by *Poires Belle Hélène* looked for all the world like canned stew and packet mashed potato with tinned pears.

'You're welcome!'

That sugary phrase was just one of the things she would have to get used to she supposed. Kay ordered a gin and tonic, paid for headphones, and settled down into the musak as the Atlantic Ocean drifted on thirty thousand feet below. Well, she had got this far without too much trouble. At least she was doing something. Those last few months in London had been like a limbo state which she was doomed never to escape, until Chuck's phone call.

She had failed to prepare herself at all for life after Oxford. In the last spring term she and Zoe had made tentative approaches to the careers advisory board. Zoe had decided to apply for a traineeship at the BBC but had never got around to filling in the forms. Kay had considered the possibility of research. There had been a lot of thinking and discussing but in the end neither of them had actually done anything. In that cocooned and rarefied atmosphere the future had seemed far away. And when Zoe had died, there hadn't seemed to be any future at all. It was only when her father had driven her to the flat in London, unpacked the cases from the car and left her on her own, that Kay had sat down and wondered what she would do the next day, and the day after that.

The flat where she was to live was on the first floor of a pastel Georgian house in Chalcot Square. Kay's father had used it as a *pied-à-terre* in London in the heyday of his career, and now that he was retired and came to London infrequently, he had suggested that rather than sell it, it would be sensible for Kay to live there. Kay had leapt at the opportunity at the time and had tentatively asked Zoe if she would like to share it with her. They had made plans to redecorate and have cocktail parties. 'Eat your heart out, Bloomsbury,' Zoe had joked. 'We'll start the Primrose Hill Set.' But, somehow, Kay hadn't got around to redecorating it on her own. It was more comforting to sit gloomily in the dark panelled front room and think what it would have been like, if only . . .

After a few weeks of doing not much else, she had decided to do a secretarial course, partly to fill her days and give her some prospect of earning money, and partly to quash the guilt she felt whenever her parents came to visit her and asked her what she was planning. They had been kind, almost too kind, supplementing her dole money with regular cheques and taking her out to tea once a month. But all their well-intentioned gestures made Kay feel even more of a failure. They would never understand what Oxford and all that went with it had meant to her, because in the final analysis it had been her liberation from them. The chasm of love and understanding that had always separated her from her family, gaped wider still when Zoe and Bob and Will were not around to fill it. She knew they talked to each other about her 'pulling herself together', but she couldn't even begin to think where the pieces of her life had gone. Even in the three months she spent up until Christmas, in a crowded classroom, tapping away on a typewriter and surrounded by girls of her own age, she had made no friends. She sat alone in the coffee bar in their breaks, while the others grouped themselves together and made in-jokes about the instructor. It began to remind Kay of school. She wondered if she would ever make friends again. Whatever way she tried to rationalize her inability to be companionable, it always came back to the same thing: she had lost everything that mattered to her. Everything that had seemed to be her right.

Bob had finally broken the few strands of confidence she had left. He had sent her a postcard saying he would be in town and would she meet him 'for old times sake'. They had met in a crowded pub in Camden, and he had drunk bottled Guinness and taunted her for drinking gin and tonic. 'I see you're as cool and unattainable as ever.' His words still rang in her head. If there had been no final ending at Oxford she knew that evening that it was over. Their conversation had been stilted and Bob had taken every opportunity to criticize her. When they said goodbye and she walked away into the grey, drizzling night she had not looked back at him once.

When Chuck rang out of the blue from America with the suggestion that she might want to get away from it all, live in New York as an au pair for his sister, it had been deliverance. After months of lethargy there were two weeks of whirlwind panic to get a visa, new underwear and a ticket. Now she was actually on the plane and New York only a couple of hours away. Some of the adrenalin that had drained from her body was flowing again in her veins. Who cared whether it was the right thing to do? It was *something* to do. She was getting away from it all and she was going to give it all she had got.

She glanced at her watch. They would arrive in one hour. Kay went to wash her face and brush her hair in the washroom and as she applied just a little lip gloss, she noticed something unfamiliar about her mouth. It was smiling.

'So tell me, what on earth did you want to leave England and become an au pair for?' Chuck's sister Ellen asked Kay

91

when she had been in New York a few days.

'Well, lots of reasons really.'

'And one of them has got to be men, right? This Bob guy Chuck told me about. He was your boyfriend all the time you were at Oxford, but you've broken up, right?'

After a week of it, Kay was just about getting used to Ellen's frankness but she felt the reference to Bob was going too far. She was saved by the baby who gave a loud bawl and Ellen's attention was immediately distracted.

'You try, Kay. No! How many times do I have to tell you not to be too gentle. Babies hate to feel you're not in control. Just handle her like she's a lump of dough or something. Her diaper, or nappy as you so quaintly call it, needs changing. Go on, have some practice. Just forget you have a sense of smell.'

Kay gingerly fumbled with the safety pins and the baby began to cry.

'Hey! Keep those pins away from her or she'll stab her eyes out. Be firm. Go on. Oh God, there's the 'phone.' Ellen marched across the room.

'That was Chuck. Says he's coming in for the weekend for a party. He'll pick you up on Saturday at about ten o'clock. Hope that fits in with your plans.' Ellen was talking at top volume before she even entered the room. 'Here, give me my baby.' Francesca was cleaned, powdered and changed in an instant. 'Here, Kay, take her. I'm going to get us a beer. It'll open you up a bit. We'll be seeing a lot of each other, so I don't want any of this English reserve. I've been waiting to hear all about you ever since you recovered from jet lag, but you're not exactly forthcoming. You like being here, don't you? Not feeling homesick or anything?'

'No and yes.' Kay laughed. 'I mean yes, I think I like it and no, definitely not homesick.'

Kay had wondered how long it would take her new employer to break down her reserves. Not long, she had concluded. In Rome you must do as the Romans. In New

York, she would have to bare her soul. Well, a little of it, anyway.

'Well?'

'I won't bore you with all the details . . . '

'You bet you won't.' Ellen beamed. 'Cheers!' They clinked glasses over the sleeping baby's head.

'In answer to your question, several reasons really. My last year at Oxford. I'm sure Chuck's told you something about it . . . '

'And?'

'When Oxford finished I didn't know what to do, careerwise. I spent a few months in London and then Chuck invited me out here to work for you and Francesca. I thought time would help sort things out a bit.'

'Things?'

'Oh well . . . ' Kay was finding this all very difficult. 'Well, I see you won't be satisfied with bare bones so . . . I had a brilliant first year at Oxford, loved my subject, made real friends for the first time, had a boyfriend – yes, Bob. It was idyllic. But by the end of Oxford everything had gone wrong. You know about Zoe dying . . . she's the first person I had ever known who had died. It shook me up. I blamed myself. I still do . . . '

'Yeah, Chuck told me you took it real hard. He was pretty broken up about it I think, but then men tend to internalize their feelings, don't they?'

'Yes, I suppose you're right. What made it worse for me was that it all happened at the same time. Zoe died. Bob and I broke up, although I sometimes find it hard not to think of him as my boyfriend, and Will, my nephew, sort of gave up on me.'

'Nephew?' Ellen's eyebrows interrogated Kay.

'Yes, he is the same age as me, nearly . . . and he used to be my closest confidant. Oh, it's too complicated to explain.'

'Really?' Ellen sounded disappointed.

'Yes, but there are other reasons why I am here too. I'm

93

determined to have a terrific time. I'm going to explore New York from top to bottom and take a very close look at your social mores.' Ellen burst into peals of laughter. 'And I'm going to get my shit together, as I suppose you'd say. So there we are. In a nutshell, that's why I'm here.'

'I'll drink to that!' Ellen applauded and then became more serious. 'Look, since you seem to be OK with the kid, I've decided to go back to work as soon as possible. In fact, tomorrow. I might as well start as I mean to go on. I think you can cope. Don't worry, it'll be fine. So, why don't you take the rest of today off and go into Manhattan. It's the last chance you'll get to see it on a weekday. Take a look at some stores, take in a gallery, get yourself a real American hamburger.'

Kay leapt at the offer. 'The only thing is, Ellen, you'll have to give me full instructions about how to find my way about. I don't understand the numbering of the streets. I had a look at the subway map and it all looks a bit daunting. I was sort of hoping that Chuck would show me around a bit.'

'You'll never find out anything from Chuck. He takes cabs everywhere, and on the salary I'm paying you, I'm telling you you won't be able to afford that! Anyway, Chuck is in Boston most of the time. Don't you have anyone else to look up in New York?'

'No, I don't know a soul here.'

'Well, the British are supposed to be reserved, but this is absurd! Don't worry, you'll soon meet people. New York's like that. I'll explain the subway and the grid system. It's much easier than London, where all the streets have names. All you have to know here is that avenues to the east of Fifth or Central Park are numbered from one to five. Although there isn't a fourth, and there are a couple that do have names liike Lexington, Park and Madison. Oh, and there's Alphabet City on the Lower East Side, but you won't go there, if you value your life. Anyway, avenues to the west of Fifth are numbered from six upwards, although

94

they have names too. Kay, you are right. When you don't know it, it is very complicated!'

Kay was more nervous than she cared to show. When the snow had let up for the first time, Ellen had taken her and the pram for a walk along the promenade in Brooklyn Heights. From there, Kay had caught her first real glimpse of New York. Right up the river from Wall Street to the Empire State Building and beyond, and down to the Statue of Liberty, Staten Island and the Verrazano Bridge. Kay had felt that she was looking at a picture postcard or a travel brochure from TWA. Everything was just as she had imagined New York to be, even the noise from the Brooklyn-Queens Expressway, one hundred yards from the apartment with its constant hum of traffic, punctuated by the wailing of police sirens. It all looked and sounded unreal. Kay hadn't been able to believe she was there. She had felt she had been transported to an alien environment.

For an English person, or indeed any foreigner, Kay decided, visiting New York was not quite like visiting any other city. Paris or Rome had an atmosphere all of their own that could not be caught on celluloid. New York was different. From the towering skyscrapers of Wall Street to the gleaming cupola of the Chrysler Building; from the flashing neon of Times Square to the steam rising from the vents in the streets; from Little Italy to Harlem, everything was just as she had always expected it to be. The hot dog sellers on Fifth Avenue, the pimps on 42nd Street, the students in Washington Square, the black limousines in Little Italy and even the denizens of the subway all looked like extras from an episode of Kojak, or as if they wandered out of the French Connection.

As she emerged from the subway, outside Blooming-dales, Kay's apprehension vanished. Not only did three people in succession ask her directions, but on one occasion she was able to give a correct answer. Her careful study of Ellen's map, and the down jacket Ellen had lent her, made her feel and look suddenly like a native. The only giveaway was the English accent. When she ventured into a small bar and asked for a cup of coffee, the waitress had looked startled.

'Excuse me, Ma'am?'

'A cup of coffee, please.'

'Oh . . . Caawfee . . . Jesus, are you English or something?'

On that first day, Kay was to see only a small part of Lexington Avenue – ten blocks of shopping streets in the driving snow, but she was to come back feeling exhilarated, refreshed and eager to explore. When she returned to the apartment, her face chapped by the wind and her eyes sparkling, she related every detail of her adventure to Ellen, right down to the purchase of her first pair of designer jeans at Bloomingdales.

'I knew you'd love it,' said Ellen. 'New York is the best place to live in the world. You thought today was good, just wait until the snow melts then you'll find out what really having fun is all about.'

'So how are you getting on with my bossy sister?' Chuck asked Kay. 'And how is she getting on with "having a baby on her own"? I bet it's more work than she thought it would be.'

'I like her enormously,' Kay said. 'I think Francesca is more than she bargained for and she's really tired when she gets in from work, but we're coping.' They were in a cab driving over Brooklyn Bridge. The hum of the tyres on the metal drainage ridges in the road, which sounded like a squadron of jets flying over, and the floodlights on the cathedral arches of the bridge and the panoramic view were mesmerizing. Kay was only vaguely aware of Chuck's questions.

'So you've settled in?'

'Yes, I'm very happy, thank you.' Kay steered clear of another emotional grilling. 'Tell me about this party we're going to.'

'Well, I'm not quite sure myself. It was just a vague invite from a friend of a friend, but I thought I'd use it as an excuse to come down and see how you've settled in, and to show you off a bit.'

'Show me off?'

'Well, introduce you to a few people and that sort of thing. Well, actually Kay, to be honest, the girl who is giving the party is someone that I've fancied for ages. I thought that if I brought you along, she might get the traditional feelings of jealousy and realize what she is missing. You don't mind, do you?'

No, thought Kay, she had no reason to mind. All the same it was a bit much to be told you were being asked along to make someone else jealous. She didn't really want to be party to a macho plot.

'You look so bored.'

The voice was that of a New York gay. Kay didn't know how she knew. It was almost like a code. Not as obvious as wearing an earring as they did in England, or having keys dangling from the belt loops of their jeans as she heard the fashion was in Los Angeles, but just as effective.

'No, I'm not bored.' How many times were people to tell her she looked bored? 'I'm just observing people from a comfortable distance.'

Kay's eyes travelled around the room. Some bizarre things were happening for sure. The room was an enormous loft in a street on the Upper West Side. It looked more like a dance studio than an apartment.

There was no furniture at all apart from an upright piano and a couple of chairs. A garish mural covered one wall, the others were bare. A group of people in one corner were passing round a mirror and sniffing lines of cocaine that had been carefully assembled by the hostess, a tall androgynous female who had painted her face into an exact replica of the cover of David Bowie's *Aladdin Sane*. A zig-zag of colour from her forehead to her chin, and her scarlet hair swept back from her face, made it impossible to imagine what she must look like when she went to work, if indeed she did. Perhaps she was a pop singer. Chuck had taken one look at her and decided hastily that perhaps she wouldn't be the ideal girlfriend for him after all. Kay had asked whether she always looked like that. Chuck thought not but found it hard to remember what she had looked like before.

'She seems to turn up at practically every party I ever go to in New York. It doesn't matter who is giving the party, from Ellen's friends to my old roommates at Columbia. I guess I must have been drunk or something to think that I fancied *that*,' he had added, and sloped off to the kitchen, leaving Kay unintroduced.

Others were dancing balletically to the music. Two men were openly necking on one of the chairs. Her eyes returned to the man who had spoken.

'Is this an unusual party, do you think?' she asked him.

'You're English, aren't you?' He looked delighted. 'I *love* the English. I'm practically English myself, you know, at least my grandfather was, I think. How lucky to have discovered you.'

Kay eyed him closely. There didn't appear to be any innuendo in his words. He was obviously genuine.

'Tell me your name,' he went on. 'You don't mind me taking you over, do you? I notice that clodhopper you arrived with has sequestered himself in the kitchen with a terrible JAP and they're eating bologna sandwiches. Gross! You're not married to him are you?'

'Chuck is in the kitchen with a Japanese lady, is he? No, I'm not married to him. Do I look like a married woman?'

'Japanese lady? What is this? Don't you know what a JAP is? It means Jewish American Princess. You can't have been in New York long. They are one of our most recognizable ethnic categories. And *no* you don't look married. In fact, you look rather virginal . . . No . . . now I see I've overstepped the mark. Forgive me, whatever your name is, and let me make amends by asking you to dance. I

98

just know you'll dance beautifully and *won't* all the others be jealous when they see me dancing with a beautiful English maiden! My name is Jerome.'

His words brought the memories flooding back. She had practically the same conversation with Simon Leach all those years ago in Oxford. It could be a good omen. That conversation had also taken place at a party and had marked the beginning of a very happy and blissful period of her life.

'Tell me all about the royal family,' Jerome persisted. 'I love the royal family. It's such a shame that we don't have anything like that in America. Except Jackie O, of course, and Nancy Reagan's trying hard. But they're poor substitutes. Do you think the royal baby will be a girl or a boy?'

'Quite honestly, I have really no idea, and I don't care.' Kay couldn't make out whether Jerome was mocking her and felt guarded.

'Oh, don't tell me that you're a cynic. I can't believe it. All that wide-eyed innocence, and underneath a heart of stone? I'm not going to let you pretend.'

'All right, you win!' Kay smiled. 'I think it will be a boy.'

'I knew it. You're a secret monarchist. By the way, have you noticed my hairstyle. Doesn't it remind you of somebody?'

Kay perused his blond coiffure. It was shoulder length at the back and swept back from his face.

'Oh no . . . it's not . . . ?'

'Yes, it is. It's the only Princess Diana haircut in New York. My hairdresser took a lot of trouble with it. I even had to buy a copy of *People* magazine with her Royal Highness on the front cover in profile, so that he could get it exactly right. It's lost on most people. But I knew you would appreciate it.'

Kay didn't know what it was about Americans, but one seemed to form an immediate superficial friendship with them. Right from the traditional greeting 'How are you?', there was something familiar about the briefest of conversations. After five minutes in the company of Jerome she had learnt the most intimate details about him, yet she still wasn't sure whether he was telling the truth. Everything he said seemed exaggerated and unusual. He had a fascination with the rich and famous, which he had managed to exploit in his career. He was working as a photographer's assistant on a magazine that dealt exclusively with describing and displaying the interiors of the glitterati's apartments. Kay liked him.

'You can tell so much from going into people's houses,' he said. 'Now, for instance, what would you say about the person who lives in this loft?' Kay shrugged her shoulders. 'What you see is a room that someone is just about to move out of. Our dear hostess was living here with an artistic type as you can see from that rather tasteless mural. He was going to paint the whole room like that, but, happily, they had a row, and he upped and left, taking everything with him. One day the room was filled with his furniture, brushes, easels and the biggest bed you have ever seen, right in the middle, like a sort of altar, and the next day, when Addy came back from work, everything was gone. He left the fridge and the piano, and a couple of pieces of clothing . . . '

'God, he sounds horrible. Was she terribly upset?'

'Addy? I don't think so. The first thing she thought of doing was having a party with all this free space. She always manages somehow, doesn't she?'

'I wouldn't know. I haven't met her.'

'Haven't met Addy? How extraordinary! But then you have only been here for a week, haven't you? I'm sorry, how very remiss of me. You must be introduced. Now I come to think of it, someone once told me she was English. I wonder if she is. You wouldn't know. She has lost all trace of an accent. I must introduce you and maybe you can persuade her to readopt those gloriously clipped vowel sounds. How exciting!'

Why on earth, thought Addy, as she tried to curl up and sleep on an armchair in the dawn hours of the next morning, did I sniff so much coke? She knew that when she woke up the mess of spilt wine, beer cans, melted ice, piles of ash and cigarette butts, would cause her a lot of grief. But her mind was racing. It had been a great party. She didn't realize she knew so many people. Those few weeks with Jean Pierre had really cut her off from the normal social scene.

Jean Pierre! How could she have fallen for someone called Jean Pierre? He wasn't even French. Where was it he came from? Indiana! It was funny when you looked at it that way. It hadn't been so funny to come home and find the whole apartment looted, but what the hell. She could put it down to experience. Again. Why was it that at twenty-three she still continued to fall in love with the most idiotic men? Jean Pierre had been pretty hopeless at everything. His paintings were laughable. The graffiti artists on the subway had a lot more flair. And the sex! He was as self-satisfied about his sexual prowess as he had been about the mural. Not surprising, really, they were both forms of masturbation.

Addy smiled. She hadn't seen that before. Pity she hadn't said that to him when they argued. Anyway, she was popular. The party had proved that, hadn't it? Hadn't someone said that Andy Warhol turned up? She hadn't seen him, but it would make a good story. She shivered. She would have to get some blankets when she moved into the new apartment. Where had she put her fur coat? She would never get to sleep feeling so cold. It was nowhere to be seen. Maybe someone had taken it. No, now she remembered, she had been advised that it would look better if kept at a constant cool temperature. She had left it in the deep freeze before the party.

It was rock hard when she managed to chip it out and she sighed as she brushed the frost from it. Ruined. And how was she ever going to get any sleep? Then, with a flash of inspiration, she turned on the electric oven, leaving the door open. She closed the kitchen door and curled up on the long wooden draining board. And that was how Kay found her the next afternoon.

Kay had left the party at about four o'clock. Jerome had found her a cab and she had arrived back at Brooklyn Heights to find Ellen feeding Frannie and singing lullabyes to her.

'Thank God you're home! You didn't come back on the subway, did you?'

'No, I took a cab.'

'So where is Chuck? Why didn't my preppie brother escort you home?'

'Well, he left a little while before me with a Barbra Streisand lookalike, and they didn't look as if they wanted to make it a threesome. But I had a great time. Met several weird people, danced a lot.'

'Initiation into New York by fire, I see. Good, I'm glad. Will you be seeing any of them again?'

'Someone said something about all going back to the apartment today and helping the girl who gave the party to clear up. Then going for brunch. I thought I would go along.'

'That's terrific . . . now, can you just grab hold of Fran and burp her for me while I change her bed?'

'Hello?'

Kay pushed open the loft door. The sun was streaming in through the large windows at the far end of the room. Outside, the snow was melting and there was a real feeling of spring in the air. A few leaves had begun to sprout on the trees on the edge of Central Park West. Children were sloshing about in the snow, trying to form snowballs from the fast melting slush, while their parents looked on. Many of them had carrier bags with Zabars written on the outside, from which they produced delicious-smelling

102

croissants and bagels. Kay's appetite was ready for the amazing brunch that Jerome had described the night before as the best part of living in America.

She had expected to find the mess almost cleared up by now. It was after midday. But as soon as she opened the door, she realized that the place hadn't been touched since the night before. There were bottles everywhere and a dustbin, which had been full of cans of beer on ice, was upturned, the contents ransacked. Some of the ice had melted in the heat of the party but had reformed in the night in great slippery puddles on the floor. There was no sign of anyone about.

'I've missed them,' Kay thought. She had no idea where they might have gone, so decided to wait and do the best she could herself until they returned. Perhaps there would be some garbage bags in the kitchen that she could start collecting some of the rubbish into.

A belt of heat hit her in the face as she opened the kitchen door. It was like opening a furnace. She had to step back and catch her breath. Something in there had the distinct smell of wet dog. But there was nothing there apart from the large refrigerator, several empty bottles, the ends of a few french loaves and, on the draining board, a body, half covered with a ragged-looking coat from which two silver-clad legs dangled into the sink. The oven door was open and for an instant Kay thought that she was the first witness on the scene of a suicide.

'Oh, my God,' she said under her breath.

The body stirred and a face appeared from under the coat. 'Who the hell are you?' it rasped.

'I'm Kay, we met last night.' It struck her as odd to be exchanging formalities with an angry face covered in smeared paint.

'Oh, hi. You gave me a bit of a shock. Have you been here all night?'

'No, I came to help clear up. We all agreed to come along and help you move out. But I seem to be the only one here as yet.'

'As yet? As ever. People are always saying that they'll come and help clear up, but you're the first I've ever known who's dumb enough to do so. Sweet of you though.' Addy made a great effort to manoeuvre herself off the draining board and she marched past Kay into the bathroom. Kay wondered if she should go. She had just decided to make a quick exit when she was stopped in her tracks.

'Bloody hell!' shouted Addy from the bathroom. 'I look like a peacock just shat on my head.' Kay burst into giggles. It was a surprisingly accurate description.

Addy sang in the shower and five minutes later appeared, scrubbed clean and wearing nothing but a very small hand-towel around her waist.

'I think I left my only other clothes in the top of that piano over there. Do you think you could retrieve them for me?'

Kay opened the piano and sure enough there was a pair of jeans and an emerald silk shirt stuffed amongst the hammers and wires, and leather ankle boots exactly the same colour as the blouse.

'Thanks a lot,' said Addy, donning them. 'For a moment when I came back into the kitchen, I thought you'd gone. Anyway, I wanted to tell you that I had a brilliant thought in the shower. Can't think why it didn't occur to me before. I'm supposed to move into my new room today. Well, I say room, but I use the term loosely. In fact, it's more like a box, but never mind. I'm sick of all this space . . . Anyway, that's not the point . . . what I'm trying to say is that this place here is not rented in my name. The landlord doesn't know I exist. So I can just leave and forget about clearing up. If anyone complains about the mess, they'll have to complain to Jean Pierre in Indiana, won't they? Do you know Jean Pierre?' She added aggressively.

'No.'

'Well, if you did, you'd know that he deserves what I'm about to do to him, OK?'

'OK.' There didn't seem any point in disagreeing.

'Well, let's go eat, then.'

104

'But don't you have any suitcases?'

'No, all I have is a bag. Now, where is it?' After some searching they found it was in the freezer, cold, but intact. 'I must have put it in there with the coat,' said Addy enigmatically. 'Tell me, since you seem to be my guardian angel of the moment, do you happen to know anything about restoring furs?'

Kay rather liked her image as a guardian angel. 'I'm afraid I don't.'

'Too bad. I was beginning to like you.' Addy laughed, took Kay's arm and guided her purposefully to the door.

Minutes later, Kay was to discover where all the shopping bags marked Zabars that she had seen in the park came from. It was a huge delicatessen on Broadway filled with mouthwatering aromas. Addy ordered two cappucinos which were frothy and speckled with cinnamon. Kay could feel the caffeine coursing through her veins. There was a moment of silence as both took stock of one another, enjoying the coffee. Then they both spoke at once.

'I'm rather hungry.'

'Jesus, I'm starved.' And both laughed.

'Look, I don't know how to put this, Kay, but I'm broke. If you want to eat, go ahead. I'm supposed to be on a diet anyway.'

'Don't be silly. I'll buy some food. I've got plenty of money on me. Anyway, you couldn't get any thinner if you tried.' Addy was tall and slim as a bean pole.

'OK. You twisted my arm. But I promise to pay you back. I'd sell you my coat, only it's probably not worth a lot now.'

They bought ham and salami and bagels and a bottle of red wine and walked back up Broadway. Addy's box was on the top floor of a seedy hotel on 100th Street.

'I'm supposed to clean the foyer and corridors of this whorehouse in exchange for the room. But I don't think they'll notice if I don't, do you?'

It was extremely grimy, but the room itself, although

105

small, had a shower cubicle and a huge double bed. There was a rail along one side with some wire coat hangers on it. And, to Addy's delight, there were a couple of blankets on the bed.

'Oh well, it's Manhattan and it's home,' she said, plunging into the paper bag.

'We don't have a corkscrew,' said Kay, as Addy took out the wine with a flourish.

'Well, that's exactly where you are wrong,' Addy replied, fumbling in the copious tapestry bag they had earlier retrieved from the fridge. 'There are many essentials of life in here, including . . . ' She withdrew them one by one. ' . . . a clean pair of knickers, a toothbrush, pills of varying kinds . . . God, I've got some Quaaludes, wish I had remembered that last night . . . photographs, my expired passport, one dollar and seventy-five cents in cash – that's if you include the subway token – and da de da da, a corkscrew!'

The next few moments were given over to eating and drinking in hasty gulps from the bottle.

'So what's a nice English girl like you happen to be doing in New York? Obvious question, I know, but we have to start somewhere.'

'I may be English but I'm not sure I fit the description "nice".'

'Hey, come on. It was only a flip remark. Besides, it's not the way I'd describe you straight off.'

'No?'

'Oh, some other time. This is getting pretty complicated. Back to the basics. What are you doing here?'

'Well, it's illegal but I'm being an au pair.'

'You can't tell me anything about illegalities I don't know. I'm English too, lived here for quite a while. My immigration slip ran out years ago. How did you come to be at my party, anyway? I hadn't met you before. Did you know that Andy Warhol called in and I didn't even see him?'

106

'God, what a shame, neither did I. Wish I had. That would really be something to write home about . . . No, I came to the party with Chuck Hamilton. I met him in England and I'm working for his sister out here.'

'Chuck Hamilton? The name doesn't ring a bell . . . I don't think I've ever met him, have I?'

'Apparently you have, several times, but . . . '

'But he's pretty unmemorable, right?'

'Well, I suppose he is but he's quite a useful soul to have around at times.' Kay could see no reason why a person like Addy should remember Chuck, but she felt a twinge of guilt at her own summary dismissal of him.

'So did you meet anyone interesting?'

'I spent most of the evening with Jerome.'

'Ah, Jerome. He's a pet, isn't he? I just adore Jerome. Pity he's gay, although I think I might convert him one day. You did know he was gay, didn't you?'

'Yes, I gathered that.' Kay was offended. Did she look *so* innocent?

'Jerome has such an interesting job. He knows where everyone who is anyone lives. He took me on a tour of New York of the famous once. Did you know that he actually photographed Bianca Jagger's apartment?'

Addy chattered on, dropping names in every sentence. A couple of times Kay thought to herself, What on earth am I doing sitting in a room above a brothel in Manhattan, talking about people I've never met with someone I don't know? But she warmed to Addy. She liked her American accent which just occasionally would slip back to English before she checked herself and used a phrase that Kay could never have heard before.

On her way to her evening bar job, Addy looked forward to the prospect of showing Kay New York. She had already decided she would see her again. She had thought her a bit stand-offish and Brit at first, but she liked her sense of humour and the way Kay didn't let her get away with her most blasé, throwaway lines. No, Kay was quite a tough cookie, but she had a soft centre. Or was it the other way round?

Addy loved doing all the tourist things and would sometimes on her free days take a trip on the Circle Line or go up to the top of the World Trade Center to look at the view. She was too cool to admit it to the people she knew, but it gave her a real kick every time she looked down on the tiny yellow cabs and the tops of other buildings and out across the rivers to Brooklyn and New Jersey. 'The closest most of us will ever get to heaven' the brochure said, and Addy agreed with it.

'You're late again, Addy.'

'Gimme a break, Joe, I've been moving house today.'

'Oh yeah. So what else is new? You move house every two days, Addy. Who is the lucky man this time? Black or white, or maybe you got yourself a Puerto Rican for a change. Who is it this time, Skip or Bill or Marvin maybe? Jesus, I don't know how you remember all the names . . . How would you fancy someone called Joe one day?'

'Oh, fuck off, Joe. You don't pay me enough to make it worth my trouble.' She expected him to laugh. They usually had this sort of banter before she started her shift, but tonight his face was sweaty and drunk.

'Sometimes, Addy angel, you push your luck. I wouldn't if I were you. Know what I mean?'

'Oh sure, Joe, we all know what you *mean*, it's just that you never do anything about it.'

'Listen, smartass, get to work. Why aren't you dressed, anyway? The girls who work here wear black pants and white shirts, in case you hadn't noticed. So get that bearskin off and go change.'

'Well, Joe, I was wondering if you wouldn't mind me wearing jeans tonight. You see, all my clothes are packed up in boxes and these are the only things I could find.'

'Well, go find yourself another job. No one serves my

customers wearing a shirt that colour.' His eyes stared at her breasts.

'But, Joe, if this night is the same as all the others, you don't *have* any customers, so what are you worrying about?'

'Listen, lady, I don't need some smartass Brit telling me how my trade is going. Either get dressed or get out.'

'Look, I've just explained to you, you dumb asshole, I don't have any other clothes . . . '

'And I'm telling you to get out.'

Addy felt scared. It was a shit job, but it was all she had.

'Come on, Joe, you can't be serious. What will I do if you fire me?'

'Go stand in Times Square with the other ladies of your sort. I don't want no whore working for me.'

'Well, fuck you.'

She turned and managed to get to the door with dignity, but outside on the street, she started quaking and had to sit down on the sidewalk. With one dollar bill left in all the world, what would she do? Of all her friends, she couldn't think of a single one she could call up and ask for money. It didn't go with the image. Addy the partygiver, Addy the socializer, Addy who was game for anything. Addy who always fell on her feet. When she had told people about Jean Pierre walking out on her, they had laughed. What a joke. What a gas. What a great excuse for a party. Nobody had asked her whether she cared. Why couldn't she have smiled and flattered Joe's ego a little? Did he *really* think she was a tart?

She became aware that someone was standing over her. She looked up. Maybe it had all been a joke. She smiled. 'Listen, Addy,' Joe said gently, bending his knees to squat beside her.

'Oh, Joe, I'm sorry,' she wailed and put her head in his lap. He began to stroke her hair.

'God, Addy,' he crooned, 'you've got such soft hair. Now, as I see it, you need me and I need you, so why don't

109

we come to a little arrangement?'

'I've got my job back?'

'No, honey, don't act innocent, now . . . ' his grip tightened around her arm and one hand started to caress her throat. Then, in a split second, she was all too aware what he meant and found herself struggling against him. And then she was running down the street, her shirt open, her coat flapping behind her. She kept thinking that she couldn't run, that he would catch up with her like they always did in dreams, but after a few blocks she had escaped him and all she could hear as she panted was his voice shouting, 'Whore, frigid bitch, bitch, bitch . . . '

She didn't remember getting back to her room, but when she had, she had stripped off her clothes and spent hours scrubbing herself in the shower. Her skin was white and wrinkled and starting to flake when she finally dried herself on one of the blankets. She lay there shivering and watching the neon Budweiser sign on the top of the building across the street flashing long into the night.

'Kay, is that you? Oh, thank God. It's me, Addy . . . how many other people have your phone number in New York for Christ's sake? . . . Listen, take my number and ring me back rightaway will you? I'll explain.'

Kay sat holding the receiver for a few seconds and then dialled.

'Four Brothers,' a deep male voice barked down the phone.

'Oh, I'm terribly sorry. I've got the wrong number.' Kay tried again.

'Yes, Four Brothers.'

'Is there someone there called Addy?'

'Wait a minute, lady . . . *Anyone here called Addy?*' Kay waited.

'Kay? What took you so long?' Addy's voice finally said.

'Addy, what's going on? Look I'm in the middle of giving

the baby her bottle. I really can't talk.'

'Oh God, please help me.'

'What's the matter?'

'Can I come over right now?'

'Well . . . yes, I suppose so . . . '

'What's the address?' Kay told her.

'I don't know what it is. I just feel dirty and horrible.' Addy had just told Kay about last night. She was sitting there in the kitchen, her hands cupped around a mug of hot milk. She had wanted brandy but there wasn't any in the house. Kay was reluctant to get involved. She was surprised that Addy had just rolled up out of the blue and expected her to pick up the pieces. They'd only met once before. She didn't even know if she believed Addy. Was this the same person sitting there, who only yesterday had bounced along Broadway at her side, talking nineteen to the dozen, gesticulating madly and throwing her head back in laughter and joy at living in New York?

'How did you manage to call me, if you had no money?'

'I bought a coffee with my last dollar and chatted up the barman into letting me use his phone. Anyway, what does that matter, for God's sake? What am I going to do?'

'I don't know what to say. I'm not used to this sort of thing,' Kay said slowly.

'Well, it's not exactly routine for me either, you know. And just in case you're wondering, I'm not what Joe said I was. Sure, I sleep around, but that's none of your business and I don't make a career out of it. Oh, I'm sorry. You've been great. What am I going on at you for?'

'Look, I'm just surprised that you rang me in the first place, but for the record, I'm not casting moral aspersions on you. The more men the merrier, that's what I always say.'

'Do you?' Addy's face visibly brightened as if Kay's statement had signified some sort of approval.

'Yeah.' Kay felt guilty that such a blatant lie had

111

obviously been the most comforting thing she had managed to come up with. 'Anyway, why did you ring *me*?' she asked.

'Oh, you were the last resort. Just everyone I called was out. The number of messages I have left on answering machines today. You wouldn't believe it.' Why am I lying like this? thought Addy.

'Hmmm, well, what are we going to do?' Kay didn't know why but she suddenly felt she wanted to help Addy. 'Shall I lend you something to wear?'

Upstairs, Frannie woke, and Kay went to settle her. When she came down she found Addy trying on her wardrobe. Anyone more different in looks to herself she couldn't imagine. Addy's hair had been bright orange at the party but now that she had washed the hairspray out completely it had turned to the softest baby blonde curtain round her delicate face. It was the colour normally only seen on small children, perfect, natural blonde. Their colouring wasn't the only difference. Addy was eight inches taller than Kay, and most of the height was in her legs.

Even in adversity Addy's taste was as difficult to please as Kay had imagined it might be. 'Very nice, but not really me,' she would say as each item was surveyed and then cast aside. Eventually she decided on the pale blue mohair jumper that had always been Kay's favourite. 'It will go OK with jeans.' And a drop-waisted dress of fine Liberty print wool, which was calf length on Kay, but a mini on Addy. 'I think it was supposed to be this length, don't you?' said Addy as she left the apartment, in quite a different mood from the one in which she had arrived.

That evening a huge bunch of yellow roses arrived for Kay with a note that read:

FOUND A JOB, IT DON'T TAKE LONG,
FOUND A MAN (I KNOW IT'S WRONG)

WHO KNOWS WHERE IT MAY END?
BUT THANKS A LOT FOR BEING MY FRIEND. (OK so I'm not a poet) ADDY.

Kay burst out laughing. Addy really was an extraordinary person.

'I hear you and Addy have become great friends,' Jerome quizzed Kay over brunch.

'Well, I don't know about that.' Kay grinned. 'Does anyone become a great friend of Addy's? I've seen her a couple of times. Do you know about this new job of hers?' They were eating Eggs Benedict in One Five, an elegant restaurant and cocktail bar at the foot of Fifth Avenue. The Hollandaise sauce was mouthwatering and Kay was attempting to savour every mouthful. A svelte black waiter with an aura of superiority that outshone the decor, brought them Screwdrivers made with fresh orange juice. The perfect complement to the meal's rich, creamy texture.

'Her job? Oh yes. Well, it's certainly a step up from that terrible dive she used to work in. Haven't you seen her yet and heard about it?'

'No. I don't even know what she's doing.'

'Well, don't look so piqued. Sometimes you don't see Addy for months and just when you were beginning to forget she existed, there she is again. She's so popular. You can't expect to have a monopoly on her, you know. Even if you are both British.'

'Oh, come on, Jerome, stop keeping me in suspense. What is she doing and how did you find out about it?'

'Well, funnily enough, it was rather bizarre. I was walking around SoHo, you know, pretending to take in some art galleries but really looking for clothes. I came to this designer store and there was a crowd gathered round the window which I couldn't ignore. In the window were two dummies wearing the most beautifully cut suede clothes. Well, very nice, I thought, but it's hardly worth staring at. And then the most strange thought occurred to me. That dummy looks exactly like someone I know, I

113

thought. And do you know, as I pushed my way to the front of the crowd, bless me if it didn't wink. Well, I absolutely squealed I was so frightened, and then it came to me in a flash. They weren't dummies at all, they were real, live people. I felt so ashamed I just had to stick my tongue out at her, and of course Addy burst out laughing, rather spoiling the whole display, I might add. The thing about Addy is that she looks just as good wearing men's clothes as women's. Rather better, I fear, and so she can do all the shifts in the window and has, how shall I put it – mass appeal.'

'How amazing! Can we go and see her?'

'Well, I'd love to, Kay, some other time. I'd rather like to stay here for just a little while if you don't mind. Don't you think he's the most gorgeous thing you've ever seen?' He leant forward and whispered across the table.

'Who?' Kay looked round.

'Oh, don't spoil my fun. The African Queen, of course.' He signalled for two more Screwdrivers and when the waiter arrived, blushed pink. 'I know, don't tell me, I'm a terrible flirt. Can't you see him just dying to know what I am doing with a pretty girl?'

In Kay's opinion, the waiter couldn't have been less interested in Jerome but she was prepared to concede that in this case he knew better.

She had only been in New York a month, but the city had changed. Not only had winter gone, but summer had set in with a passion. Washington Square, snow covered and empty when she had arrived, was now buzzing with roller skaters. Everyone was wearing tracksuits of all shapes and colours. The sun shone and music blared from every shop. Everyone seemed to be in a hurry, to shop, to jog, to roller-disco. To enjoy life. It was all so different from the sedate dreariness of the flat in London or the cool, serious corridors of Oxford. Here Kay found she had limitless energy. Looking after Frannie in the day was tiring, but

114

when Ellen arrived back from work, Kay would change her clothes and go out walking. She gradually extended her knowledge of Brooklyn, daring each day to go one block further into areas she didn't know.

The news that blared twenty-fours hours from WINS – All News All The Time, giving constant reports on muggings and murder – failed to deter her. Kay was becoming street-smart. She could almost sense where the danger lay, and that made her outings more exciting. She was also getting hooked on being so free. After work she could do what she wanted when she wanted. On Thursdays she would take the subway in to Manhattan and wander around the department stores, blissfully trying on outfits she wouldn't have dared touch in London. It was all so new, so welcoming. The last time she had gone to Lord and Taylor, it had been filled with potted azaleas, luscious, dark pink tropical flowers reflecting in all the mirrors. Kay had found herself pinching the leaves to see if they were real. On weekends she would stroll up Fifth Avenue where a parade of some sort was always taking place, or walk around the Metropolitan Museum or the Guggenheim. Everything from art to ice cream was accessible. All she had to do was reach out and take what was offered.

Much to her surprise, she made friends with ease. Jerome rang her most afternoons 'just to hear your English voice', and the other people she encountered were equally eccentric and equable. A girl called Maria had offered her a cigarette one afternoon as they sat on a bench on the promenade. Each had a pram beside her.

'Good-looking kid that.'

'Thank you,' said Kay, who was beginning to feel a certain motherly pride in Frannie, 'but it's not mine.'

'You're kidding! This one isn't mine either. I'm just looking after it until I get my career sorted out.'

'So am I. What do you normally do?'

'Oh, I'm trying to be a rock singer. I've got a gig tomorrow night at CBGBs, do you want to come?'

Kay had gone. CBGBs was sleazy and dank, but Maria sang energetically through a worn-out PA system, and afterwards had introduced Kay around. Kay had been out to dinner and to the movies with that group of people on several occasions. Even Ellen was surprised at how quickly Kay had become a native New Yorker. 'You've got more friends than I have!' she said with mock jealousy.

It was seven o'clock when Kay arrived at the store where Addy worked. After leaving Jerome she had wandered round the Village and SoHo until it had got dark. The shop didn't close until nine and, realizing this, Kay had tried to make her excuses and come back later. Addy was having none of it. She greeted Kay like a long-lost friend, introduced her as 'my best buddy' and was now talking to her as if they really had known each other since time immemorial.

'So what have you been doing with yourself, and why haven't you been in touch for so long? I was beginning to think you had given me up.'

'Well . . . ' Kay was surprised. These were the questions she had meant to ask Addy. 'I've been looking after Frannie all day. It's a lot easier now the warm weather's here. We're becoming great friends. When I get bored Ellen brings home manuscripts for me to read, which is great fun although some of them are really badly written.'

'Novels? She's an editor, isn't she?'

'Yes.'

'Lucky you. Have you found any bestsellers? Could I read some, do you think? Does she pay you extra?'

'No, but I quite enjoy doing it. But sometimes it's quite demoralizing when you see some of the trash people have spent their lives working on.'

'But how do you know it's trash? I mean, didn't people think Eliot was trash in his time?'

'George Eliot or T. S. Eliot?'

'Well, probably both I should think. Anyway, I meant

116

T.S. George was a woman, after all.'

Well, thought Kay, I underestimated you. What was Addy's background? She couldn't begin to imagine.

'My father's a professor, you know,' said Addy smugly.

'Oh really, what subject?' But Addy refused to be drawn.

'Anyway what do you do when you're not changing nappies and reading manuscripts?'

'I'm gradually discovering New York. I've met a few people. Went to a gig the other night . . . '

'Good. Been to Chinatown yet?'

'No I haven't.'

'Because that's where we're going. You know you're there when you start seeing phone booths with pagoda roofs – look!'

The shops were still open and buzzing with people. Like everywhere else in New York a variety of smells wafted around: garlic, warm bread, charcoaled meat, stale urine, cats, rotting garbage.

'I'm starving. You wouldn't think that standing round in a shop window all day would make you so hungry,' Addy said as they wandered through the streets. 'People come along and gawp at you, munching their hot dogs and falafels. The other day a child stuck his nose right into his hamburger when he saw me licking my lips. I think he thought I was a great big doll!'

'Isn't that the idea?' Kay laughed.

'I suppose it is. We're meant to move around just a little bit all the time, and we have various set poses that we end up in. What was I doing when you came along?'

'You were kissing the other model, sort of wrapped round his body.'

'Oh God! No, Kay, actually that wasn't one of the poses. No, that was Howie, my current man, and the owner of the store. How embarrassing. The poses are

117

meant to be rather asexual really. Oh dear. You haven't met Howie yet, have you?'

'No. Is he nice?'

'Well, nice isn't really the word for it. He's absolutely gorgeous. I just can't remember being happier. It was love at first sight, you know, as soon as I walked into the store. But I have to be careful with this one. I don't want to lose him, but I don't want to lose my job even more.' Addy looked sad. Her pale face with its huge blue eyes could change in a second. At one moment it would be ecstatic and playful, the next, a picture of woe. Her doleful look was all the more poignant in contrast to her clothes and appearance.

'I love your outfit,' said Kay, slightly bewildered by the change in Addy's moods.

'Yes, it is lovely, isn't it? I've got a great arrangement with Howie. One week he pays me in cash and the next I can take home the clothes I've been wearing. Suits me fine. As you are aware, my wardrobe was severely depleted by unhappy circumstances recently. This outfit was last week's window design.'

'Does he pay for your hairdresser too?'

'Hmm, well, that was last week's window design too. I can't decide whether I like it. What do you think?' Addy's hair was swept up from her face into a pony tail that seemed to perch on the top of her head like leaves on a pineapple. It was fastened by a blue plastic bow. The effect was to fan out all the ends into a semicircle of about three inches in height, from the top of one ear to the other. The hair on her head remained the same pale blonde, but the ends had been dyed in rainbow colours, reaching from the blue of the bow to a bright red at the op. People were literally stopping to stare at her, clad in skin-tight denim jeans, a huge flying jacket over a handpainted T-shirt, and the rainbow hairstyle.

'How did they get it to go like that?' Kay couldn't resist asking.

'It's only vegetable dye. It'll wear off in a couple of

washes. I'm wearing a gold wig this week anyway. But what do you think? Shall I keep it like this?'

'I think you'll get awfully sick of it.'

'That's what I like about you, Kay, you don't bullshit. To be honest, I'm sick of it already. I used to love it when people looked at me in the street, but now I get that all day and in my free time I just want to fade into the background. Tell you what, why don't we go to the hairdresser's together next week and get a whole new look? I've got Saturday off.' Kay had worn her hair in the same style for years, a finely cut pageboy, and she couldn't see any reason why she should change it now. But carried away by Addy's enthusiasm she agreed. She liked the easy friendship she was falling into with Addy. They had a natural rapport.

'I'm ordering because I'm paying,' said Addy as they sat down to eat. 'Anyway I've been here before, so I know what is divinely delicious and what is just averagely appetizing.'

'You can order if you like, but I'm going to pay half,' Kay said firmly.

'Certainly not, I won't allow it.' For a moment Addy slipped back into pure English. A trick, Kay was to learn, that always signified that she was about to impart a great truth or an emotional scene. 'Anyway if it weren't for you, I wouldn't have any money. I don't forget my debts.'

'But you don't owe me anything, except I would like my dress back at some stage.'

'Kay, listen, you were very kind to me for no reason at all, and I've been embarrassed to call you up and thank you properly. I don't know what you must think of me, and for God's sake don't tell me, but I'm telling you, I always take people for granted and I'm trying hard not to with you, so you'd better let me pay.' Addy waved her chopstick threateningly. 'Right. One Peking duck. Yes, I do mean a whole one, with double pancakes. One whole fish with hot sauce and some lemon chicken with rice.'

119

At the end of the meal a waiter arrived with a plate of biscuits. 'What are these? I couldn't eat another thing,' said Kay.

'They're fortune cookies, of course. The best part. You don't have to eat it, just break it open and there's a message inside. Hurry up, what does yours say?'

'THERE ARE TWO SIDES TO EVERY STORY' Kay read. 'Well, I don't see the significance of that. What about you?'

'Oh, I had this one last time. It's a bloody fraud. SOMETIMES YOUR HEART MUST RULE YOUR HEAD. Mine always does anyway.'

'And that, no doubt, is why you keep getting it!'

The salon was Wedgwood blue and white and filled with trailing ferns and palms. There they sat, staring at their reflections. For once their eyes were level. Kay's grey, Addy's blue. Addy winked. Kay winked back. 'Just tell me one thing, Addy, how can we afford a place like this?'

'Don't worry, we've got it at half price. I had a word with Jerome. He knows one of the stylists, if you know what I mean.'

'Oh no! I don't want to look like Princess Di!'

When they emerged, Addy looked as if she had walked off the front cover of *Vogue*, her shining baby blonde cap gleaming in the sunlight, the delicate but distinctive features of her face bared by cropped temples. Kay, with her long fringe and twenties' bob, could have been cast for a leading role in *The Great Gatsby*. 'Aren't we pretty?' she said gleefully.

'We're beautiful,' agreed Addy. 'Let's have lunch.'

They stopped to eat in a restaurant on Columbus and 80th. 'I think it's warm enough to eat outside,' Addy remarked, drawing up two chairs to an umbrellaed table and ordering salads and white wine. 'By the way, I've been meaning to ask you. What do you think about sex?'

'Sex?' repeated Kay, not sure that she had heard properly and wondering whether this particular spot was the best place for a discussion.

'Yes, you know, sex.'

'Well, I don't know what you mean.'

'Oh, come on, Kay, don't look so innocent. I'm not proposing that we go to bed together if that's what you're thinking. Although it might not be such a bad idea, seeing as we're both so pretty today,' she mused. 'OK, OK, joke! But seriously, do you sleep around?'

'I haven't slept with anyone in New York.'

'God, haven't you? How long have you been here? Six weeks? Well, I suppose I didn't have that many in my first six weeks, but we'll have to get you started.'

'Addy, what are you really trying to say? If you're worried about me, don't be. Don't you dare try to fix me up with a date!'

'Well, actually, I wasn't. The fact is, I'm a bit worried about my own sex life.'

'Howie.'

'No, that's over really, in the romantic sense, anyway. We still get on. That's just it – I never seem to keep any one man for more than about two seconds. Each time I start off with someone new, I think this is it. I won't be unfaithful. I'll work at this relationship. And then I run into some other guy and end up spending the night with him. I used to think it was fun, sort of naughty, but I'm not even sure whether I enjoy it any more. Then, the other day, this shrink I had this one-night-stand with told me I was heading for trouble.'

'And what Joe said hurt, right?'

'Yeah, I suppose so. What's the point in being a liberated lady, if everyone thinks you're nothing but a whore?'

'So why do you keep doing it?'

'Don't know. Insecurity? That's what the shrink said. Ahh, here comes our lunch.' The conversation dropped while they munched on lettuce leaves and alfalfa sprouts. 'Can't stand this stuff, unless it's drenched in blue-cheese mayo,' said Addy, emptying the sauce boat on to her plate.

121

'Actually, I've only ever slept with one person properly,' ventured Kay. She still felt uncomfortable talking about intimate details.

'You're joking!' Kay shook her head and blushed. 'You mean you've never wanted to screw anyone else? Was he really *good* or something?'

'Well, it was good. We used to do it all the time, at first.'

'So what happened?'

'It finished. It was wonderful in the beginning but then things just started to go wrong. He was too possessive, I suppose, and I just didn't care for him enough. Perhaps these things can't last. I don't know any more. It's sad to feel like that about someone and then not to.'

'And how long did this doomed affair last?'

'Three years or so.'

'Three years! Jesus, that's a lifetime. Thirty lifetimes as far as I'm concerned. I'm lucky if anything goes on for a month. Even when it's really something, it doesn't last . . . ' Addy's voice trailed away.

'Sex can be destructive, can't it?' said Kay. 'I think in the end it destroyed some of the best friendships I had, not just the one with Bob.'

'But did you come? Did you really come for three whole fucking years?' Addy had been leading into the question she obviously wanted to ask since she had brutally launched the conversation.

'Well, yes. I think so.'

'Honey, did you or didn't you?'

'No, not every time. Most of the time. Is that so strange?'

'I never come. Well, I have, but only in dreams and you know . . . I know what it feels like. But it never happens during real sex.'

'That's extraordinary. Why do you do it? Do they enjoy it?'

'Don't be so personal!' Addy could look many things, but rarely embarrassed. 'I put on a good show. I don't think they notice. I don't think they care one way or the other.'

122

'Addy, that's awful. I thought I was inexperienced but . . .'

'You've got it. That's the problem, you see. I don't think I should be doing it. The old Catholic guilt, I suppose, but it has just become a way of life. Maybe I'm just searching for Mr Right.'

'Is there such a person do you think?' Kay asked thoughtfully. 'I've never really talked about sex like this. I didn't know you were a Catholic. In fact, come to think of it, I don't know anything about your background.'

'But you still like me, don't you?'

'Yes, of course.' Kay was always surprised that when she asked Addy about her life before New York Addy would change the subject.

'Haven't seen the inside of a church for years,' Addy mused. 'Anyway, let's have some dessert. That's why I picked this place, you know. It's not all rabbit food.' She was once again her happy extrovert self.

They went inside, where Kay was to witness the most astounding edible sight she had ever seen. There were hundreds of different delicacies. Every kind of torte, gateau and mousse. Each one an intricate work of art. Around the dishes were arrangements of fresh fruit and strawberries falling out of little melon baskets with handles carved out. In the centre of the table was a mountain of perfect caramel profiteroles glistening with whipped cream rising about like a tornado.

'Well, I'm in a mood to destroy that particular phallic symbol!' said Addy. And they both plunged in, serving themselves huge portions and eating greedily until they both felt sick.

The conversation they had that day did not seem to affect Addy's behaviour in any obvious way. For the rest of the summer, Kay was deluged with phone calls from her, telling her of her new conquests. Addy seemed to have the ability to fall in love with every man she encountered. 'This is really it,' she would say, but two days later she would be in despair. Kay didn't meet half the men, their entrance and exit from Addy's life would be so brief.

But one of Addy's encounters particularly interested Kay. One lunchtime she got a call from Addy and knew instantly by the tone of her voice that she had met another man.

'Guess what?'

'No, what?'

'I had a great screw last night. Well, medium to great really. Thing was I managed to act real cool this time. I guess it was because I knew I'd never see the guy again. His name was Rupert. Great name, hey?'

'What happened?' Kay tried to concentrate but her eyes kept wandering back to the manuscript Ellen had given her to read. She had heard this kind of conversation from Addy so many times before.

'Well, it was like this . . . I was at the Odeon and I got talking to him, you know how it is. He's a journalist or something and he invited me to a party. Some party, I can tell you, at the Algonquin. You know that schmuck Paul Ritz, the one who's always on the Carson show talking oh so seriously about his work? It was in his honour. You can't say I don't mix with the rich and famous, can you?'

'Paul Ritz?'

'The very same. But that's not the point. After the party finished it was real late and you can guess the rest . . . nice suites the Algonquin has . . . '

'How was Paul Ritz? I met him once . . . '

'Him. Oh, he's a jerk. Listen, you're not supposed to be interested in him. I'm telling you about Rupert, remember?'

Addy talked on, but Kay could only remember her own meeting with Paul Ritz. She felt a twinge of jealousy that Addy had been at a party of his. She wanted to know all the details.

124

'. . . So Rupert and I ended up screwing in the elevator
too. I kind of didn't care too much how it was because I
knew he was off to England today, and do you know
something, Kay, it really helped. Perhaps that's what I
ought to do in the future. Get involved with men I know I'll
never see again. Sounds crazy, doesn't it? I mean, how can
you get involved with someone you're never going to see
again . . . ?'

'What was Paul Ritz doing in New York?'

'Oh, Rupert said he was on a publicity tour for some
documentary he's done for NBC. Something about cocaine
addiction among the rich and powerful . . .'

'Sounds interesting. Did you talk to him at all?'

'You've got to be kidding, with tall, dark Rupert
around? Anyway, the way everyone licks Paul Ritz's ass
really gets up my nose. I mean, what is it about him? I
thought he was supposed to be an expert on coke. There
wasn't a single gram in the joint. If you want my opinion,
that man is a fraud . . .'

Kay giggled. She realized that she would get no more out
of Addy about Paul Ritz, and she listened as Addy
proceeded to relate every detail of her night with Rupert.

For a while Kay enjoyed the role of confidante but then she
began to feel impatient. Addy's behaviour was so irratio-
nal. How could she do the same thing again and again? Kay
wondered what would happen to her if she were not there
to pick up the pieces. But she worried about Addy. It was
dangerous to pick men up at parties or in singles bars. So
far, Addy had always teamed up with men who loved her
and left her, but Kay worried that one day she would take a
fancy to a pervert and would end up bleeding in the gutter.

She wrote a story with Addy as the central character and
called it *Addy's Latest Man*. She showed it to Ellen. Kay
thought it was the best thing she had ever written in her life.
It managed to capture the vulnerability of her friend
beneath the brash exterior.

'No,' said Ellen. 'It just doesn't work. The girl is completely unreal. Nobody would believe it.'

When Addy read it, she cried. 'It's so sad . . . Why does the heroine get murdered? And why did you call her *Addy*?'

Those were fascinating days for Kay. Getting to know Addy would almost have been enough to make life enjoyable, but there were so many other things. She felt truly independent. She liked the happy-go-lucky friendships she had found in New York. She had learned to accept people as she found them, without judging them with the critical eye she had used at Oxford. In an environment where people lived for the moment, intellectual analysis was inappropriate.

In the daytime she read more and more manuscripts for Ellen. Ellen liked her work and suggested she should go into publishing. At last she had found something challenging which she could consider as a career. She began to look forward to the future positively, which only emphasized the differences between her and Addy. She loved Addy dearly but she knew that her own character was not suited to the eternal hedonism that characterized her friend. Kay knew she could not drift forever. This realization made her all the more eager to enjoy the summer months in humid Manhattan. Her freedom had a finite length to run. Kay did not know quite when it would end. But end it would.

They discovered that the hotel Addy lived in had a roof accessible from the fire escape outside her window. At weekends they would lie burning on the tarry felt, discussing life and love and planning the evening's enjoyment ahead of them. Kay lost count of the number of parties they went to and the jazz bars they discovered. Each Saturday she could be sure that Addy would have found a new group of people to hang out with. Each weekend brought some new adventure.

The epitome of the mad Manhattan experience for Kay

126

was when a black playboy who dealt in cocaine insisted on taking her out for a night on the town. They drove from club to club in an avocado-coloured limousine driven by Walter, the white chauffeur. There was a television and a cocktail cabinet stocked with a seemingly endless supply of Jack Daniels. Skip maintained a gracious distance from Kay but their conversation was flirtatious and salacious. When she remembered that night one dreary London evening later that year, Kay wondered how she could have enjoyed herself. But in New York, in a limo, she had felt perfectly at home.

'Not Skip!' Addy had laughed as Kay narrated what had happened. 'I bet you a hundred bucks that he told you he could give you an orgasm by massaging from the waist upwards . . . '

'How did you know? That was going to be the witty climax to my story!'

'He says that to all the girls,' smirked Addy. 'And by the way, it's not true.'

Only two events made Kay stop and think about home. The first was the Falklands War. It came as a great shock to realize that Britain was at war. The fact that she was in America made it seem even more unreal. She and Addy found there was outrage amongst the liberal New Yorkers at the British imperialist stance. For several weeks, they kept a low profile and even Kay's New York twang became stronger.

The second thing was a letter she received from Bob. A fourteen-page epic declaring his undying love, asking her forgiveness and pleading with her to go back and live with him. He said he had realized that they had differences but that in the end they were made for each other. He was living in the country, near the sea, just as they had dreamed. He was starting a new life; wouldn't she come and share in his bliss? For an hour or two Kay felt tempted to settle for that life he described so eloquently. After all, she hadn't met any other man that she liked in the same way as Bob and it was almost a year. Perhaps she never would. Perhaps she did love Bob. But she couldn't imagine being with him for ever, or even for a few months. It was that sort of commitment he was asking for. The letter was sweet, like a Valentine. But it made it all the more obvious that he would never understand why they had split up and how much he had angered her. He wasn't ever going to be able to understand that and that was why they couldn't be together.

Addy sensed that something was wrong. 'What's the matter, Kay, you're not your usual self?'

'I've heard from Bob. He wants me to go back to England and live with him. Here, read it.'

'What a lovely letter. He's really in love with you. God, I envy you. But you're not going back to him, are you?'

'No, I'm not. But it has confused me. I thought I was over him and I'm not.'

'It's something to do with sex, isn't it?'

'Well, for once, you obsessive, you're right! It's something that really worries me. Sometimes I think I'm frigid. All the men I feel most comfortable with here are gay. Not just Jerome, but all the men I know here. I'm really nervous when someone makes a pass at me. I don't know what it is. I just don't want to be intimate with anyone else. Bob's just about the only man I've ever fancied. The only man I've been to bed with. I can't imagine sex with anyone else. Besides, I miss being in bed with someone. It would be nice . . . '

'I know exactly how you feel.' Kay looked at her and laughed. 'No, really, Kay, basically I'm a monogamous person.' Addy looked serious for a second and then burst into peals of laughter. 'By the way, have I told you about Billy? Got our first date tonight. Black, beautiful *and* the perfect gentleman.'

'Do you have the time, lady?'

Addy's eyes narrowed. 'Not for you, big boy,' flashed across her mind. She'd better check the enemy out before she opened her big mouth, especially in this place. She turned gracefully. A small man, in an ankle-length, torn raincoat stared up at her. He was grinning. At least that's what she took the contortion of his mouth to be. Another looney. She sighed and crossed one leg elegantly in front of the other. Then in her best, plum-in-the-mouth English she intoned, 'I say, why don't you buzz off now, there's a good chappy.'

It was perfect. Her clipped diction even took her by surprise. But it worked. It was the last thing on earth he expected. The leer disappeared and turning on his heels he walked away. 'Mother-fucking son of a bitch!' floated back. But it seemed more directed at himself than her.

Addy looked at her watch. 10.30 p.m. She was impatient. The theatres were turning out and if she waited any longer she would be alone in Times Square, alone amongst the pimps, pushers and winos. Her eyes wandered around. Everything was moving, the flashing neon Sony advert, the crude cinema advertisements, the wailing traffic and the people. What a hellhole. What had happened to Times Square? It used to be exciting, sordid but vibrant. The garish lights, slouching bodies, the hum, the stench of baking pizza, distasteful but real. But not tonight.

'Hey, lady.'

Addy spun round with her most hostile expression. 'Hey, Billy, you big, black bastard!'

'Cool it, girl. Jesus, you're jumpy tonight.'

'Yeah and so would you be if you'd been waiting in this dump for half an hour like a prostitute with no tricks.'

'Have I ever told you you're beautiful when you're angry?' The frown disappeared from Addy's face and she smiled. The old clichés were still the most disarming, and Billy had a lovely, self-mocking way of delivering them. She reached out both arms and he caught her and swung her round in a great bear hug.

They were a striking couple as they walked arm in arm towards Billy's double-parked white BMW. Addy looked like an elegant American footballer, six feet of silver grey, in her Norma Kamali sweatshirt and tights. All legs and shoulders. And Billy. Addy had told Kay he was the only man to make her feel secure because she could rest her head on his shoulder without bending her knees. He was ridiculously tall with Jamaican good looks and always an open smile. He drove like a maniac downtown, joking and writhing in his seat to the continuous beat of WPLJ.

'Do I get an explanation of why you were so late tonight?' She should have known by now not to ask that of Billy. She felt annoyed with herself and then annoyed with him. He had arranged to meet her in Times Square of all places and then he had been half an hour late. She was cold and angry. She often felt let down, disappointed, suspicious, disillusioned, but rarely angry with other people. And with Billy, never. He was for the good times. He was the joker, the dude. He was sexy. She thought she was in love with him.

'No explanation, honey.' He flashed her a quick smile.

Mickey's bar was a brownstone two-storey building on the corner of a partly demolished street in Tribeca. Surrounded by wasteland and the skyscrapers of Wall Street, it looked like a Hopper painting pinned to the bottom of the World Trade Centre towers. Addy had always loved it, ever since Billy had taken her there on their first date.

She looked on as he greeted all his friends standing round the bar. It was the same scene. The stone floor, the loud jukebox. She sat on a bar stool and Billy ordered two White Russians – glorious concoctions of cream, Kahlua and vodka that summed up for Addy in one sickly mouthful everything that was decadent, extravagant and fun about New York. He handed her a glass and stroked her thigh. She sipped slowly and watched Billy immediately involved in a pool game, his hips swaying to the sound of late '60s Motown.

She had seen it all before so many times, heard the barman's wisecracks. She sighed. Usually she would be leaning against the bar, chatting and smoking innumerable cigarettes. But tonight she did not want to join in. For the first time she was an observer, watching the multicoloured New Yorkers at play, an outsider not a participant. After years in New York of heightened emotion, laughter and *carpe diem* she felt sober and bored. She couldn't even be bothered to pretend. The bar was crowded but she felt alone.

'Carpe diem.' Here she was thinking of something her father used to say. That had been his phrase when his unspoken exasperation at her lifestyle would give way to open contempt. 'You'll come to your senses sooner or later,' he had shouted like a threat.

She could hear his barking voice. She raised her glass to her lips. 'Well here's to you, Dad. To the man who spoke Latin better than English, at least to his daughter.' For a moment the bitterness was replaced by a twinge of sadness. She wondered how they were getting on. Poor old Mum. Well, in two months she'd have an excuse to ring her. She always called home at Christmas. Home.

She watched a drunken couple take to the open space between the tables and attempt to dance to the thumping music. Kay would like this bar. She ought to bring her here. Kay had never met Billy. Addy did not want to share him in any way. He would be fascinated by Kay, her flawless skin and English accent. He'd probably try and get her into bed with him. But she couldn't imagine it, not Billy and Kay. Kay would like him, but she would disapprove of him in that disdainful way of hers. Suddenly Addy wished Kay was there.

Their clothes lay scattered on the floor. Billy had always said that making love used equivalent caloric energy to jogging seven miles in Central Park. On that calculation they had just done a twenty-one-mile marathon.

131

'Addy, honey, you're beginning to fuck like it's going out of fashion.'

They lay there entwined, sweating and silently sharing a joint. The air in the room was chill and they shivered, too exhausted to pull up the covers.

For hours, Addy was wide awake, gazing at the neon Budweiser sign across the street. She could not stop thinking but there was no coherence to her thoughts. Billy slept heavily, but from time to time his breathing became fitful and Addy was jolted involuntarily. Then he woke up and looked down at her, expecting to see her half asleep but her eyes were open. 'I'll take a shower with you, Billy,' she said, getting out of bed.

They both stepped into the cubicle, almost embarrassed to touch, as if this act were too intimate. Billy turned on the shower and started washing himself, quickly and efficiently. Addy stood with her eyes closed. The incessant noise of the water hitting the enamel floor and perspex walls had driven her into a trance. Then she knelt in front of him, gripping his ankles, the stinging water pounding on her back.

She began to lick his inner thighs and belly with long unhesitating strokes, gradually creating a circle of salivary sensation, and all the time trying not to gulp the hot, chloriney water that was streaming down his legs. He stood utterly still, taken aback by her initiative. Then he was her captive, overtaken by sheer pleasure. Her chin collided with his erection and they both laughed spontaneously, relieved that the uncanny intensity had been broken.

He hoisted her to her feet and turned her around, spreadeagling her against the cubicle wall, like a cop doing a bodysearch. In one exquisite thrust he entered her. She felt every nerve-ending in her body screaming with raw sensation, and her body was rigid as he slid in and out. Each second that he left her, she craved him back, and when he returned more and more roughly, she felt full of him, as if she would burst with two people trying to get inside her. He

132

prised her arms from the walls, turned her round and
folded them around his neck as he picked her up. She
gripped her feet under his buttocks and looked into his face
with urgent expectancy. A final thrust. She yelped as she
felt him pouring into her and he soothed her still-demand-
ing gasps with luxurious kisses. They stood there with her
body melted on to his in the stream of the pouring water – a
liquid mass.

'That was some shower, honey,' he said, turning off the
water and wrapping her in a large white towel. Then he
dumped her on the bed like a parcel.

'Hmmm.' The understatement was the climax of their
relationship. Billy would go back to his wife now and she
would not see him again for a while, until he became bored
again. Sometimes she didn't know how much that worried
her, but tonight it mattered a lot.

She lay there watching him methodically putting on his
jeans, tucking in his shirt and tying the laces of his shoes.

'I sometimes think I ought to go back to England,' she
said thoughtfully.

'You're kidding. Why?' He showed no real interest but
she wanted to explain, if only to herself.

'I'm twenty-three. I'm an illegal alien. I work as a
mindless mannequin all day, and I get high when I finish my
shift. I don't think, I have no responsibility. I love New
York, but I can't survive in my self-imposed vacuum any
longer. I have to start doing something real. And I couldn't
survive in New York if I became committed to something
or someone. What I have going for me here is that I'm
footloose and fancyfree . . . and English, I suppose. A real
expatriate. I'm going back to England to see if there's
something different there for me.'

God, she sounded American. She'd be talking about
finding her roots next. She looked at him, and as she had
expected, Billy was obviously bemused by her outpourings.

'You'll hate it there, sweetheart.'

'Probably.'

He didn't seem to know what to say next. 'Well, honey, what we have is real and it is fun too.' He was consciously mocking her words.

She stuck her tongue out at him. 'But it isn't "real fun",' she countered.

He laughed, put on his battered leather jacket and opened the door. Then he turned and looked at her. 'Good luck.'

Addy heard him bouncing down the stairs. She wondered if she would cry but found she couldn't. Really, she had become so casual about everything. Numb.

On Hallowe'en night, as Kay prepared to sit down to a traditional pumpkin pie supper with Ellen and wait to be invaded by an army of trick or treaters, a telegram arrived for Kay from her mother. Her father had suffered a heart attack and was very ill in a London hospital. Her mother didn't ask it, but Kay knew she was expected to go back to England.

She didn't want to go home. She wanted to extend her existence in New York just a little while longer. She felt cheated of the culmination of her hedonism. She had so much wanted to spend Christmas in the city. It was difficult to leave Ellen. They could find someone suitable to look after the baby easily enough, but Kay felt she hadn't fully reciprocated all the efforts Ellen had made to give Kay a home. She would miss Frannie too. That warm little bundle of a child who was just beginning to crawl and burble noises that sounded so much like talking. And Addy. How could she imagine life without Addy?

She had insisted that Addy not come to the airport with her. She hated goodbyes and, to her surprise, Addy had put up no arguments. They had said goodbye after a night spent cruising all their favourite bars and nightclubs. Addy had helped Kay up the stairs to Ellen's apartment and hugged her quickly. Despite her drunken state, Kay had been

134

surprised at how coolly Addy seemed to be taking it. She had felt slightly hurt but proudly held back her tears. She wondered if she would ever see Addy again.

'LAST CALL FOR TWA FLIGHT 703 TO LONDON HEATHROW.'

Wearily, Kay began to make her way to the plane from the departure lounge. She looked back for a moment as she reached the gate. There seemed to be a commotion at the entrance to the lounge. A tall figure dressed in scarlet was being rigorously searched by a security officer. Addy. She was dressed in a long, tight skirt and a square-shouldered jacket with three large white buttons to the waist. A white pill-box hat balanced on her blonde head with a red net veil to her nose.

'Addy!' Kay shrieked.

'Kay. Hi. This isn't a love-in, by the way. I'm just being frisked. I made the machine bleep. They seem to think I might be a terrorist. Me? I've told them it's just my magnetic attraction . . .'

'But what the hell . . . ?'

Addy snatched her handbag from the security officer and threw her arms round Kay.

'You didn't honestly think I'd let you go back on your own, did you? Listen, I'm pig-sick of the Big Apple. Come on. We'd better hurry if we're going to get that flight. If you knew the problems I've had getting a seat next to yours.'

'You're coming with me? Why didn't you tell me?'

'One, I only decided yesterday, and two, it's more fun like this, don't you think? Hey, look a little pleased to see me!'

COMING HOME

LONDON

'You know, it really is great to be home,' said Addy, sinking into the long leather Chesterfield that filled one wall of Kay's living room.

'What's that?' Kay walked in from the kitchen.

'I was just remarking how good it feels to be back in the old country. Did you manage to get through to your mother?'

'Yes. She sounds a bit tired, but all right. Father seems to be out of danger for the time being at least. I'll go to see him tomorrow.'

'So he's going to be OK? That's great, Kay. I'm so pleased for you. Hey, what's up?'

'Oh, nothing really. It's just a bit of an anticlimax. Not that I wanted him to die or anything, but I've come all this way home, and now it seems there was no real reason to . . .'

'But you wouldn't have wanted to stay in NY much longer, would you?'

'No, I guess not. I suppose I'm just worried about what next. I mean, Addy, what are we both going to do?'

'Oh, don't worry. Something will turn up. It always does,' said Addy reflectively, sighing and putting her feet up. 'This is a great sofa, you know.'

A few moments later, Kay noticed that Addy had fallen asleep. She walked over to the Chesterfield, pulled Addy's stilettos from her feet and threw a blanket over her. It was at moments like this that Kay envied Addy. She was, in many ways, a child of nature. When the mood took her she would laugh, when she was unhappy, she would cry, uninhibitedly and copiously, and when she was tired or worried, she would sleep. Sometimes in New York, Addy had slept twenty hours at a stretch and when she woke, she would ring Kay, apologize for missing an arrangement and make the excuse that she needed to 'sleep herself out'. When she decided to leave New York it was on impulse, but she wouldn't regret it. For Addy there were no regrets because she didn't try to analyse. Sometimes Kay wondered whether Addy ever thought at all. She obviously hadn't considered the question of where she would live when she returned. She had assumed that she would share Kay's flat. Kay couldn't decide whether to be slightly irked or even annoyed. But after a lot of thought she came to the conclusion that for once she would give in to her predominant feelings, just in the way that Addy did. She was tremendously happy about the arrangement, and flattered.

When she visited him in hospital the next day, Kay was shocked to see her father looking so old and vulnerable in his pyjamas. He had always seemed old, but now he was a frail, elderly man who grasped her hand with the desperation of one who knows he will die. She sat by his bed and tried to make conversation, but she began to feel that old discomfort with him and she was irritated by everything he said.

'I expect you're ready to get going again now after your extended holiday.' He smiled at her.

'I was working actually, father.'

'Yes, well, you'll want a proper job now . . .'

'Whatever a proper job may be. I'm not thinking of going into the City you know.' She was ashamed to feel herself slipping back into the resentful little girl role she thought she had shaken off. 'I'm going to get a job in publishing.' She tried to make an effort to be positive.

'That's the girl, Kay. I expect that pays well.'

'No. As a matter of fact it doesn't. But money isn't going to rule my life. In fact, I'll probably have to start as a secretary.'

'Well, if that's what you want, I suppose there will be no

stopping you. I can't see you as a secretary though. Far too bolshy. I wouldn't have employed you as my secretary.'

'Thanks a lot. I wouldn't have wanted to *be* your secretary. You always treated them like dirt.' Kay could feel tears of fury welling up inside her. Why didn't he encourage her just a little?

'No, no.' Her father was chuckling to himself. 'Far too bolshy. Just like your mother.'

Kay looked at him closely. Surely he wasn't going senile. If he thought her mother was bolshy he was quite demented. She had never spoken out of turn to him in her life. Perhaps he was still drowsy. Kay watched him dozing gently and then noticed her mother coming down the ward towards them. She ran to greet her.

'Hello, mother!' She tried to give her a hug, but as usual her mother looked embarrassed and flustered.

'Hello, dear. You're looking well. How did you find him?' Her mother motioned towards the bed.

'Oh, I think he's going to be OK. Seems a bit weak and tired, but the old business acumen is still there and he still manages to annoy me whatever he says.'

'Oh, Kay.' Her mother's look rebuked her silently.

'Sorry. I know I shouldn't care any more, but he always seems so disappointed with me.'

'He's not at all. He was so flattered when I told him you had come all the way back from New York to see him. Now stop being silly. He looks as if he's off for the night now. Why don't we have a coffee somewhere and you can tell me all about it.'

They walked out of the hospital together into the cold November air. It was fresh after the warm fug of disinfectant in the ward.

'I hear Will has popped down to see your father a couple of times. He's doing very well you know. The hospital does seem to think highly of him.' Her mother looked at Kay for a reaction but there was none. Kay had forgotten that Will was a student at that hospital. She had forgotten a lot of things about Will. The memory of him sent a brief flicker of regret through her mind. She wondered whether Will ever thought of her these days.

'Did you speak to the doctor?' Kay asked, changing the subject.

'Good news. They think your father is out of danger for the time being. They'll be sending him back to Sevenoaks in a few days.'

'Oh, that's good.'

'What about you, darling? Will your American friend be staying with you? You can both come back to Sevenoaks with me, if that would be easier for you. I've got to get things sorted out for your father. He'll need a bed downstairs to rest in the day and I ought to clean the place up. You know how he is. But I have been dashing up here and back every day since he's been in hospital and I just haven't had time.'

'Poor you. Would you like me to come down and help?'

'No, dear, you'd probably be in the way. I'll be perfectly all right.'

Kay felt excluded and wondered briefly why she had bothered to come back. Her mother wouldn't admit to needing her, even now. But she tried to put a brave face on it.

'OK then, I'll stay in London. I'd quite like to decorate the flat. It looked so dismal when we got back last night. Anyway, I'll be able to come to see father for the next couple of days while he's still in hospital. And I've got to get a job as soon as I can. In fact, to that end, I've already bought a copy of the *Evening Standard*.'

'But will you find a suitable job in there?' Her mother looked concerned. 'You don't have to try for anything, you know, darling. We can quite easily support you until you find something you really want to do.'

'That's kind of you, mother, but I really need to get my act together.'

'Oh really, Kay, I hope you're going to lose that awful American accent soon.'

'Oh, for Heaven's sake, mum!' They both laughed.

'Hey, let's have a coffee.' Kay suggested and pulled her protesting mother into an Italian coffee house on the Tottenham Court Road. 'Wow, this is just like Little Italy.'

'Oh, Kay, you didn't go there, did you?'

'Of course I did.'

'But isn't that the place where the Mafia live?'

It was obviously going to be pointless trying to tell her mother anything about New York. If she thought Mafia when she heard Little Italy, goodness knows what she would think of the time when Addy had borrowed a friend's convertible and taken Kay on a 'cruise' round Harlem, or the time when they had dressed up as groupies and got in backstage to see David Bowie at a private gig, or the nude barbecue they had been to at Jerome's summer time-share on Fire Island. How could she begin to describe cavorting in a heart-shaped pool with several gay men? How could she begin to describe Addy?

'Did you enjoy yourself there, Kay?' her mother was asking. 'You seemed to be having a good time from your postcards.'

'Oh yes, I had a wonderful time.'

That was it. All that would be said on the subject, probably. Her parents were mellowing with time, but the distance between them remained. Her mother seemed to know that too. She wasn't relaxed in Kay's company. She never had been and Kay wondered if she ever would be. Kay was relieved to part from her at the tube station. She had thought that New York had made her communicate better, but as far as her parents were concerned, that had been wishful thinking.

When Kay had tentatively remarked on their arrival back that the flat could do with a lick of paint, she hadn't imagined that Addy had taken note. But when she arrived back from the hospital the flat was already covered in dustsheets and Addy, wearing a boiler suit and a spotted scarf Mrs Mop style round her head, was at the top of a stepladder sloshing paint on to the ceiling of the living room.

'Hi. The ceiling is always the worst bit and as I'm tall I thought I'd make a start and get it over with. I thought it would be nice if this ceiling looked like the sky, since it's so high, so I bought this lovely blue shade emulsion. The thing is that it doesn't matter whether the paint goes on evenly because that adds to the impression of clouds, if you see what I mean. I've got white for the walls and some green gloss, because I thought we could paint some palm trees over by the window. A sort of mural. Jean Pierre taught me how to paint. That's about the only thing he did teach me. You don't have to be much of an artist to do it. Oh, by the way. I bought you a surprise – over there.'

Kay pulled the brown paper off a large rectangular package to reveal two brightly striped deck chairs.

'Apart from the Chesterfield, there's not a lot of furniture here, so I thought to myself, buy some deck chairs and have this room like a beach!'

'But, Addy, it'll look like a cocktail bar.'

'Yes. Great, isn't it?'

In the next two weeks they spent a lot of time redecorating. Addy's concept of interior design, as she called it, was to make each room have a theme. She proved to be a talented scrounger both in the local shops and from building sites and skips. The beach room was as fresh and colourful as a Hockney painting, Kay's bedroom turned into 'the library' lined with grey-and-white-striped wallpaper and bookshelves. Addy constructed a bed on stilts in the tiny spare room and painted it with pink gloss. Her clothes, on an open rail she had 'found' outside a department store, formed the main decoration and she managed to persuade a local electrician to create her a full-length mirror surrounded by lightbulbs.

'Addy, you are such a narcissist!' Kay said when she was allowed to see the full effect. 'A bedroom like the dressing room of a Broadway star. Don't you think you'll get sick of it?'

'Well, perhaps. But just think when we're rich and famous. They'll want to interview us in the Sunday colour magazines and we'll be prepared. As a matter of fact, I think we ought to invite the Sunday mags in right now. We could set up as interior decorators. What do you say?'

Although Addy wasn't serious in her suggestion, the lack of success in getting jobs was beginning to prey on them. Kay had a couple of interviews with publishing companies and literary agencies where she was told she was too ambitious and probably over-qualified, but there seemed to be no way in apart from as a secretary. She had no direct experience of office work and could not hope for anything more prestigious until she did.

Addy got the opposite response from most of the jobs she applied for. She was unqualified for any office job. When she finally managed an appointment as a receptionist in an advertising agency, she was sacked after two hours for cutting off calls on the switchboard and refusing to let the managing director past the reception desk until he produced identification. She got one night's work per week in a nightclub called the Camden Palace, but apart from that, they were living off money that Addy had saved in New York and it was running out. By the end of November they had both decided to apply for absolutely anything that came up, in order to make ends meet. They were reduced to eating very simply and one drink per week in a pub.

One Saturday morning Addy burst into Kay's bedroom at six o'clock in the morning.

'I can't stand this poverty any longer. Let's just blow all our money for next week today. It's going to be a lovely day. Let's do something special. Where can we go to be really decadent?'

'Oh, for God's sake, Addy.' Kay rubbed her eyes and

looked at her clock. 'Calm down. What do you want me to suggest? Lunch at the Savoy or something? We'll regret it when we get the bill.'

'No. I'm thinking of a day out. Let's go to Oxford and have some champagne on a punt. What do you say?'

'The punting season is over. We can't afford champagne. But I can see you're going to get your own way, so let's go.'

Kay had forgotten quite how beautiful Oxford could be on a clear autumn day. It was nearly the end of the autumn term. She felt oddly disorientated to be viewing Oxford as a visitor rather than an insider. It was hard to imagine that for three years this town had been her home. She found she could spot the students in their various years. 'That's a St Hilda's fresher,' she would say, pointing, or 'He looks like a Balliol PPE second year'. When Addy asked how she knew, Kay found herself slipping easily back into the old student snobbery that had been a way of life just a year ago. 'Oh, *nobody* except a fresher would wear a college scarf, *nobody* but a Balliol leftie would have such dirty jeans . . .'

'The odd thing is,' she said as they sat down for lunch in Browns, 'that they all look so young.'

'Yes,' said Addy, 'but they all look pretty tasty too. You never told me that this place was packed with beautiful young men . . .'

'Well, it doesn't seem like that when you're here. Zoe and I used to have a saying. When we were here there were about four times as many men as women, and when we arrived we thought we were going to have a ball. But Zoe and I came to the conclusion that if you took four typical men, one was gay, one played rugby with the boys, one had a girlfriend in London, and the other was a spotty natural scientist. That sounds so Arts snobby, but it was really true!'

'But you didn't do so badly, if I recall. Your nephew and the delicious Bob.'

Will and Bob. They had become a memory in the way that Oxford had. A strange nostalgia-tinted piece of the past that no longer seemed appropriate.

'It was so easy with Bob . . . ' Kay mused, stirring the thick malted chocolate milkshake she had ordered for old time's sake, and now didn't feel she could stomach. 'Do you think he was just the exception? Won't it ever happen with anyone else?' She was filled with a sense of passing and gloom. But Addy didn't seem to be listening. She had made eye-contact with the bartender and was in a world of her own.

After Addy had tried and criticized practically every cocktail on the menu, but decided the bartender must be bisexual, if not gay, they left Browns and walked down St Giles. The sun had gone in and a damp grey mist chilled the air.

'Where do you want to see now?' Kay shivered and wrapped her tartan box jacket closely around her.

'No more colleges,' said Addy, 'they all look the same to me. Isn't there a river in Oxford, with punts and Pimms and things?'

'Yes, but only in the summer. Let's go to Magdalen Deer Park.'

They wandered down the Broad and stopped outside the Sheldonian. Addy gazed at the building and the statues on pillars around it.

'What are those very ugly heads? Dons or something?'

'No, I think they're meant to be Roman Emperors . . . '

'Well, what the hell are they doing here?'

It was odd to be called upon to explain the things one had taken so much for granted in student days. Momentarily, Kay was irritated by Addy's intrusive, childish behaviour.

'Don't know.'

'You don't know much about this place, considering you were here for three years, do you?'

'Well, in that sense, no. It's much more to do with

147

atmosphere and traditions when you're here.'

'Like?'

'Well, for instance, Blackwells. That bookshop over there. I think it is supposed to be the biggest and best bookshop in the world. The sort of British Library of bookshops. But when you're here, nobody really buys books there. It's the place where you hang out and spot famous people signing their new publications. I met Paul Ritz in there when he was signing *Embassy*.'

'Oh yeah, that creep. And how did you find him?'

A flood of memories washed pleasantly through Kay's mind. That had been one of the highlights of her time at Oxford.

'I liked him. He took me out for a drink and I wrote an article about him . . .'

'You know, I can see why you're so frustrated, Kay. It was all so bloody easy and privileged here. You met Paul Ritz and you wrote an article about him, did you? Where else apart from Oxford would you ever get a chance to do that? I think it must be a terrible education for kids. They come here and they are taught to think that the world is their oyster . . .'

'You're right. Everything else is downhill after here . . .' Kay was disappointed to be denied her anecdote.

'But that's exactly the wrong way of looking at it!' Addy stopped and eyed her seriously. 'This place isn't real. It's like toy town. Everything else isn't downhill. It just is. And this place *isn't*. Do you see what I mean?'

And that, thought Kay, is the sort of distinction that I, with my Oxford education, should be able to make. But Addy didn't even think about it. It just came to her as an instinct.

'Now where is this fucking deer park?' She was already yards ahead.

They ambled along the path by the Cherwell. There was nobody about. The mist hung heavily over the marshy fields.

148

'This is where Bob and I came just after we had first made love,' Kay ventured.

'And Kay, he turned out to be a loser. I know what you're thinking. But you can't go back. I've been thinking about what you said earlier. I'm sure your reminiscences of him are unreal too. You and Bob were like Oxford. You were like a dream. You were like a story in a slushy magazine. I'm not saying that you won't ever have tingling feelings in your stomach again about a man, I'm just saying that they don't mean anything. Love is like dyspepsia, painful but you get over it.'

'Addy, you are talking the biggest load of rot I've ever heard, even from you. But you're right about Oxford and you're right about Bob. I shouldn't have come back, but it was your idea, don't forget. And now let's go home.'

On the train on the way home, Kay felt immensely relieved. It was a good thing to exorcise old ghosts. Addy's attitude was cathartic. Crudely cathartic, almost emetic in fact, but somehow comforting.

'Addy, where do you get all your worldly wisdom from? How do you know a hundred and one things about the human psyche? What were you doing when I was naively prancing around with Bob in Oxford's hallowed halls?'

'The thing is, Kay, I wouldn't want you to think that I'm some sort of guru.'

'Nothing was further from my mind.'

'No, I know, but you're always so over-impressed with other people's views. I just say what's on my mind. At least, I do to you. Other people I have a problem with. I just think that after three years with Bob you have gotten so used to bullshit that you set too much store by honesty.'

'Sorry.'

'Don't be sorry. Anyway, do you really want to hear how I spent my misspent youth?'

'Yes.'

'Well, I suppose about the time you started here, I first

arrived in London, after I ran away from home. No, that's another story. My growing up was in London. I lived above a pub in Soho. I made friends. On New Year's Eve we danced in the fountains of Trafalgar Square . . . '

'Now who's being nostalgic?' But Kay was fascinated. It was the first time she had ever heard Addy prepared to talk about her past.

'But it's all true! It must have been longer ago than I just said. I was only sixteen, sweet sixteen and never been kissed – well, never been laid anyway. I discovered sex and nearly became a pop star.' Addy told her story so nonchalantly and straightforwardly that one believed every detail until one stopped to reflect for a second on her words. Addy's anecdotes required total suspension of disbelief. Kay sometimes thought she would write a novel about Addy, but when she tried to write down past conversations she always failed. Addy's stories needed her own idiosyncratic telling of them. She had a rare quality of dramatic presence. Kay listened intently as she persevered.

' . . . My life is full of nearlys and this was an almost nearly. This band used to come into the pub. They played pubs in the East End and had just started to do a few gigs in Soho nightspots. They were called Ruby Shoeshine and were trying to revive mod music and all that. One night we were all sitting around getting drunk and Brian, the drummer, said he thought I'd look neat in one of their suits. So I stripped off and he stripped off and I put his suit on. I looked so good they decided to have me dressed up with them on stage. I had to sing a few lines too. Speak them, anyway – well, growl them would be a better description. I thought it was such a great idea I packed in my bar job and moved in with Poke . . . '

'Poke?'

'The lead singer. Appropriately named too. He couldn't believe I was a virgin. The first time we were really stoned. It all happened quite easily and I thought it was so funny I just laughed and laughed. I thought, is this what I've been

saving myself for? The earth didn't move. Needless to say
. . .'

'So why aren't you a rock star now? You sing terribly but that's no disqualification.'

'Poor old Poke had an accident on his moped. He was stoned and he just drove into the back of a delivery van. Lucky he wasn't killed, but he was in hospital for a while. That threw us all. We were just getting it together. We had even been reviewed in the music journals. By the time Poke came out of hospital there wasn't much left of Ruby Shoeshine . . .'

'So what did you do?'

'Just drifted for a while. I got a couple of waitressing jobs. I hate waitressing, but I get good tips. I didn't know what else to do.'

'Oh, poor damsel in distress. No Sir Galahad?'

'Who needs it when you can have an African potentate?'

'Oh, come on, Addy, there is a limit to what I'll believe.'

'He was real, I'm telling you. I was in a nightclub, a pretty trendy one, and I bumped into him. I think I'd served him the day before in one of the restaurants I worked in in Covent Garden. He was called some incredible unpronounceable name, but I called him Charlie. He was interesting and different from my usual boyfriends, and rich! He had a flat in Notting Hill Gate, a little *pied-à-terre* he called it, and he said if I wanted to move in I could. He was a student at Cambridge, but his family had this place in London which was empty most of the time. He said I could look after it for him. He took me back there one night and I stayed, and in the morning he asked me again. So I said yes. It was amazing, Kay. The flat was in one of those grand Georgian squares and had vast, high-ceilinged rooms with antique furniture and the walls dripping with old masters. I was so free. I had the place all to myself except when Charlie came down for the weekends. Every time he asked whether I wanted to sleep with him. Actually asked me! But it wasn't heavy. He was really the only man

151

I've screwed who I felt was a friend too.'

'But Addy, what happened? He sounds so nice.'

'Oh, he had to go home in the end and get involved in politics there. But he helped me get my next job. He knew the woman who ran Creme-Creme. You know, that really exclusive boutique in South Molton Strect. Victoria Hetherington Down. She was looking for an assistant who could show the clothes too. Little old me apparently fitted the bill. It was hard work and Victoria was a bit of a stuck-up cow, but we got along fine. I was star mannequin. I loved it. People would ask me out to the theatre and opera and stuff and loads of parties. Victoria didn't mind as long as I wore Creme-Creme clothes. She was very good-looking but she never seemed to have any men around. She had dark red hair and a wonderful voice, deep and throaty and sexy. She was powerful in a funny sort of way. To her customers how they dressed made them or broke them, so she was quite an important lady . . . '

'So why didn't you stay with this auburn bombshell?'

'Well, I blow everything as you know. But in this case it wasn't exactly my fault. She asked me to go on a trip to New York. We spent a lot of time choosing winter lines. I had to try on all the clothes and walk up and down all day in front of her. She always used to look so admiring. I began to think she was looking at me, not the clothes. She was the sort of person who needs to touch you the whole time when they're talking to you, just a hand on your arm or something. Several times she came in and watched when I was changing. Once, she told me I was beautiful. Even then the penny didn't drop. When she told me she was in love with me I was flabbergasted. Nobody has ever said that to me in any serious way. Usually men say it when they feel they have to, after fucking, but she really meant it. I was completely freaked. I was so naive I said I was sorry, but I just didn't feel that way about her. Then we both got all embarrassed and she told me to forget about it. But the next day she came in in a mood and said, 'You know, Addy, darling, sometimes I think you could do with a change of image. What do you think?' I just shrugged and asked if that meant she was giving me the push. She looked shocked and said she wouldn't dream of being so crude. But that was that. Yours truly, all alone in big, bad New York.'

'Oh Addy, you poor thing.' Kay wanted to give her a hug, she looked so woeful.

Then Addy laughed. 'Oh hell, that's life really, isn't it? I mean you just don't know what will happen next. I guess it's quite exciting!'

Addy's words took on a prophetic quality when they arrived back at the flat to two letters.

'Oh God, you'll never guess . . . !' Kay started jumping up and down. 'I've been offered that job at the literary agency . . . you know, the one where I had that interview and I thought I had been too pushy. Well, I've got it. What does yours say?'

'It's the big time, Kay, I'm going to be a model again.'

'I didn't know you were applying for modelling jobs.'

'Well, I was too embarrassed . . . On Thursday I saw this scrappy little ad in the *Standard* for a modelling agency called Below the Belt and, I thought, that sounds like me. Turns out they deal only with legs and bottoms. You know those catalogues of underwear? Well the next time you look at one, remember, I'm the bum inside the pink lace. It's good money though. What do you think?'

'Take it. Trust you, Addy. That is the most outrageous job I've ever heard of.'

'I didn't think I'd get it. I had to strut around in bikinis and things and the guy there wrote something on a clipboard. When I left I peeped at what he had been writing and it said 'nice legs', so I scrawled 'shame about the face' underneath. Thought I'd blown it. When do you start?'

'Monday. You?'

'Monday too. It's a new beginning. I wonder how soon it will end?'

Nine-thirty and the phone was already ringing. Her first phone call in the office.

'Richard Hawthorn, please,' the voice barked.

'I'm sorry, he doesn't seem to be in yet. Can I help?'

'Can you help? Who, my dear, are you?'

'I'm Mr Hawthorn's assistant, Kay Trevelyan, actually. It's my first day.'

'I see. Well, when do you expect him in?'

'Err. I'm not sure.'

'That's a good start. You're no good to me, I'm afraid. I want to speak to my agent. Tell him I rang.'

'Yes, but who . . . ?' The line went dead. Kay felt herself flushing. What was she doing here? For an instant she wanted to leave, run out of the door and never come back.

'Cheer up!'

'No, I was miles away, that's all.'

Two women, secretaries to the other agents at John Solomon, shared her room. Sharon, an eighteen-year-old cockney blonde with perfectly painted fingernails, and Anna. Anna had worked for John Solomon for years. She was one of those women of a certain age. Her smile was over-friendly and her watery eyes, surrounded by just too much turquoise eyeshadow, looked at Kay as if to say, 'I'll be your friend, but will you be mine?' Kay instantly felt guilty when she looked at her and decided promptly not to get too involved with her immediate workmates.

'I'm sure that Kay is just adjusting to our happy little family here, aren't you Kay?' Anna said. 'It must be a bit of a comedown after Oxford University. Richard told us you were at Oxford.'

'Yes, I was. But that was some time ago, now. I'm quite used to the real world, if that's what you mean.'

Anna turned back to her typewriter as if she had been rebuked. Kay regretted her sharpness. She had not meant to sound so confident and abrupt. She quickly forced a smile and turned to Sharon.

'So what's your lord and master, Richard Hawthorn, really like?'

'He's yours too, you know, or weren't you told?'

Sharon giggled, but Kay knew she had said the wrong thing again. She tried to persevere.

'Did he say when he would be in?'

'Richard? Doesn't usually get in 'til about eleven. He's OK once you get to know him. Doesn't half have his moods though. Really changeable . . . know what I mean?'

Oh God, thought Kay, I'm surrounded by morons and doomed to work for a monstrous chameleon. In her first moment alone in the office she decided to ring Addy at her new job.

'How is it?'

'Terrible. How's John Solomon?'

'Awful. Boring and tedious . . . '

'Got to run, Kay, looks like we've both got a great future behind us . . . '

Kay laughed. 'Too right . . . '

'In my view, things are never *too* right. They are right or wrong. Good morning.'

Kay swivelled round to see her new boss Richard Hawthorn looking down at her. His expression was severe, but there was a twinkle in his eye. Her phone rang again, but he snapped it up before she could reach for it.

'Hello. Yes, speaking . . . ' He talked and fumbled for a cigarette in his tweed jacket pocket. He shuffled from foot to foot as he spoke, but his voice was firm and relaxed.

'That cleared that up. Good.' He handed the receiver back to Kay. 'Welcome to John Solomon. Sorry I wasn't here to greet you in your first hours with us. I'm sure Sharon and Anna made more of a welcoming party than would have been within my competence. Any problems? Messages? Tell what crises and traumas fate has landed on my doorstep.' He flashed her a brief smile as she handed him a list of callers.

'Good, good. I see Janine Smythe has called three times.

She can wait. Yes. That seems to be under control.' He picked up his briefcase and walked into his office. Clouds of smoke trailed from his room as he talked on the phone.

At one o'clock he summoned her in. 'Ahh, there you are. My lunch guest is waiting downstairs. Can you show him up? Oh, and Kay, if I may, we're all on first name terms here, ask him if he'd like a drink.'

When Kay had imagined what her job would be like she hadn't thought that one of her tasks would be general waitress, but she had watched Sharon and Anna running around making coffee for their respective bosses most of the morning, and now Richard was asking her to be a barmaid. It had been difficult to persuade herself that she must get into publishing as a secretary, but it had seemed the only way to get a foot on the ladder. She had been prepared for typing, taking dictation, filing and other menial duties, but not for being a lackey. What possible reason, apart from macho ego-boosting, could there be for asking her to pour drinks? Kay stamped downstairs to the reception area, frowning.

A slim, dark-haired man stood with his back towards the stairs. Kay realized that she had forgotten to ask Richard his lunch guest's name, but as the man turned, she recognized him instantly.

'Paul Ritz. I didn't realize . . . How do you do?'

'Hello. Richard's free now, is he?' There was no sign of recognition in his distinctive, sad dark eyes. Kay tried to think of something to say but 'we've met before' sounded so corny. And how would she explain her position? Paul Ritz wasn't the sort of man who had time for secretaries. He had only just managed to tolerate her as an aspiring journalist. But she had to say something. She held out her hand.

'My name's Kay Trevelyan and I have just started as Richard's assistant.'

'Kay Trevelyan.' He looked at her closely. 'I remember names. Tell me where we've met before. I'm not so good at places.'

'Oxford. A couple of years ago.'

'Ahh yes, indeed. Well, something is coming back now. But you've changed surely? Your hair perhaps? And now you've come to apprentice yourself to Richard. Good. Where is he?'

'Oh, just follow me upstairs.' Kay was mystified. Either he remembered her or he didn't. She wracked her brains to find something suitable with which to continue the conversation. What she came up with sounded banal.

'Have you been abroad? I heard you were in New York this year.'

'Yes, I don't seem to have stopped travelling since *Embassy* was published. Lecture tours, documentaries and then the film. But I'm back in Europe now for a little time at least.'

Kay led him into Richard's office.

'Paul! Welcome. You've met this little lady, then . . . '

'I have, but Kay and I go a long way back. She's the little devil who wrote that piece about me in *Isis*. Don't you remember, Richard? I recall you thinking it was good copy. I'm afraid, with all due respect, I didn't agree . . . '

Kay returned his smile. So he did remember. She had always wondered how he had reacted to her article.

'Good Lord, what a coincidence!' said Richard. 'I do remember something like that. Now, Paul, will you have a whisky before, or just during and after lunch? Thank you, Kay.'

She realized she was expected to leave quietly and she resented being dismissed so perfunctorily.

'Goodbye, Mr Ritz,' she said, holding out her hand. 'It was nice to see you again.'

'Take care, love.' Ritz winked at her as he shook her hand and she was flustered with annoyance. Both men were as bad as each other. Patronizing male chauvinist pigs. For the umpteenth time that day Kay was firmly convinced that a secretary's life was not for her.

* * *

A joking camaraderie was so much part of his relationship with Richard Hawthorn that, when he gave it any thought, Paul Ritz could never remember when their professional dealings had become a friendship. Richard, for all his mannerisms, was a good friend and an entertaining companion. Ritz felt a sense of warmth at seeing him again after such a long time. Since leaving Oxford, where they had been arch rivals, and even before Richard had become his agent, it had been their custom to have a regular slap-up Chinese feast, but it had been impossible to continue this tradition since the publication of *Embassy*. Ritz had not stopped in London for more than a couple of days for the last two years, his assignments had been so plentiful, pressing and, thanks to Richard's silver-tongued negotiation, lucrative. Richard was a first-rate agent, one of the best in London, and in some ways Ritz recognized that it was Richard who had made Paul Ritz into the success he was. He had planned his career carefully, urging him to specialize in the beginning, and building on the name he had made during Vietnam into a top-class journalist. It was Richard who had suggested him for television, and even *Embassy* had stemmed from one of Richard's famed insights – the ones that occurred to him halfway down his second bottle of claret. Ritz was happy to see him again and laughed loudly as he finished an anecdote about a rival agent.

'They call him a legend in his own lunchtime!' Richard guffawed. 'Paul, even *I* couldn't contemplate spending fifty thousand pounds per annum on lunches alone!'

A blank-faced waiter arrived with a trolley of *dim sum* and they helped themselves liberally. The conversation was as predictable as the menu. Over the *dim sum* Richard would be jolly and loud. During the main course he would sit quietly and listen to Ritz's schedule and his ideas for the future. An intelligent if drunken discussion would ensue over the lychees and mangoes.

'And what do you think of that young wench I've just

employed?' Richard lecherously bit into a deep-fried *won ton*. 'Quite a little cracker, is she not?'

'She's a pretty girl.' For no good reason that he could think of, Ritz was reluctant to get into a girlie conversation today, but he caught a flicker of disappointment on Richard's face and continued for his benefit: 'Quite a goer, I should think, although there is something a little bit prim about her. Have you got some wicked ideas, Richard? Surely you're too old to contemplate . . . .'

'My dear boy, nothing was further from my mind. I look and admire, but I don't touch any more. Playing with fire in her case, I should think. Underneath that ice-maiden serenity, a blazing furnace. No, I rather thought I caught a little *frisson* of something between you and the girl, but if, as you say, you're too old . . . '

'I remarked that you were . . . '.

'Quite.'

One of the standard jokes between the two men was their age. Richard was less than a year older than Ritz but appeared much more. Time and drink had taken their toll on him.

'She's certainly not the lamb I saw in Oxford. Very much more sophisticated. But we are not here to discuss the fair sex.'

'Ssshush, my dear fellow,' Richard's voice was heavy with irony. 'Never let me hear you say that in a public place again. Paul Ritz must be seen to be always discussing sex, fair or not. Tut tut. Ahh, here come the sizzling dishes. Now tell me what you've been up to.'

Ritz successfully negotiated a sliver of peppered beef with his chopsticks. He felt inordinately impatient with the bantering chitchat. 'I'll fill you in on the details some other time, but what I really want to ask you is how you think the world would react to another book from me.'

Richard's reaction was as he knew it would be, immediately and spontaneously enthusiastic.

'With open arms, Paul, you know that surely. But have

you the time or the inclination?'

'Inclination certainly, time I think I must make for myself. I've come to the end of most of my commitments and, quite frankly, I'm bored with living out of a suitcase, even if it is a Louis Vuitton suitcase.' He smiled. Richard liked acknowledgement of the riches he was responsible for amassing for his client. 'I haven't stopped since *Embassy* and I think I have diversified too much for my own good. Now that the television thing in American is sewn up and I only have one commitment to that ghastly Christmas round-up programme, it seems like the right moment to pause and have a rethink.'

'Of course, there's no need to justify it. I think it is a very timely suggestion . . .'

But now that Ritz had started he wanted to finish, as much to clarify his own thoughts as to satisfy his agent. One of Richard's most valuable uses was as a sounding board. Generally Ritz's life was so hectic that he rarely stopped to think of what next. All his assignments were planned and executed with clockwork precision. Articles were written to deadlines, flights booked, interviews scheduled, but recently he had become tired of the pace and the organization. He felt he had in some sense relinquished his freedom.

'I have lost the impetus to do as much as possible,' he continued. 'I have the increasing feeling that my work has lost its substance. Everyone wants me because I'm Paul Ritz, not for what I write. I'm not having a menopausal crisis or anything, Richard, but I need to do something I find more satisfying, more solid.'

'I quite understand and approve, for what it's worth. What I can contribute is this. I could get you commissioned this afternoon, but I doubt that's what you want. That would, of course, be an extension of what you're talking about – selling a book on your reputation. What I would prefer to do is show a nice detailed outline of the book you have in mind. I presume you do have a book in mind?'

'I have a very nebulous idea, but a blockbuster if I get it right.' Fighting talk, but Ritz was nervous.

'Perhaps at this stage we should wet our whistles with a little more booze?' Richard waved at the waiter. His sense of timing was immaculate, perfected after twenty years of salving the anxieties of sensitive authors. Ritz was glad of the opportunity to collect his thoughts. He was conscious that perhaps for the first time in his working life, he really needed someone else's blessing on his idea. It was nebulous. He had thought about it on and off for three years and still he was not sure whether he was chasing a wild goose or a real story. But it stayed with him and kept cropping up in his thoughts. He wanted it to work. He sipped his whisky.

'I want to write about people who have defected. And before you say "hardly original", I'll add two words – without trace.'

Richard sighed and poured himself another glass of wine. 'I'm sorry, Paul, if this stuff has gone to my head, but I honestly don't see what you are getting at.'

'Nor did I, at first, but then it all became clear. You see, we all assume that we know about defectors because as soon as they get to the Soviet Union they give a press conference. Half their use is to embarrass Britain in the eyes of the CIA. We know all about Burgess, Maclean and Philby now, because the Russians chose for us to know. But what if many others, not necessarily major political spies, but small potatoes, scientists, technicians and people like that went over? Certainly the British government might suspect but wouldn't necessarily want anyone else to find out. The Soviet Union would have no reason to expose them if they had specifically got them in to do a job, would they?'

'So, in effect, you're proposing a West-East brain drain?'

Ritz smiled. Richard was quick and he could tell immediately that he liked the idea. 'Exactly.'

'Good God, Paul, that's a fascinating idea, and right up your street. What on earth made you think of it?'

Ritz took another sip of his drink. 'Do you remember when I was in Central America in 1980? It doesn't seem like three years ago but it must have been . . . '

'*Behind the Scenes* was a fine piece of writing. One of your best.'

'Thank you. I think you're right. I was moved by what I saw. I think some emotion does produce better work from me. But one of the people who touched me most, I didn't write about. She didn't want me to, and I didn't want to press her. But I felt she had a story to tell. I had enough material and I didn't pursue it. She's an Englishwoman living in the Nicaraguan forests and working as a nurse. She had been there a while, I'm not sure quite how long, but unlike most of the ex-pats she deliberately separates herself from the other whites. The extraordinary thing was that when I met her, far away from the rest of the British community, we vaguely recognized each other. She was a contemporary of ours at Oxford. One can't get away from them, you know, however far you go. I don't think you would have come across her. She was what you would have called a leftie. I didn't really know her myself, but we had a tutor in common and I knew her face. It is not a face one could easily forget . . . '

'But where does she come into your book idea?' Richard interrupted. 'I'm sorry, Paul, I don't follow. She's a beauty is she, this lone nurse?' He leered.

'Not now, no. It's not what your one-track mind is thinking. She was a beauty. Now, well, she has a powerful presence and a smile to move hearts. But she has aged.' Ritz found he couldn't sum her up adequately in terms of looks. 'But perhaps I'm getting sidetracked. She's an interesting woman, but there's hardly a book in her. It was something she said. We were chatting about book possibilities. I'd just finished *Embassy* and was ready to go on the next one. I got sidetracked there too of course . . . '

'And what did she say?' Richard was impatient for the facts.

'She brought up the concept of betrayal. It started me thinking . . . '

'But is there anything in your theory? Have you done any research?'

'A little. I've done a lot of thinking about how to go about it without alerting anyone, and I think I can manage it. Of course, I may find nothing. It's a risk I've got to take. I think we ought to keep it under wraps until I've got a lead or two, don't you?'

'You mean I can't even mention it to Roger Montgomery when I'm lunching him tomorrow?' Richard was teasing. Roger Montgomery was renowned as the most indiscreet publisher in town.

'I think not.'

'You know, Paul, I've got a feeling it's going to work. It's so obvious. It's one of those ideas that makes you think "Why hasn't anyone thought of it before?" and that sort of idea is usually a winner. Strange how these things crop up. From an old Oxford chum too . . . '

'Then you really think I'm on to something?'

'Of course I do.' Richard paid the bill and stood up. 'You have wasted three years as far as I'm concerned. Get to work!'

'OK,' said Ritz. 'Well, I'll be able to get in two good weeks before Christmas then I'm off to Paris for a few days. I'll keep you in touch if there's any progress.'

'Going to stay with your lovely sister? Do give her my love.'

'I will. Are you having the usual bash at New Year?'

'Yes. Why don't you come along, if you're back in London? It should be fun.'

'I'll try,' said Ritz and disappeared into the throng of Christmas shoppers.

Kay looked at her watch. The afternoon was dragging. She seemed to have run out of things to say to Sharon and Anna and she still felt demeaned after her encounter with Ritz.

'Don't let that swine Paul Ritz get you down,' Sharon had remarked. 'He makes life hell for everyone around here. Always ringing up from all over the world and reversing the charges. Don't know who he thinks he is.'

'Well, he is pretty important. He must make a huge amount of money for the agency,' Kay had ventured, and Sharon had glared at her.

'Don't care if he's Jesus Christ Almighty, there's no need for bad manners,' she had said through tight lips, and Kay had felt she herself was being rebuked as much as Ritz.

'How long do Richard's lunches usually last?' she said.

'With Ritz? Forever! I doubt that Richard will be back today . . .'

'Which goes to show, Sharon, how wrong you can be. Usually are, in fact.' Richard stood in the doorway. 'Kay, can you come into my office now and bring a notepad please.'

Kay followed him in and shut the door behind her. Richard was on the phone telling the switchboard girl to hold all calls. Then he put down the receiver and turned to her with a wide smile.

'Look, I'm sorry to do this to you on your first day here, but I've just had the most fascinating lunch and I'd like a few letters to go off to publishers this afternoon. I'm going to be conducting what is called an auction. That means I offer a book project to various publishers and ask for the highest offer by a certain day. The only thing is that in this case I'll be putting my own credibility on the line too. In effect, there's no book, it's what is called a sight-unseen auction, but I think that I can hype up the mystery enough to get as good an offer as if there were. Don't look so disapproving, my dear, I'm not conning anyone. I'm just taking a slight gamble . . .'

He went on to explain his conversation with Ritz and the reason why he thought it would encourage his author to continue if he had a commitment to a publisher. He remarked that Ritz had obviously been unsure of the

164

project for three years and needed a push to get him going now. He assured her that Ritz would approve in his heart of hearts if he knew what was going on. It was often the case that an agent knew what was best for the author, before the author himself did.

By the end of their conversation Kay was at fever pitch with excitement. To be helping to sell a book by Paul Ritz on her first day at work was more than she had dreamed possible. She was delighted that Richard had taken her into his confidence. He had instilled her with the feeling that they were working together and she was learning so much about the business in so few minutes.

'One of the most important things for you to learn is discretion, Kay,' Richard finished up. 'You may sometimes think that I am being totally indiscreet, but what twenty years in this job has taught me is to know who to say what to. For the time being your best bet is silence. I don't want a word of what I've just said going out of this office. Not to Sharon, Anna, your boyfriend or anyone else. The walls have ears and one has to be careful. But I'm sure it's superfluous of me to tell you this. You seem from our brief acquaintance to conduct yourself well. If there are any questions, ask me. I'm sure you're clever enough to realize I'm not the ogre these girls think. Now, let's get going.'

Kay spent the rest of the afternoon deciphering her rushed shorthand and typing the letters Richard had dictated. Richard had a way with words. The letters to publishers were a subtle manipulation, promising the book of the century without mentioning anything of substance. She found herself enjoying typing them.

On the stroke of five-thirty Sharon and Anna gathered their handbags up and left the office. Kay sealed the signed letters and persuaded the postboy to open up the franking machine and add them to the evening's first-class post. She felt satisfied at having done a good day's work, and was tidying her desk when Richard poked his head round the door.

'How wonderful not to have taken on another clock-watcher.' He beamed at her. 'Sharon and Anna find it difficult to raise their well-upholstered bottoms from their chairs all day, but when it is five-thirty they move as if they're making an attempt on the land-speed record.'

Kay laughed and lit a cigarette. Her first that day.

'And a smoker too! I know I shouldn't encourage it in the young, but it is nice to find a companion in vice. You've coped very well today. I think you deserve a drink. How does a cocktail at the Connaught grab you? I've got to meet Jerry Mildenberg, the most fatuous American publisher, there for dinner and I need a little refreshment at the unconscionable prospect of three hours with him. Would you join me? Come on, we'll hail a cab.'

'Well, you have rather been thrown in at the deep end today, but I need someone who can take some pressure,' Richard said when they were seated at a table. 'What will you have?'

'A tomato juice, please.' Kay didn't think that alcohol would be a good idea. She had spent the lunch hour reading through the authors' files in an attempt to assimilate background details. She hadn't thought about eating, but now she felt empty.

'Oh, come now. Don't be shy. You look as if you need something much stronger.'

'No, really, a tomato juice is what I would like. Make it a double if you want.' But Richard was already on his way to the bar.

Kay sat down in an armchair and surveyed the Connaught lounge. She was glad she opted for looking smart but trendy that day. A plain navy wool suit with a white silk blouse and a navy-and-yellow striped tie. Addy had approved of its demure schoolgirl appeal that morning. Kay knew that Ellen would have approved of the suit, but perhaps raised an eyebrow at the tie and that had been exactly the impression she wanted to create. Proper, but individualistic.

She was slightly discomfited to become aware of a tall man lolling in the sofa opposite and unabashedly staring at her. She wished Richard would hurry up. It was difficult to avoid the stranger's gaze. He was dressed entirely in white, from his bow tie to his shoes. Crisp raw silk against a pallid complexion, but even at this distance the blue of his eyes was striking. Those eyes, that angular but pretty face reminded her of someone, but somehow the straight dark hair was wrong. And there was no look of recognition in his blank stare.

'Is that androgynous creature over there bothering you?' Richard looked down at her.

'No, I don't mind.'

'You really don't mind either, do you? You seem to be a pretty tough young lady, if I may be so bold as to make a personal comment at this early stage.'

'I wouldn't describe myself as tough. Determined, maybe. And for the record, I'm not the young lady type.' Kay frowned, but seeing the look of utter surprise on Richard's face, turned the frown into a self-parodying glower.

'Well, thank goodness for that. I thought for a moment that ferocious look was meant to kill.'

Kay took a sip of her drink. It had lots of ice, lemon and Worcester sauce in it. And vodka. She coughed. Richard was obviously used to having his own way. He seemed to be waiting for her to say something but she decided not to rise to the challenge.

'So tell me,' he asked after a short silence, 'What do you want from John Solomon?'

Kay was slightly taken aback by the directness of his question. Her natural instincts told her to defer to him or manoeuvre the conversation until she was surer of what he was really asking. But her talks with Ellen about getting a job in publishing had taught her to be assertive. Being a secretary was a way in, but where most women failed was that they began to see themselves in a purely secretarial role. The trick, Ellen had said, and it was a difficult one, was to expect to be treated as an equal while not exceeding the bounds of subservience the job required.

'To be honest, Richard, (it was always best to drop first names into the conversation, she had read in a book Ellen had edited called *Getting On*), 'I want to use John Solomon as a stepping stone. I'm prepared to work hard for you for one or two years at most, and learn as much as I can about the business, but when I feel I'm ready, I'll want you to help me get a job at a higher level, either inside or out of John Solomon.'

'Well, well. I see that Ellen Hamilton, who, by the way, gave you a sparkling reference, wasn't wrong about your zeal. I'll want to see if you're any good, of course, before I set you up. And I do require total commitment and hard work, but *ceteris paribus* I think we have a deal. Would you like another drink to clinch it?' Kay giggled. She was flushed with the success of her first negotiation and the alcohol was, as she had predicted, coursing through her blood.

'Something a little stronger than tomato juice?' he enquired.

'No, I think the same again, thank you. It is one of the strongest tomato juices I've ever tasted.' She thought she detected a look of approval as he strode to the bar.

They spent another pleasant half hour chatting about the business, and Richard described his clients to Kay with brief, thumbnail sketches which Kay was to learn in the next few weeks were beautifully accurate, for all their economy. The authors he represented were mainly of the commercial variety. Modern romantic novelists, a couple of big thriller writers and several cooks. He said he hoped she wasn't expecting Booker Prize-winning literary calibre, and when Kay admitted that she would like to deal with some creative writers he told her firmly that she had a lot to

168

learn. All professional writers were creative, and creative usually meant neurotic and demanding. It didn't really matter whether the book was a literary masterpiece, or a Marks and Spencers guide to home decorating, the same processes were involved and it was the job of a literary agent to support the author and get them the best deal possible. But, he added as if softening the blow, if she knew of any literary geniuses, he would be glad to take them on.

'Now tell me,' he concluded, 'from your vast experience of one day, and the benefit of listening to me for half an hour, what do you think you will find most exciting about the job?'

'Working with Paul Ritz.' The words were out before she realized it, and Kay cursed the alcohol for making her sound like a fan.

'Indeed!' Richard chuckled. 'Of course you've met him before, haven't you? I'm afraid he isn't usually the best-liked author of my girls. But perhaps he'll be different with you.'

Kay disliked the implication that she was one of his girls. Surely if men were secretaries they wouldn't be referred to as boys. 'And why is that?' she asked coolly.

'Well, I'm sure Sharon would tell you it's because he's arrogant and "full of himself".' He mimicked Sharon's twang perfectly. 'But really it's because they fall in love with him, you see. They seek intimacy with him, they tell their friends with pride that they have made coffee for him and they outrageously bat their eyelashes in his direction. But the fact is that Mr Ritz is surrounded by so many talented, rich and beautiful women that he really doesn't notice. He has what one might call an *embarras de richesse* as far as the fair sex is concerned. Understandably my girls are jealous and feel betrayed.'

Kay was furious at his outrageous chauvinism and felt bound to stand up for women. 'Well, perhaps he ought not to flirt with them in the first place, if that's the case,' she snapped, knowing as soon as she had said it how ridiculously she was conforming to the stereotype Richard had described.

'Perhaps not, perhaps not.' Richard grinned at her. 'But I'm sure you are far too surrounded by your own admirers to be bothered with our famous playboy.'

Practically the same words that had fallen from the lips of Ritz himself all those years ago in Oxford. Did they secretly know about her lack of success with men? Kay began to feel she was the victim of a male conspiracy. But she was determined not to show it.

'Quite,' she said, smiling. 'Now I think I had better leave you to your boring dinner. I'll see you tomorrow. And thank you for the drink. It was most . . . educative.'

She left Richard with his mouth hanging open with surprise. Certainly Kay would learn a lot from him. But perhaps she could teach him a thing or two as well.

Those first two weeks at John Solomon lived up to the promise of the first day. Richard concluded his auction with a record sum and took her, appropriately, to the Ritz for a champagne celebration. Kay buzzed with energy and a sense of purpose and each night she went home bursting with things to tell Addy.

One night she came in to find Addy lounging in the bathroom. 'Hi, come in and shut the door,' she called out. 'I know it's fresh oxygen but it's ruining my sauna effect.'

Addy lay sprawled in the bath, one leg inelegantly dangling over the side. The steam was rising from the surface of the water and her skin was a delicate shade of pink. She looked like some strange shellfish cast up by the sea on a Caribbean shore. A cut-glass goblet perched next to the soap dish.

'Have some bubbly. There's more in the fridge.' Addy waved a languid hand. Kay took a sip.

'Mmm . . . so what are you celebrating then?'

'Nothing at all. I nicked it from the Palace.'

170

'You stole it? From the Camden Palace? But you've only had that job a month.' Addy still had her one night a week job at the Camden Palace to supplement her modelling income.

'Oh, they're so dumb they wouldn't notice. Anyway, I deserve it. Your job might fill you with enthusiasm, mine's a pain in the butt!'

'What about the glass? It's beautiful. Where did you steal that from?'

'Oh, come on. Gimme me a break. It's a family heirloom. It was my great-grandfather's. He was an eccentric Victorian explorer and, according to family legend, that's where I get my wildness from. I'm also supposed to look like him, devastatingly beautiful, you know. My granny had a portrait of him and I do, if you take away the beard that is.'

'How romantic!'

'You bet. He came to a terrible end too. He should have been eaten by a rampaging lioness or drowned in the waters of the Blue Nile. Do you know what happened to him? He was short-sighted and refused to wear glasses. Vanity, you see. One day, squelch, right under a passing tram.'

'Addy, you're preposterous!'

'It's true. You can laugh . . . Granny used to tell us. She said we should be grateful for the fact God gave us good eyesight.'

'And are you?'

'You bet. I can spot a man a mile off.'

Addy wriggled a pair of suede shorts over her hips and scowled at her image in the mirror. An uneven trail of talc led from the bathroom to her dressing table. Kay sat perched on Addy's bed looking down at her applying make-up with quick, efficient strokes.

'You know,' said Addy, 'I'm not sure whether I like my body or not. I guess it's got some good points. I think it's a bit ambivalent myself . . . Just listen to me. I wish I didn't hate myself so much sometimes. I mean, do you ever stare at yourself in the mirror and think, Christ, who is this?'

'No, can't say I do, and I don't think you need to either. You look great.'

'Why is it we're so different, eh?' Addy swung round. 'I mean, take men. You don't seem to care whether you have a man around or not. You really wait until you find someone you like, even if you do sometimes make mistakes, like that Bob guy! But me, I'm a lost cause. I just can't keep away from them! Seriously though, Kay, don't you miss them, I mean don't you ever feel like a screw?'

Kay felt embarrassed. 'Yes, I suppose I do sometimes, but . . .'

'But, you see, you just coolly say, "but" . . . I couldn't be so self-disciplined. That's what you are, Kay, really controlled. I mean, I wouldn't mind if I even enjoyed it, you know, screwing. Sometimes I think it was a nasty joke God played on us, don't you?'

Kay felt irritated. Since they had come back to London Addy had had an endless string of boyfriends and at times she had felt a twinge of jealousy. It seemed a long, long time since there had been a man in her life.

'I don't understand you, Addy. You meet some really lovely men. Why do you always talk as though you hated them and sex? I almost envy you all your affairs. At least you've had lots . . . You're the one who's the *femme fatale*.'

'Huh, sometimes I feel about as *fatale* as an after-dinner mint . . . as someone once said. Anyone can have men. They're suckers.'

'Well, right now I wouldn't mind a man in my life.' That was quite an admission. 'The only men in my life are Richard Hawthorn, Paul Ritz and the postboy. He's a real sweetie!' Kay laughed.

'Who, the postboy? Well, as long as you're not talking about Paul Ritz. Every time I see him on the box I want to puke.' Addy pulled her tongue out at her reflection.

'I really don't see why you're so rude about him. He's really not that bad. He's supposed to be a highly desirable bachelor, don't you know. Richard showed me a copy of *Cosmopolitan* where he was listed as one of the top ten most eligible men in the world.'

'Jesus, Kay, just listen to you, anyone would think you were sweet on him yourself. You're not, are you?'

Addy stared intimidatingly at her. 'You're blushing, Kay. Christ, I should have known it. Every time you tell me about your job you mention him. Look, kid, forget it. Don't give him another thought. In one word, get over it, it would be a disaster, capital D. Go join a nunnery.'

'You can't count and I don't know what you're talking about. He's one of our most important authors and he happens to be very good looking.'

'Well, just keep on looking and keep it at that.' Addy blew a kiss and bounced out of the door to a date with an out-of-work actor she'd met the night before.

Kay lay back on the bed staring at the ceiling gloomily. She knew without a doubt that Addy's date would end in some trauma or other, they always did, but she couldn't stop feeling envious. At that moment she longed for a man to touch and put her arms around. She climbed down from the bed and walked despondently into the front room. At least there was her work to enjoy, she supposed.

When Addy wasn't around, the flat seemed very quiet. Kay turned the radio to Radio 3 and tried to work up the energy to get out the vacuum cleaner. The living room floor was strewn with magazines and brimming ashtrays. Kay disdainfully picked up a pair of shiny green running shorts Addy had discarded. Addy was like a whirlwind and Kay found it difficult to remember what life was like before she had taken over. But it somehow seemed inevitable she should be there.

Since their day in Oxford Addy had revealed a lot more about her background and it had moved Kay. She did not believe everything Addy said but she realized just how much Addy's tough exterior belied the truth. They had a lot more in common than she had ever imagined. Kay now knew that she was part of Addy's support system and Addy was part of hers. They needed each other.

They had established an easy routine in the flat which reminded Kay of her flat-sharing days with Zoe. In fact, Addy sometimes reminded her of Zoe, her brashness and *joie de vivre*. At the back of Kay's mind this had become a further reason for wanting to be affectionate with Addy. She had never forgiven herself for Zoe. Whenever she thought of her dead friend she felt great loss because she had never demonstrated her affection for her.

In their first few weeks in London Addy had sometimes been unusually low and despondent. Kay had only seen her like this after one of the innumerable break-ups of a relationship, when Addy would be sad for twenty-four hours and then point to all the obvious defects in a former lover's character and proclaim what a lucky escape she had made. Kay had thought Addy was worried about her future. Whatever it was it did not last for long and as soon as Addy got the modelling job she resumed the mad, zany act Kay knew so well.

She spent Sunday mornings roller skating in Chalcot Square, zipping and weaving between benches and litter bins with several of the local kids whooping and squawking behind, while Kay sat reading the papers and occasionally watching her from the window seat.

The biggest surprise was when Addy started to cook. In New York she had eaten out or grabbed a pretzel as she walked down the street. Now, when Kay got in from work on evenings when Addy was in, she was greeted by a smell of cooking and Addy would be sprinkling herbs and spices into a casserole muttering to herself, 'Yeah, let's have a bit of that, why not?'

One evening she announced to Kay that she had decided they ought to become vegetarians. They were watching a TV programme on how battery hens were kept and the conditions which farm stock for slaughter lived in. 'Christ, it's disgusting, Kay. Just look at that. I mean, can you

174

believe it? Look at that poor cow!'

And that night she produced a bean goulash and proudly dumped it on the table. The beans were not properly cooked and the sauce was bland. Kay took a few mouthfuls and then burst into giggles. For a moment Addy looked crestfallen then she picked up the casserole and disappeared into the kitchen. Kay heard her tipping it down the waste disposal unit. When she emerged again she had two enormous doughnuts on a plate. 'Emergency reserves, just in case,' she muttered, cramming a huge bite into her mouth.

As the nights drew in and the weather became progressively colder and wetter, Kay would look forward to returning to their flat and curling up on the bed in her warm, dove-grey bedroom. She thought of Chalcot Square as 'their' home and enjoyed the rare evenings when Addy was not going out and they would listen to records and mix innumerable cocktails, discussing their days at work and laughing.

It often occurred to Kay how different their daily existence was. Addy's exploits modelling seemed so far removed from the frenetic routine at John Solomon. At times when she felt worried about the amount of work she had to do or when she had had a conversation with an author that she felt she had not handled well, she envied Addy's nonchalant attitude to her job. Occasionally she would feel irritated when she tried to explain to her why she felt pressurized or concerned about how well she was doing, and Addy would laugh and dismiss her as a perfectionist. But she was constantly amazed at how well they got on.

One evening Kay was reading a manuscript when Addy wandered into the living room and flung herself into a deck chair.

'Jesus Christ, I'm hot!'

'What the hell are you wearing? I know you haven't been to the launderette for weeks but this is ridiculous!'

175

'Well, I always was kind of trashy.'

'Well, don't complain to me about being hot when you've chosen for some bizarre reason to wear a plastic bin liner.'

'But that's the whole point – I'm meant to be sweating out poisons. It's my new health kick, a lot easier than excrising!'

'But do you have to purify yourself here? You look ridiculous lounging on a deck chair in a black bin liner.'

Addy shrugged her shoulders. 'I could go and put on the latest in jade satin crotchless knickers, if you'd find that more tasteful. You know, last night on my date I decided to wear stockings. Jesus, Kay, have you ever worn them? I felt like a Barbie Doll, every time I sat down I thought the suspenders would pop and my stockings would fall down, and the worst thing was, when I got undressed, the jerk I was with pissed himself laughing. I mean, I thought underwear was supposed to be a turn-on not a wind-up.'

'So what was so funny?'

'I guess it was what I had on over them. I decided to wear my black Pierre Cardin evening jacket and trousers, you know the ones I filched from Henry, as of "Isn't it heavenly, darling, simply perfect" fame. Well, I had this stunning suit on and my suspenders and stockings underneath, real silk too, and then I decided to wear my Calvin Klein Y-fronts on top. Well, they kind of went with a man's suit, I thought. You remember I showed you them last week, they're the latest in sporty underwear.'

'Addy, you're crazy!'

'So I gather from the reaction I got . . . anyway, seriously Kay.' Addy's expression took on a pleading quality. 'There's something I've been wanting to ask you, a big favour. You know at Christmas . . . Oh, Jesus, I hate asking this. Thing is I was going to spend it skiing with some old friends, and they've kind of let me down. I know you'll be going home and I wondered – well, can I come with you? I mean it would be really depressing being here on my own with a turkey cutlet and these fucking deck chairs, don't you think?'

'Well, I suppose so . . . I mean, yes, of course, only it'll be really boring, Addy. I'm only going because I promised I would, Father being ill. You know what it's like. If you're sure you really want to, I could ask. But don't say I didn't warn you.'

'Your parents can't be as bad as all that. I just don't believe it. Your Mum sounds a real sweetie on the phone.'

Kay pulled a face. 'I suppose she is. Well, she will be to you.' Kay was lying. She wasn't at all sure how her parents would react to Addy.

PARIS

Christmas was for families. He never really thought of himself as having a family except at Christmas, which he had spent for as long as he could remember with his sister Gina. He had left her struggling to pluck and clean the fat Christmas goose, his offers to help having been firmly turned down. He always thought of Paris as a restful city. He knew few people here and even in the Christmas bustle he found it a haven.

Bright sunshine cascaded down from the clear blue sky, drawn like a magnet to the frozen puddles. It hurt his eyes. In their frosty sparseness the Jardins des Tuileries were magical. He drew a deep gulp of frozen air and it sunk to his stomach. As he walked through the park towards the ice-covered fountains he could hear the shrieks of children skating on slippery pathways. He shivered in the cold and buttoned up his leather trench coat.

He was glad of this opportunity to walk anonymously and think. The cold air would clear his head and allow him to order his thoughts. Last night he had drunk too much whisky and his tongue felt thick with the stale alcohol. Gina had warned him, 'Paolo, tomorrow you will regret this drinking, this whisky is not good for you. You will see.' She had been right.

For years he had come to spend Christmas in her small flat on the Ile St Louis. He always looked forward to it. A few days of calm and relaxation, an escape from the fray. He enjoyed the fuss Gina made of him, her ceaseless chatter and eruptive giggles, her mocking castigation of his lifestyle, their verbal jousting and teasing familiarities, the ease of her care and affection. Gina's flat was, for a few days, a home.

178

He quickened his step past couples strolling arm in arm. The women elegantly decked in furs, their faces alive with warm lipsticks and pinked cheeks. The distinctive Parisian waft of expensive perfume. Occasionally he met their eyes glancing inquisitively at him. These days he was unmoved by even the most beautiful face. A young couple ran past him giggling as they tumbled into an embrace. It was a long time since he had looked into anyone's face like that. He had given up the pretence of romance a long time ago. But at times like this he regretted his hardness, the cynicism that separated the bedroom from the rest of his world. He had made loving into one kind only, between the bed sheets. It was safer that way and that was the way it was with him now, he couldn't imagine anything else. Being in love was for the young, he heard a voice in his head mocking him, the naive. Besides, he didn't have the time. Paul Ritz sat down on a bench.

On reflection, he was pleased with the work he had done so far. Richard had done well to give him the extra incentive. The book had assumed a concrete shape now that he had a deadline to work to. He had learned a lot in these two weeks, but he was slightly troubled that there was no definite substance. With *Embassy*, he had always known his aims and his research had been a collection of proof. But this book, whose working title was *Gone – Without Trace*, was more difficult. Before he could get anywhere with his research he had to know that his thesis was right. By its very nature this was practically impossible – he was looking for people who no longer officially existed and he didn't even know their names.

His strategy was to obtain twenty-year-old lists of personnel from major industries and government research establishments and follow up their careers to the present day. Several of his more useful contacts had given him clues as to where to look. He had managed to eliminate thousands of the names quite quickly and he had a few hopeful leads. Names of people he could not trace or who had died under suspicious circumstances. Some of their families, friends and disillusioned colleagues had given him enough reason to think he was on the right track. But still he had to find that first big name.

Yet he was sure it had been the right decision to pursue this book. His mind had been envigorated and he had worked with an enthusiasm he had not felt since writing *Embassy*. That night even Gina's lavish Christmas preparations could not fully distract him from his mental notes.

'I see that you cannot stop thinking about your work,' she said, 'so I'll have to ask you about it, then perhaps you will talk to me for more than one sentence.'

Gina snorted and threw back her head. She was sitting in a huge tapestry armchair, a glass of brandy in her hand. He watched as she looked down and swirled the brown spirit slowly round the rim and then her eyes returned to his face.

'So, what are you up to now? It must be this book those stupid publishers have paid so much for. What is it about? Is it exciting? I want to know everything.'

He was sitting cross-legged on the floor. He leant backwards to allow the sofa to support his back. 'If you ask fewer questions I would have more time to give you answers, *cara*.' He grinned as a flicker of annoyance crossed her face. 'Patience, patience. I would like another whisky, if I may.'

She was always like this when he told her about his work, eager, interested and as impatient as a child. He felt a wave of affection. Gina waited and the sound of the *Messiah* filled the room. With a gesture of annoyance she leapt up and lowered the volume.

'Well? Tell me . . . I see now, Paolo, why you are so restless, so . . . ' she clenched her fists and then splayed her fingers like a spring unwinding, 'so wound up. I thought it was a woman, I should have known better. I thought, I hoped, you were sick with love, Bah . . . ' She laughed.

'Lovesick. No, I would have thought by now you'd have known me better. You're quite incorrigible in your urge to marry me off. I'm sorry, but I am devoted to my type-writer.'

'Oh, you're so boring. You do nothing but work, work all the time. You arrive last night, you say "I have to work". You go for a walk then you hardly speak at dinner. It is all work with you.'

'That is not quite true, cara. I always give you my undivided attention. I thanked you for the beautiful meal and I gave you your Christmas present.'

He had bought her a complete set of Dickens novels. He had had them bound in soft kid with silver lettering. 'To improve your English,' he had said as she closed her eyes and he put the huge parcel on the table in front of her.

'Books, books, books.' She nodded her head emphatically. 'All I ever hear about is books. But you won't tell me about *your* book. Why not?'

'Because it's in my head, tangled like your spaghetti. There's so much to work out yet but I know where I'm going. In broad outline it's about betrayal. I want to write about defectors who slipped from the West to the East without anyone knowing. The great brains, the scientists, the technicians. But it will not just be about revealing these so-called traitors, but their reasons, their motivations and also about their friends, lovers and families, how it affected them. It has great potential if only . . . '

'If only?'

'If only I can make one big breakthrough, then I'm sure the rest will fall into place.'

'Paolo, it's Christmas . . . you look so sorry for yourself, the real writer's anguish. Your soul is bleeding.' She burst into peals of giggles. 'Oh, Paolo, it is not so serious, is it?'

'As you find it so amusing I think I'll say no more. I think you should amuse me now, little sister. Tell me what's been going on in your life.'

'Little sister! Paolo, I'm only three years younger than you . . . ' Gina launched into a cascade of Italian. It was still the language she was happiest in, but Ritz, who had never lived in Italy, found it difficult to pick up every word, although her extravagant gestures and outrageous mimicry made her meaning clear.

Gina had come to Paris from Calabria when their mother died. In the two years since then, she had metamorphosed from a rather plump Italian into a svelte, smart Parisian on the outside. How, Ritz couldn't imagine with the amount she ate.

He had helped her get a job in the Paris office of *Upmarket*, an international glossy, and had bought her a small apartment on the Left Bank. He hadn't seen her enthusiasm lasting and had wondered how she would compete in this new world, but he had thought the apartment a good investment and a *pied-à-terre* for himself. But he had underestimated her. She had learnt French in a matter of weeks and had worked hard to revive her childhood English. She had begun to come up with original ideas for the magazine. Her latest one, she told him now, was a series of portraits of sexy men doing unsexy jobs. The first in the series, Pin-Up Politicians, had been well received and she was working on Pin-Up Priests. It was proving more difficult to find material for this, she joked.

Paul admired his sister's courage. But all his family had been resilient, if nothing else. His father, Giovanni Rizzoli, had arrived in London after the war, a penniless Italian immigrant. He had married their Irish mother and had worked his way from waiting tables in an East End café to owning two restaurants in Chelsea. How strange it was that two parents, both uneducated and practically illiterate, should have produced journalists as children. When Paul won his scholarship to Oxford, his father had said that he had now achieved his life's ambition and had taken his wife, daughter and fortune back to his native Italy. He had been killed, just a year later, driving his first Alfa Romeo saloon. Gina, just sixteen then, had remained in Calabria with her mother, growing to love the sunshine and enjoying an indolent life. She had tended her mother as she died of cancer. Paul often felt that he should have shared that burden. Gina had never had a life of her own as he had, and in those last years she had seemed to lose the remnants of her youth to worry and duty. But Paris had rejuvenated her. She looked more like thirty than forty. Ritz was proud of her.

'And what about *amore*?' he asked her. 'Tell me about your love life.'

'I knew it!' Gina squealed. 'All this talking about writing and all you are interested in is sex. You are still an Italian, Paolo! I have lovers, don't you worry. Not as spectacular as you, no doubt, no one in particular. I want to be free a while longer. I am not so innocent any more. I have how you say "lapsed" a little. No! I won't give you all the details. You must tell me about you.'

'But I've told you. There is nobody. I have decided to give up the playboy life . . . getting too old I suppose. Have you noticed my grey hair?'

'Oh, you are ridiculous! You are as handsome as ever. Your hairs are not grey. And only last month I saw a photo of you with that movie star – what is her name? You can't fool me . . . '

'That was just work.'

'Always work, work, work. Maybe you *are* getting old.' She reached across and tweaked his nose. 'Don't lie to me. You are never without women. You are a ladykiller.'

'A rather inappropriate choice of words.' Ritz's smile faded.

'Ah, Paoletto, I'm so sorry. You know my English. I didn't mean . . . Mama Mia, what a fool I am! Do you still think of Susan, since so long?'

'Don't worry.'

But his nonchalance belied his feelings. He did think of her still. Yes, Susan Howitz would have been quite an old lady now. She had refused to tell him her age, but he had read it in the papers afterwards. Thirty-six. She had lived twice as long as he when she died. He couldn't remember how it had started, but from their first tutorial, he had fallen in love with her. Far from being the experienced man of the world his contemporaries had thought, he had been a seventeen-year-old virgin and she had seduced him, with her mature intelligence, her socialist principles, her Rubens body. He could remember exactly the sensation of running his fingers through her long, glossy hair and the musky smell of incense in her flowing Indian dresses. For a year, he had been her pupil in every way. But as his confidence grew, he would taunt her with the arrogant words of youth – 'I'm your protégé! Your unpaid gigolo!' How could she have let him say things like that? He had grown to despise her tolerance. He had dated other girls, the prettiest students of his year, and flaunted them in front of her.

When she committed suicide, he had thought it was all because of him. Arrogance again. He had grown to realize over the years that his actions had only been a catalyst to her fundamental manic depression. But the guilt still nagged at him. The playboy role that he had assumed and acted to the full in all those years since Oxford had been almost a punishment.

Yes, he thought of her often, and now he laid the responsibility for her death at her own door, and, in indulgent moments, blamed her for what she had done to him.

'Paolo, I'm sorry. I didn't realize. It has been so long. I had forgotten.' Gina's mothering voice and eyes full of concern distracted him.

'Don't apologize, you didn't mean anything, I know. It doesn't matter.' He managed to smile.

'Paolo, *tesoro*, you ought to find yourself a wife.'

'Before I grow too old?'

'No, be serious for once. Because you need love and affection, and a home.'

'Do I indeed? I have survived without one for twenty years. I think not. But, my dear Gina, you are still an

Italian Catholic peasant through and through.' He mocked her accent. 'You'll be offering to say prayers for me next.'

'But, Paolo, I always say prayers for you. Everybody needs prayers, even you. Next time I'll say a prayer for your book too.'

'I think it may need it.'

SEVENOAKS

Mrs Trevelyan was waiting for them at the station.

'Hello, Kay, darling. You must be Annie.'

Her mother couldn't quite contain her surprise at Addy's outfit but smiled bravely. Addy had decided to wear the scarlet, slit-skirted suit she had worn to fly back from New York in. 'You see, Kay,' she had explained, 'it's my travel suit. Going home with you and seeing your folks will be interesting, a bit of adventure like coming back to London.'

Kay had thought her a little optimistic to hope for an interesting Christmas with her parents.

'It's *Addy*, mother. Addy George.'

'Not to worry, Mrs Trevelyan, I've been called a lot of things in my time.' Kay hoped Addy was not about to catalogue them. 'My real name is Madeleine, but I'm afraid it's just too long and Catholic for me.'

Kay was surprised. She had, she supposed, always realized that Addy couldn't have been her Christian name but she had never thought to ask. There were still so many things about Addy she didn't know and for a moment she was piqued that Addy should volunteer a secret to her mother, of all people, quite so readily.

'I've got the car outside.' Her mother was strolling ahead with Addy. 'Your father didn't come, Kay dear, it's rather cold for him and he didn't want to miss the Christmas service from King's College.'

Why was it, thought Kay, that ever since she could remember she always felt she was putting her parents out. As she sat in the front seat next to her mother she felt exactly as she had all those years ago when her mother drove her to school or to her friends' houses. Like a burden that had to be carried around out of duty. In those days, she had expressed her feelings in the occasional tantrum. Now she just bottled them up or felt guilty.

'I expect it's very different from New York for you.' Her mother was really being banal.

'Addy is English you know, mother. Countryside and gardens aren't all new to her.'

'Ah, I see. What part of England do you come from?'

'Well, my family lives in Newcastle . . . '

That too was news to Kay. She had never been able to draw Addy on her family. In New York she had often tried to probe but Addy had been defensive. She could see her now sitting on a swing in Central Park wearing running shorts and a sawn-off T-shirt, saying, 'I'm not interested in what's gone, it's here and now that counts, Kay. Live for the moment. That's what New York's about.'

That had seemed right then. It was only when she had come home that Kay realized it wasn't so easy. You could only ignore people and places that had shaped you when you were completely divorced from them, but not when you went back to old haunts, like Oxford, or when you went home for Christmas. Then you had to face them and work out ways of living with them or their memory. Perhaps Addy couldn't face her parents and family yet. That was why she was here in Sevenoaks and not in Newcastle. Kay wondered in what sense Addy's coming home would ever be a homecoming.

'Here we are.' They drove up the gravel drive and parked outside the large house. There were fairy lights in the oaks that flanked the drive and a Christmas tree stood in the front room window bedecked with red tinsel and multicoloured ornaments. Kay's parents had obviously gone to some effort which was not wasted on Addy.

'How absolutely lovely!' she said as she clambered out of the back seat, and Kay noticed that traces of her American accent had completely disappeared.

'Mr Trevelyan, I presume.' Kay's father stood in the door and shook Addy's hand. 'How wonderful to see you looking so well. We've all been so worried about you. But I see I don't need to even ask whether you're fully recovered.'

Kay's father beamed at Addy's outrageous flattery, and Kay couldn't suppress a giggle. She had been dreading her father's reaction to Addy, but here she was practically sweeping him off his feet.

'Well, I think we'll go up to bed now if you don't mind.' In the bright light of the house, Kay's mother looked tired. 'If you're hungry, Annie, then I've left some soup in the kitchen and Kay will heat it up for you.'

'But make sure she doesn't burn it! Culinary expertise was never one of our little girl's gifts.' Mr Trevelyan chuckled.

'I think I'm quite capable of heating soup,' said Kay coldly.

'I've made up a bed in the spare room, Kay, so if you'd be kind and see your friend has everything she needs.' Mrs Trevelyan's voice was conciliatory.

'Thank you so much, Mrs T.' Addy shook both parents' hands before they disappeared upstairs. 'Jesus Christ, I need a drink,' she whispered to Kay as soon as they were out of earshot. 'Does your culinary expertise run to knowing where your mother keeps the cooking sherry?'

Kay laughed. For a moment she had thought Addy was going to be on their side. 'I can do better than that. They may be old-fashioned but they like a little tipple from time to time. I can offer you port, brandy, Madeira or Tia Maria.'

'Hmm, sounds nice. How about a cocktail of all four? Let's live dangerously! By the way, is this a smoke-free zone?'

'No, no. They hate me smoking and they think I've given up, but go ahead.'

Addy took a swig of her drink and pronounced it sensational. 'We'll have to think of a name for it,' said Kay. 'How about *Family Christmas*, strained and shaken but not stirred?'

188

Addy laughed. 'God, you're a fork-tongued bitch, but I know what you mean. To me your folks seem pretty nice, innocuous, middle-class people, trying their best. But to you I know they're blinkered bigots who don't understand.'

'That's very perceptive and philosophical for you. Have you missed your vocation as a snap-judgement shrink, or indeed a clairvoyant?'

'Ha, bloody ha! No. It's just easier when you're on the outside. I know exactly how you feel because if I'd gone home for Christmas, I'd have been the same – but a million times worse. I wouldn't have been able to see why. Anyway, I know a lot about your parents from what you've told me and there's nothing about being misunderstood I don't understand, if you see what I mean. You think you've got it bad – mine are Catholics *as well*. That makes it even worse.'

'Why?'

'Well, let's put it this way.' She hesitated and delved in her tapestry bag. 'This is the way my parents saw me.' Addy took a photograph from her wallet. 'You've never seen that before, have you?'

The girl in the photograph was about fifteen. She had long silvery blonde hair and a demure smile. She was wearing school uniform. Kay knew she was being shown something very precious. 'Is this really you?'

'Yup. Before I became a skinhead.'

'What?'

'Yeah – the first of my little rebellions. I'll tell you about it sometime . . . '

'Why not now? Oh, go on. I don't want to go to bed yet. Besides, you're seeing my family and I think it's only fair to tell me about your mysterious past.'

'Do you really wanna know? OK, but we've got to have another drink . . . Well, it was like this. Basically, I just never fitted in at home, like you. My parents didn't have time for me, especially my father. He's a professor of Greek and Latin at the University. He was always working,

189

writing books and lecturing. He expected me to do really well at school. He hated my Geordie accent, really hated it and threatened to send me to elocution lessons! I went to the local Catholic comprehensive. There were all these nuns looking like penguins waddling about in black robes and rattling their rosary beads. I hated it. It was so formal and strict. I was really tall. Prepubescent but head and shoulders above the other kids. I was in the top stream to start with but they were all real goody goodies. I just switched off. When I got sent down a form Mum and Dad were summoned to see the chief penguin, Sister Josephine. They were all so disappointed in me. I was letting everyone down. Get the picture? I fell in with the bad girls in the lower forms. I was their hero, the weirdest and the wildest of the lot. And the most vicious. We used to hang around the bike sheds smoking and plotting. I could always come up with the most disruptive plans.'

'Is that when you became a skinhead? I still can't really imagine you as a rough, tearaway type, not like that anyway.'

'Well, I was. Until then everyone thought I was going through a "phase". I was a bit of a tomboy and all that. They thought that soon I would grow up and become a nice young lady. But when skinheads were all the rage I went and got myself skinned. Poor Mum, when I told her I was going to get my hair cut she was so sweet. She thought this new interest in my appearance heralded my "growing up". She even gave me the money for the hairdresser. I was literally scalped. I looked like a golden coconut. When they saw me, Mum started to cry and Dad, well, Dad nearly had a heart attack. I was hauled into his study and he shouted and shouted. My pocket money was stopped and I was made to wear a hat when we went to church.'

'But what happened at school?'

'I was expelled.'

'What?' They were now, Kay felt, getting into the

realms of fantasy, but she listened. 'So you were expelled, were you?'

'Yup . . .Oh, not because of my hair, well not exactly. Sister Josephine had me in her room and bellowed at me about how she couldn't understand how a girl with all my advantages and intelligence could behave in such an unchristian way, upsetting my parents, disturbing the discipline of the school. And what was worse was when she tried to get all confidential and matey. Was there something wrong? I could tell her. I just stood there thinking what a silly cow she was. Then she said she thought it very strange that a pretty girl should want to shave all her hair off. I just looked at her kind of innocently and said, ''Well, Sister, I just wanted to be like you . . . sexless, ugly and bald.'' '

Kay roared with laughter.

'You may laugh, but I was sent out and made to stand in the corridor. I don't know what made me do it but I decided to have a cigarette. Well, that was the final straw. The fire alarm went off. It was smoke sensitive. Pandemonium and all because of me.'

'So they chucked you out?'

'The last thing on earth I wanted to do was go back, I can tell you. Anyway, it was the summer holidays and I spent all my time with the gang. We went around shoplifting and smashing up telephone boxes. Perhaps Dad was right all along. I really was a juvenile delinquent. But I got bored. One day I just got on a train and arrived in the great metropolis, London . . . You know the rest, well, some of it – the pub, the pop group and all that.'

'But what about your parents?'

'I rang Mum and told her I wasn't coming home and I wouldn't tell her where I was. I promised to ring home often to let her know I was OK. She begged to be allowed to come down and talk it over with me. But I just put the phone down.'

'Your poor mother.'

'I know . . . it all sounds callous. But I did keep my promise to Mum. I do phone her sometimes. In fact, I'll phone her tomorrow, if that's all right.'

'Of course it is. But won't they mind you're not spending Christmas with them?'

Addy's mouth tightened, and Kay realized she had said the wrong thing. Hastily she added, 'It's funny, isn't it? Our backgrounds are sort of similar in a way. But I've never really rebelled. In a sense, I didn't need to, I don't think I care so strongly for my parents as you do for yours. I just feel we don't have much in common. It makes me sad. If I were to run away they probably wouldn't notice – well, they would but they'd just think, oh there she goes, as bolshy as ever. The one thing I regret is not the pressure of their expecting too much, but that in the end they don't really love me enough to expect anything. It's as if I've been foisted upon them and they're doing their best, and that's about it as far as they're concerned.'

'Jesus, what a pair we are. All maudlin and soul-searching on Christmas Eve. Let's have another drink and cheer up. Don't know what's got us like this. Come on, Kay, here's to us.'

When Kay woke the next morning she realized they had both been very drunk. Her head was splitting and she remembered painfully that they had left an ashtray full of stubs and four half-empty bottles on the kitchen table. When she went downstairs in her dressing gown the kitchen looked as pristine as ever. Her mother was basting the turkey.

'Happy Christmas, Kay!'

'Happy Christmas, Mum. Look, I'm really sorry about the mess. You've cleared it up. Addy and I just got talking and, well, you know . . .'

'Oh, don't worry, Kay. Annie seems to be quite a girl. Quite a smoker, too. We want you to have a nice Christmas . . .'

192

'. . . and if you choose to enjoy yourself by drinking us dry, then we'll just have to turn a blind eye.' Her father had appeared at the door.

'Oh, Oswald, please.' Her mother turned round.

'Just joking, darling. Kay enjoys a little joke, don't you, Kay?'

'Yes, father, and I'm sorry.'

Addy came downstairs humming a carol and wearing pink. Pink drainpipe jeans, pink sweatshirt, pink sneakers and a pink headband.

'Happy Christmas everybody.' She kissed Kay and then bent to kiss Kay's mother and father in turn. They were obviously overcome by this spontaneous display of affection. 'I haven't missed the present-giving ceremony, have I?'

'No, no, we were waiting for you, young lady. A very fetching outfit you're wearing, if I may say so.'

Kay coughed. She wondered what her father would have said if she had been wearing it.

'Come on, Mrs T, get that apron off and let's have a drink.' Addy produced a bottle of champagne from behind her back and opened it, spraying the tiled floor with bubbly foam and they all drank a toast.

The morning passed off with a jolly, exuberant atmosphere instigated by Addy and carried off with great aplomb. There was only one sticky moment when Kay opened her present from Addy – a pair of black silk camiknickers – and her father commented that they would be better left in their wrapping paper.

After a huge and jovial Christmas dinner at which Addy produced a box of large gold crackers and insisted they all wore paper party hats, they sat and sleepily watched the TV. Kay was bored and about to get a book to read when *Current Affairs* came on. It was the Christmas edition of a popular news programme. The presenter introduced Paul Ritz in a Paris studio. Kay sat up and began to watch the screen. He had a slot on the programme in which he talked

193

in a witty and hard-hitting manner about the year's political machinations. It was a satire on personalities, funny and informative. She watched fascinated as he held forth in his soft, lilting voice, his handsome face completely impassive.

'Oh, God,' Addy yawned. 'Paul Ritz again. Why doesn't he go write that book of his you're always talking about and get his mug off my screen. I mean, fancy having him to watch on Christmas Day and all the way from gay Paris. He's such a prick!' Kay glanced at her sleeping parents. Her father stirred and opened his eyes.

'You have to admit he's a good journalist, Addy.' Kay turned to her father. 'Paul Ritz is one of our authors. The biggest name on our list.'

'I must say I feel some sympathy with Addy's point of view but I don't think I would express it in quite her colourful manner.'

'What do you mean?'

Before Mr Trevelyan could answer, Addy interrupted. 'Well, look at him, sitting there basking in his own brilliance. Huh, I bet icc wouldn't melt in his mouth.'

'I think that's unfair and besides that has nothing to do with his journalistic ability. He's a very talented writer.'

'Kay's not exactly objective in this matter, Mr T. He's her pin-up, isn't he, Kay?'

Mr Trevelyan smiled. Kay was red with anger. She felt humiliated. Her professional assessment had been waved aside and she had been made to look like a small, lovesick schoolgirl in front of her father.

'Well, my dear, you could do worse.' Her father winked conspiratorially at Addy.

'You're both being ridiculous!' Kay exploded.

Mrs Trevelyan sat up. 'Now, now, what's going on? Now, Oswald, you two musn't argue on Christmas Day, goodwill, remember. You should see your face, darling. It reminds me of when you were younger. You should have seen them, Annie, like a pair of angry bantams . . . Now, how about a nice cup of tea?'

'I'll make it, Mum.' Kay tried to control her voice.

'No, no, darling, I'll do it. I feel like stretching my legs.'

It was just after that Addy seemed to go quiet and fidgeted in her chair. Suddenly she was very much like a little girl.

'Is anything wrong, Annie?'

Kay thought her mother must be going deaf. She had been told Addy's name several times.

'I wonder if I could ring my parents, Mrs T?'

'Of course, the phone is in the hall, or you could use the one in the bedroom . . .'

'No, the hall is fine, thanks.'

Addy left the room and silence fell. The spirit of camaraderie could only be maintained when Addy was there. Kay's mother started to fuss about the wrapping paper on the floor, and her father debated smugly whether he would allow himself one more liqueur chocolate Addy had given him before lunch. Kay picked up and pretended to read a biography he had given her, but she was concentrating on the very American voice drifting from the hall.

'Yeah . . . it's real cold out here. I'm at a friend's. We're having a swell time. We're going skating this morning on the lake in Central Park . . . I'm fine and you, how are you all? Did you get my presents? The kids like them? Great . . . sure . . . wish I was with you too, Mum, maybe next year. Yeah, job's great, New York's as wonderful as ever, everything's fine. Have to go, Mum – friend's phone bill. Happy Christmas!'

The phone pinged as Addy put it down. 'Shit!' she shouted and ran upstairs.

Addy was lying face down on the bed in the spare room punching the pillow with her fists.

'Jesus, Kay, I'm sorry. I'm so selfish. I didn't realize. I was going to tell them I was back, then I just couldn't bring myself to do it – I thought it would hurt them even more. And I couldn't bear the questions – How long have you been in England? Where are you living? What are you going to do? All that *shit*. Jesus. I don't know myself. I don't know why I came home. My mother even said how close I sounded. Do you think she knew? Christ, what a mess.'

'It's OK, Addy, calm down. You'll be able to face them one day. It takes time. You've just got to do it step by step. Come on, don't worry about it. You're doing OK. You can always visit them when you feel up to it.'

'Kay, you're so sweet. I don't know what I'd do without you.' Mascara poured down Addy's face. 'You're my family, you know. Yes, you really are!'

'And you're mine, in a funny sort of way.' Kay smiled and held her hand.

'Shit,' said Addy. 'We may have the excuse of Christmas but we're a right couple of turkeys ourselves . . .'

Apart from the small hiccup of Addy's phone call home it had been one of the happiest Christmases Kay could remember. Addy had the ability to make people have fun. She flirted with Kay's father and had struck up a friendship with Kay's mother. Kay had heard them chattering over the washing-up, almost like old friends. Her mother had obviously been overawed at first, but as she grew more confident Kay heard her questioning Addy about her family and admonishing her gently for her behaviour.

'You must remember that your mother is probably very worried about you. It's none of my business why you don't want to see them but they're probably not as condemning as you think. They probably have as many regrets as you . . .'

It had stunned Kay to hear her mother waxing lyrical about personal subjects. She was usually so inhibited. Annie, as her mother still insisted on calling her, had struck a chord. Later she heard her mother say, 'You're similar to Kay in a way . . . all huff and puff and devil may

196

care, but underneath you're not like that, are you?'

To which Addy had replied, 'I don't know, Mrs T, I just don't know . . .'

When they left on Boxing Day to go back to London it had been an emotional parting and even Kay had waved fondly at her parents standing in the driveway as the taxi drew away.

'They look so old,' she said to Addy.

'Yeah. They're old but they're OK, your folks. Your mother's a sweetie, even though she gave me a bit of a moral earful, and your father's pretty ill. Bet he was a bit of a disciplinarian when he had the strength to be. Still . . . thanks Kay.'

'For what?'

'For letting me stay in your flat, for putting up with me, for a happy Christmas and for a happy year!'

LONDON

It was New Year's Eve and snowing hard. There was that silence that seems only to exist in the snow. Kay felt deliciously isolated standing in the street. It was almost as if she were the only person in the world. She took a deep breath and walked up the path. In the dim light of the porch she could just see that her watch said nine o'clock.

Richard Hawthorn opened the door. 'Kay, my dear, come in out of this frightful snow. All alone? I did make it clear you could bring someone?'

'Yes, you did, Richard, but I decided not to.'

'Ahh. We'll have to do something about this determination of yours to remain single.' There was a note of triumph in his voice.

'Don't put yourself out.' Kay took off her coat and smiled.

Richard put his arm around her shoulder. 'Goodness me, Kay, you are quite a siren when you decide to be and you look absolutely gorgeous.'

She had never looked so beautiful. That was due, in part, to Addy. Kay had intended to wear something inconspicuous, but Addy had insisted that Kay's first big literary party merited a new dress and to hell with the cost. In fact, she had paid and told Kay to consider it a Christmas bonus. They had chosen it the day before in an expensive boutique just off the King's Road. It was the ultimate little black dress. A plain, strapless sheath of ebony velvet with a wide velvet belt. Addy had lent her long, fake diamond earrings but she wore no other jewellery, leaving her shoulders and neck completely bare.

Richard made a visible effort to stop staring and gently took her arm and ushered her into the long high-ceilinged lounge. There was a Christmas tree in the corner, tastefully decorated but its branches were drooping and some of the needles had begun to fall. The rest of the room was empty apart from a group of people, none of whom Kay recognized, standing in a circle in the opposite corner. Kay wished she had chosen to arrive a little later. She hated being one of the first at parties.

'If I can just interrupt for a moment . . . ' Richard shouted, he was already slightly tight, ' . . . for some introductions. You've probably spoken to most of these people on the phone, Kay, and I'm sorry that they look so disappointing in the flesh. Anyway, this is David, Colin, Marjory and Mike. And this, everyone, is Kay.'

'And how do you know Richard?' said Marjory.

'I've just started working as his assistant.'

They looked her up and down and then resumed their conversation as if she wasn't there. She felt a sudden draining of confidence. She had learnt since starting her job that however hard you tried if you were a secretary, no one wanted to know. Sometimes she wondered how she would get on in this hierarchical world.

'Didn't we talk the other day about that book jacket?' she ventured to Mike, whose voice she recognized from the phone. He had seemed very friendly then.

'Did we?'

'Kay, my dear, the drink is in there if you want to get some for yourself . . . And if you wouldn't mind going round with refills for the others . . . '

So that's it, thought Kay, there's no such thing as a free party invite. Richard was trying to assert his authority and put her into a role.

She thought what Addy might say: 'If you want a cheap waitress, go to a catering agency.' Even 'Up yours', but Richard required more tact. One minute he was a charming admirer, the next the watchful boss with put downs at his fingertips. In the office she had learnt to deal with him. They had built an understanding since the first day. They worked well together and both had sought and found each other's limits of tolerance. In social situations their relationship was less practised. Kay had attended a pre-Christmas party with him and felt very young and almost at a loss for words. She was having the same feelings now. She decided she needed a drink and went into the kitchen. She poured herself a large gin and tonic and was plonking in ice cubes angrily when Richard returned.

'Ah, here you are, Kay. Alone again. Have you met my honoured guest? But of course you have, how could I be so forgetful. Paul Ritz, Kay Trevelyan.'

'Hello, love.' Ritz smiled so warmly at her that Kay had the greatest difficulty in trying to remember all the warnings from various sources she had had of him.

'Quite the little glamour-puss tonight, isn't she, Paul, out of office drab?' Richard's teasing voice cut through her.

'Lovely and enchanting,' Ritz replied.

Kay decided she despised both of them. 'Let me get you a drink,' she said sullenly.

'Come and meet the others,' Richard said simultaneously and added sarcastically, 'Whose party is this?'

'I think the young lady's offer sounds more appealing,' said Ritz.

'Oh well, then, I'll leave you in her capable hands but, Paul, you'll have to say hello to David Moriarty. He has mortgaged his firm for your book after all. I think he deserves an audience. But I can see you're preoccupied. Ta ta for now.' Richard went to answer the door.

'Gin and tonic?'

'A lovely thought, but I only drink whisky,' said Ritz, and Kay could feel his eyes on her shoulders as she turned to pour the drink. 'How are you getting on with dear old Richard? I expect you're used to his little jokes by now?'

Kay couldn't decide whether Ritz was being condescending or genuinely sympathizing with her embarrassment. She plumped for discretion. 'Very well, actually.'

'Good, good. It's about time he got someone decent to

organize him. But I'm still mystified by your reasons for wanting to be his secretary. On our encounter in Oxford I had a feeling you were all set to join me in the dirty world of journalism.'

'Did you?' Kay laughed. She didn't believe he had given her so much as a thought. But it was convenient for now to have her like him. 'I suppose my ambition has changed direction, that's all.'

That wasn't exactly true but it was easier to explain. Her ambition to be a journalist had somehow died with Oxford. Before New York she had lost all her confidence, been so deeply depressed that she hadn't thought she was capable of anything. New York had changed that and the publishing world had been accessible. It had seemed right and it was right. Kay knew she could be good at it and that it inspired her. It had been tremendously exciting selling Ritz's proposed book. She wanted to hear all about it as she had only heard Richard's version, but she was hesitant to ask him about it since she didn't know what his reaction had been to Richard's clandestine auction. She decided to play the *ingénue*.

'You must have been delighted with the advance for your new book? It's a lot of money.' Understatement of the year, thought Kay. A cool half-million to be paid in thirds – one third on signing the contract, one third on delivery of the book and one third on publication.

'Yes, Richard did very well – now I'll have to write the damn thing!' Ritz relaxed for a moment and laughed, and Kay could see all too clearly what a clever trick Hawthorn had played. Paul Ritz was quietly delighted. Richard had judged him supremely well.

'I'm looking forward to it,' Kay said politely because she thought it the right thing to say.

'Thank you for that vote of confidence and, of course, for all your good work. I know an auction requires a lot of work from all parties. Now, how about another drink?'

Kay poured him another whisky and herself a large gin

201

and tonic. She wondered why he didn't leave her alone. Surely they had talked as much as professional etiquette required. The party had begun to come alive and Richard had put on some loud dancing music. She shifted from one leg to another, imagining he was about to make some excuse and leave her. Faces kept popping round the kitchen door, expectantly waiting for him to greet them.

'Let's circulate a bit,' said Ritz, and she jumped as he took her arm. 'But not too much. I do find these occasions a bore and naturally I want to use my name and reputation to prevent anyone else monopolizing the most beautiful woman in the room.'

Kay gave up thoughts of professionalism and attempts to second-guess him. After all, it was New Year's Eve. If the most beautiful man in the world wanted to be with her it was his problem.

Everyone's eyes were on her as they moved around the room. Kay sensed they were all asking, 'Who is Paul Ritz's new woman?' David, Colin, Marjory and Mike were much more willing to talk when Ritz was standing next to her, and even Richard seemed bewildered by the turn of events but he was obviously enjoying the reflected glory.

'We seem to have what is often called a natural rapport,' Ritz whispered when they found themselves alone for a couple of minutes.

'Do we?' She felt as if she were playing a role at his side, but she was warming to his ridiculous flattery and at least he seemed to have a sense of humour about it. She found him compellingly attractive.

When he asked her to dance she realized he had deliberately chosen a slow number and she was nervous. He put one hand on her waist, held the other delicately by her side and led her round the room avoiding the other couples. She was horrified to find herself wanting to move closer to him, to feel his breath on her cheek, to narrow the space he had so formally put between them, and she found it difficult to hang on to her cool facade or to stop her hands

202

from shaking. But he continued talking as if nothing was happening. His voice had a soft lilt that she found envelopingly sexy.

'What is your accent?' she asked him.

'My mother was Irish and my father was Italian. Good Catholic stock. I think the accent is what is known as international. I've lived in so many countries and I pick up a bit of the local dialect wherever I go. That's what happens to us rootless ones. What about you, love, are you rootless or are you too young to know what that means?'

'Oh, rootless, I think.'

She noticed his wry smile and realized he was suppressing a laugh. Suddenly she felt she was being manipulated. He must be forty at least, possibly more. She was literally young enough to be his daughter and he probably thought of her as a sweet little girl, perhaps a pretty toy to play games with. Someone he could gossip about with his fellow journalists in El Vinos, or some other dingy, male haunt. The gin she had drunk swished about in her head and his attentions became uncomfortably embarrassing. She struggled to recall what they had talked about and could remember nothing. For a second, she lost her balance and trod on his foot in an attempt to steady herself.

'What is it, love?'

'Excuse me a moment.' She walked away with deliberate steps, the sort she knew she only took when she was aware of being drunk. When she reached the door she ran upstairs to the bathroom.

She sat on the edge of the bath for several minutes, trying to control all the thoughts that raced around her spinning head. She hated being drunk. She had made a fool of herself. They must all be downstairs at this moment laughing at her. Richard sniggering, 'You're wasting your time, Paul, old chap, she's as pure as driven snow,' and Ritz replying, 'That's what really turns me on.' A roar of laughter confirmed her thoughts. She was panic stricken. She splashed her face but the room wouldn't stop going

203

round. Someone was banging at the door. She lunged at it and walked slowly down the stairs, gripping the bannister.

Someone had turned on the television at full volume just in time to hear the chimes of Big Ben strike twelve. There was a cheer and the man she was standing next to turned to her and kissed her wetly. His kiss lasted for eight of the chimes which rang in her head as she struggled to extricate herself. On the ninth, she heard Ritz's voice saying, 'Do you mind?' And, feeling like a pawn in a male game, she felt his mouth on hers and his hands on her back. She responded hesitantly, inching her fingers down his spine and feeling his skin tentatively under his silk shirt. His mouth was soft, their kisses brief, as if they were tasting each other. Once or twice he drew his face away and looked at her questioningly and sighed. She pulled him closer to her body and kissed him insistently. She could feel her nipples harden under the stiff bodice of her dress and an all too long absent warmth between her legs.

But all too soon they were drawn apart into a linking circle rasping, 'Should old acquaintance be forgot . . . ' And then there was a rush of kissing and hugging from all sides. Kay even found herself in a clinch with Richard.

When she recovered her balance she looked blearily for Ritz. He was standing by the Christmas tree in earnest conversation with a group of people around him. She was standing on her own and he kept catching her eye. His look was one that she recognized but had not been aware of for a very long time. It was the same look that Bob and she had exchanged at the height of their romance. That knowing look across a crowded room, that nod of understanding which says, 'I'm bored with all these people, let's leave and go to bed.'

'Ah, there you are, Kay.' Richard approached and stood directly in her path of vision. She giggled as she saw Ritz shift his position slightly to regain eye contact with her. 'Have you enjoyed yourself?' he asked.

'Of course, very much.'

204

Richard started to describe what a terrible hangover he would have the next morning, and they began a bantering competition along the lines of 'What was the worst hangover you've ever had?'

Her attention was distracted as she saw Ritz making his way across the room but she turned quickly back to Richard.

' . . . anyway, my dear, being the ever-caring employer, I've found you a lift home. Mike lives in Hampstead, so you won't take him out of his way.'

'Oh, but really, I'll take a taxi, I don't want to inconvenience anyone . . . ' Kay faltered.

'A taxi from Fulham to Primrose Hill at one o'clock on New Year's Day? You're very optimistic. Come now, there's no need to be so diffident, my dear. I can assure you Mike's not as drunk as he looks, are you Mike? There, you see. You'll be in perfectly good hands . . . '

Kay didn't know what to do – to protest further would seem churlish. She glanced despairingly at Ritz who had picked up the last couple of sentences and was smiling broadly. He raised his eyebrows and shrugged. Kay turned to Mike with the most composed smile she could muster. 'Well, if you're sure you don't mind?' she said and went to get her coat.

She was glad that Mike didn't seem to want to make conversation in the car on the way home. She imagined he was more inebriated than Richard had indicated and was intent on concentrating on the road and driving very slowly, watching in his rear mirror for any police cars that might be around. 'Good party' was all he muttered several times as the car slithered from one side of the road to the other.

Kay stared as if mesmerized by the snowflakes. But her blank face betrayed a wealth of confused thoughts rushing about in her head. She couldn't decide whether she had imagined what had been going on between her and Ritz. Had he been flirting or was there something more to it?

Had she been too obvious? Was the whole thing an elaborate practical joke concocted by Richard Hawthorn? Was it possible that Ritz did fancy her – or even more? Were her feelings for him a silly crush or was she falling in love? What if she had insisted on staying, what would have happened? Did Richard suspect what might have been about to happen and was that the reason he had packed her off? What would she say to Addy? She wished Addy had been there to either verify or tell her she was being stupid. After all, what was a kiss? A lot to her because she hadn't been kissed like that for years, but to Paul Ritz? He probably didn't even remember it. Why was she so hopeless with men? Why didn't she ever know what was going on? She must grow up.

By the time they reached her road Kay had resolved not to say anything to anyone about the evening. It was obviously all in her imagination and she wasn't going to make any more of a fool of herself than she already had. She would just tell Addy she had had an interesting evening.

But Addy wasn't home yet. The flat felt empty and the heating had gone off. The bright beach room looked stark and idiotic with the curtains open and snowflakes falling past the windows. Kay sat in a deck chair sipping a cup of tea when the telephone rang. She assumed it would be a drunken call from Addy, but it was her mother.

'Mum, how lovely of you to call. I just got back and was sitting here being sad and trying to make some resolutions. Happy New Year!'

There was a pause. 'Kay, darling, I'm sorry, but I had to ring you as soon as I knew. I didn't want to wait.'

'Mum, what is it? Has father had another stroke?'

'Darling, he's passed away. Your father is dead.'

206

GETTING ON

NICARAGUA

He had come so far. So far to find her and so far since he had begun his research.

It was only three months since he had broached the subject of his book to Richard Hawthorn in that bustling restaurant in Soho, three months since the idea had finally crystallized. And yet in the first two of those months he had almost given up. He was looking for missing persons and had found none. They had indeed vanished without trace. But somewhere in his consciousness he had known they existed, and then the names began to emerge, like ghostly signposts on a foggy road and finally that name had appeared like the tail-lights of the vehicle in front indicating the way. Carleton.

She had been clever, oh so clever, feeding him the bait, hooking him so gently he had not realized he was wriggling on the end of a long, invisible line. It would lead him back to her, back to the Nicaraguan jungle, to Elizabeth Carleton. Had she done it in an unguarded moment of impulse? How many times would she have thought about what she had done? He could see her face, her tiny body, as clearly as if she were there. For a moment he imagined her saying, 'So, Paul, you have it. You have discovered my secret.' And then her face crumpled in pain. He did not want to cause her pain.

Paul Ritz leant back in his chair, his feet balanced on the windowsill. His pen fell on to the floor but he left it and continued to stare through the black, uncurtained hotel window. The notebook in his lap was covered in doodles with a few words written here and there. There was no point in planning any further. He knew the questions he had to ask. Tomorrow he would confront her.

He wandered to the bar, his shoes squeaking on the polished stone floor. He wanted a drink. He was nervous. But he must trust his intuitions. He had learnt so much of Carleton, but none of it would mean anything without her confirmation, confession. It was always the same with a good story, the search, the contact, the adrenalin and this, the grand finale.

And what a place for it. The hotel Santa Maria with its elegant white frontage, which rose dramatically and incongruously out of the verdant forest. Its newly painted facade and bright bursts of flowers breaking the dank solemnity. It had been like an eerie oasis at the end of his long sweaty car journey. A momentous journey filled with searing images since he had touched down in Managua airport with its straggling sheds and narrow runways; the dust and disorder; groups of soldiers in green fatigues with machine guns slung loosely over their shoulders. Some of them almost children with old eyes in smooth, unlined faces; market stalls leaning haphazardly against every possible wall; women dressed in bright, nylon clothes; children begging and offering cigarettes; the soldier leaning against a wall who had stared at his smart, uncreased suit and spat noisily on to the pavement.

Managua, a dilapidated and gently decaying capital, but a proud city. FSLN daubed in black and red paint; bold posters telling the people to work hard, to continue the success of the revolution. No one can forget the past because it is so much part of the present. He had seen it all before, but this time the slogans haunted him.

In one small village Ritz had stopped to stretch his legs. In the corner of the square they were roasting a pig on a spit. Fat dripped on to the crackling flames and the smell of burning flesh in the heavy afternoon heat was nauseating. Ritz walked towards the church. Inside, the air was cooler and fragrant with burning wax. There was a statue of a madonna in front of the altar. She was made of cardboard and painted in bright colours. Even from the shadows of the aisle she looked alive and vivid. Was her smile benign, or were her curved lips warning him? He had lit a candle as a gesture to appease her.

'So you've come back?' The proprietor poured Ritz a whisky. 'I think you like it here.'

Ritz smiled. He liked the hotel well enough, but not what he was about to do.

She was sitting on the raised veranda, her back to him, a mug of coffee on the table in front of her steamed in the warm morning air.

'*Gringo, gringo, gringo.*'

She turned as she heard the children's shrieks. A smile of welcoming recognition lit her eyes but instantly lapsed into despair. He was right. She knew why he was here. 'Cesar!' she called, half rising.

A tall Nicaraguan appeared, his face soaped, and sensing her distress laid a hand on her shoulder. Ritz halted at the bottom of the steps weakened by their solidarity.

'So you have returned.' There was a tremor in her voice. 'It's all right, Cesar. I know him, he has come to speak to me.' The Nicaraguan looked into her face, as if to reassure himself she was telling the truth, then walked inside.

'Why didn't you write to tell me you were coming?' she asked.

'Because I suspected you would run away, as you have run before,' Ritz replied.

'So you know?'

'I know what happened. I want to know why.'

She talked for hours until the midday sun burned down on the veranda and sweat trickled over her cheeks like tears. She had told him more than he had ever imagined she would, not just about Carleton, but how she had become involved, her ideals, her motives, her betrayal and those who had betrayed her. He found he did not need to question, her confession was so exhaustive. It was almost as if he had prised open a Pandora's box and all the dark

211

secrets flowed out with abandon. Amid the cold truths he warmed to her honesty and shared in her regrets.

'And now you will take all my past away with you. What have I left?'

'Your future? If I take it, perhaps you will find your peace of mind.' Nothing he could say seemed to comfort her. 'Elizabeth,' he said gently, 'surely now that all the secrets are out, it will help put the past behind you.'

But she burst into sobs. 'Some things, Paul, you can never put behind you. They live on.'

LONDON

'What kind of tea would madam prefer? Earl Grey, Lapsang Souchong or Waldorf Special?'

'Thank you, but I'll wait. I'm expecting someone.' Mrs Trevelyan sank back in the chair, luxuriating in its leather-cushioned seat. As she stretched her legs, the crisp white tablecloth brushed against her calves. She felt tired, exhausted. It was the first trip she had made into London since her husband's death. The shops were crowded and she had walked around in a desultory way, not really concentrating on anything she was looking at. She hated shopping at the best of times. But she had wanted to fill up some time before meeting Kay. These days there was so much time to fill . . . No doubt she would get used to it.

'Mother, sorry I'm late. I got held up. How are you?' Kay bent quickly and kissed her. She had caught her mother unawares, lost in her thoughts. How old she looked.

'Thank you, darling, I'm well really. Sit down and we'll order.' She looked up. Kay was standing behind the chair. Those grey eyes. That smile. How generations repeat themselves. No, she must not think of that. Since Oswald died she could not stop thinking about the past. Memories, images from years gone by, would flash before her eyes like a film running at top speed. She seemed to have no control. She smiled apologetically.

'Mother, mother . . . you were miles away. You look really tired. You shouldn't have come up to town to see me. I was planning on coming to you in Sevenoaks this weekend anyway.'

Kay had been out to Sevenoaks several times in those months since her father's death. She had made a real effort to give her mother support. It hadn't been easy. She had seen her mother cry before but never so distraught. There had always been her father's imposing presence, silently condemning such foolish displays of emotion. For the first time she had seen her mother turn to her. But even after sharing their grief together they were still not relaxed with each other.

'Look, Mum, I must just pay a visit to the ladies. I won't be long, I'm starving.'

Mrs Trevelyan watched Kay walk away. How she had grown up. The bossy tomboy with the swinging Beatles bob had vanished, as had the solemn eighteen-year-old they had put on the train to Oxford, terrified but determined not to show them, smiling but a little too bravely.

It was one of those flashes of realization, heightened by the calm of the Waldorf tearoom. She saw Kay as the other people in the room might see her. Strikingly pretty, fresh-faced, assured, holding her head high as she walked past the waiters in their formal black tails and bow ties. There were so many things she did not know about Kay, thought Mrs Trevelyan. So many memories.

It was in this very room that she had told Oswald that they must take on another child. It had been her decision and she had persuaded him. It was perhaps the only decision she had made in her life for both of them and she had needed neutral territory to break it to him. It was their duty, she had said, they had to do it for decency's sake.

There had been a band playing then, up there on the platform. The tables were still set with delicate china and silver and the marble floor still gleamed under a scattering of faded Persian rugs. The clinking of cup on saucer and fork on plate seemed to fade, swallowed up in the vast rectangular tearoom. With its sunken floor it was like a large, stone conservatory, she had thought so all those years ago.

'Mum, are you OK?'

'Darling, I'm sorry . . . I must be tired – all that walking around the shops.'

'Addy sends her love, by the way. She was in two minds whether to come or not but I thought you might prefer it to be just the two of us. She's exhausting, I know.'

Her mother smiled. 'I like Annie. She's a nice girl . . . no, now what do you call her?'

'Addy. She told you. It's short for Madeleine.'

'I must say I prefer Madeleine though I have to admit it's not quite her, is it? I suppose Addy is quite a pretty name too. How is she?'

'She's well, very busy.'

'Well, I'm glad you two are sharing the flat together. Do you know, darling, I never once asked Addy at Christmas what she does. Does she work?'

Kay knew her parents had tactfully avoided asking Addy, suspecting it might be outrageous.

'She's a model.'

Kay waited for a look of disapproval but her mother smiled encouragingly.

'I expect she likes the attention. Yes, I can see her as a model. She's got a very pretty face, quite a beauty really. It's a pity that she doesn't dress, well, a little more tastefully but I suppose I'm just being old-fashioned. All those bright colours . . . '

Kay could not bring herself to explain that Addy's face was not her main selling feature. They smiled at each other.

'How's work, dear?'

It was the first time her mother had ever asked her that.

'Oh, fine, hectic but I love it. Do you remember I told you we represented Paul Ritz? Well, one of my jobs is trying to keep tabs on him. He flies all round the world, at the moment he's in Nicaragua of all places. He's writing a top-secret book. It's really exciting being involved.'

Kay had been such an unruly child, Mrs Trevelyan thought, so energetic and demanding. When she was very young she had talked incessantly and thrown tantrums if she did not get enough attention. Now here she was, open, direct and confident. She had grace and poise. She nodded encouragingly.

They had not realized what they were taking on with Kay. When Oswald finally agreed, she had said, 'We've done it before, so why shouldn't we do it again?' She had even looked forward to it. But they were too old. It had not made them younger as they thought it would. There had always been the preying fear that history would repeat itself and so they had been guarded. Too guarded she supposed now. She had really wanted to be loving and unbegrudging but she could not trust this child because of what had happened. Soon it was too late. Kay had turned from a loud, precocious five-year-old into a quiet, brooding, six-year-old. Thank goodness for Will. She had been too tired and too old to do anything about it. Will had done so much for Kay. He provided the young friendship she had so desperately needed.

'Tell me, have you seen Will recently?' Mrs Trevelyan pulled herself out of her reverie. 'You must see each other a lot now you're both in London. He came to see me last week. He's such a lovely boy.'

'No, no I haven't. We're both so busy. We just haven't seen each other.'

'Well, dear, I mentioned I'd be meeting you today and he said he might pop along.'

The night before the funeral Kay had suddenly realized she would see Will there. Those few days had passed in a daze. There had been a lot of things to organize and she hadn't given it a thought. Addy had indirectly reminded her when she had asked who would be at the funeral and offered to go with Kay. Kay had appreciated the gesture but said no. The family gathering would be awful anyway. Her sister, Dorothy, would be there. She had flown in from Chile as soon as she had received the telegram. Obviously, Will would be there too. The irony of it. The last time she had seen him was at Zoe's funeral.

She had meant to write to him when she was in New York

216

but she hadn't been sure whether he had meant it when he'd said he never wanted to hear from her again. After their argument that day on the river she had been angry with him and then she had tried to forget about it. They had grown apart anyway. He had never been able to accept her relationship with Bob. Then everything had happened so quickly, Zoe's accident, splitting up with Bob, the pressure of finals. Before she knew it she was in New York and Oxford seemed another planet. She had been too absorbed in sorting herself out to think of Will.

But he had not been at the funeral. He was doing his elective two months of medicine in India, and Dorothy had decided not to ask him to come all the way back. Now Kay was nervous at the prospect of seeing him for the first time with her mother there.

'Well, as he's not here yet I expect he's been too busy,' Mrs Trevelyan was saying. 'But you musn't lose touch with him. I always felt he was such a good influence on you.'

'You make him sound like a saint. He's really very human.'

'There's no need to be so touchy, dear. I wasn't implying any criticism of you.'

A waiter approached with a pot of tea and a plate of tiny cucumber and salmon sandwiches.

'Mum, I'm sorry, I didn't mean to snap. Everyone kept asking after him at the funeral. It nearly drove me potty.'

'Well, you used to be such good friends, darling. I suppose you've grown out of each other. I must say, I sometimes thought you were too good friends to be true.' Kay looked down at her plate. 'Anyway, before I forget, I have something to give you. From father. I found it when I was going through his things. Here, isn't it beautiful? He treasured it.'

There were tears in her mother's eyes. In the palm of her outstretched hand was a heavy gold fob watch with her father's initials on the back.

'Oh, but oughtn't Dorothy to have it? I mean, she's the eldest.'

'No, he didn't mean it for Dorothy. Many years ago it was for someone else really, but now you must have it.'

'Oh . . . it's beautiful. But I feel funny accepting it.'

'Well, I'm giving it to you, darling. Father wanted one of you to have it.'

'Well, if that's what you want . . . '

Kay felt guilty. Her father's death had shaken her more because of the upheaval and her mother's grief than because she would miss him herself. She had ended up crying out of shame. Because she felt she should want to cry more for him. She had told Addy. 'I feel so awful. I must be really weird not to feel more about my own father. I just don't feel like I should.' She had started to sob and Addy had put her arms around her.

'Hey, come on. It's not a crime you know. So you didn't get on that well. Tough. He'd probably have loved you if you hadn't have been his daughter. Families are pretty screwed up like that. I'm telling you!'

'Oh, Mum, I'm sorry. I don't know what to say.' Kay reached across the table and squeezed her hand. 'At least you and father were happy together. You've got happy memories.'

'Yes, I was very lucky in that, very lucky indeed. Do you know, we married over forty years ago. That's such a long time and now it's all over. Well, we mustn't live in the past, must we?'

Kay ate the last sandwich and wiped her mouth with a napkin. 'Listen, Mum, I've been thinking . . . I'm not very good at saying things like this but I've made up my mind I want to. If you decide you don't want to be in Sevenoaks any longer in that big house you must come to London. We could find you a flat somewhere. I'd like that. What I'm trying to say is that I wish we knew each other better. Oh, I've embarrassed you now.'

'No, darling, that's very sweet of you.'

'Well, now I've started I might as well get it over with. What I wanted to say as well is that I wish I'd got on with father better. Listen to me, I even say "father". Most children would call their fathers "daddy". I don't know why we didn't get on very well. I keep thinking about it. Do you think it was me? Was I a very difficult child?'

Mrs Trevelyan looked down at her lap. 'Yes, I'm sorry. It must have been very difficult for you having such old fogeys as parents.'

'No, I didn't mean that at all. It was all those rows I used to have with father. Do you remember? I always felt he disapproved of me in some way. We used to argue at the dinner table. Everything I said he used to disagree with. I know it's natural to argue with parents but I just feel there was something more to it than that. Was there?'

Mrs Trevelyan could feel her heart thumping. What was she to say? Perhaps now was the time to tell everything. But she could not. She was too old to turn back the clock. Better to go on as before. She cleared her throat. 'You mustn't remember father like that. He was very fond of you. I know that. He just wasn't very good with young children . . . '

They were suddenly aware that somebody was standing beside the table.

'Granny, how are you?' They looked up in surprise.

'Will, darling. How lovely of you to come. We're all together like old times. You remember when we used to have tea in town, as a special treat.' Mrs Trevelyan was holding Will's hand. Kay stared up at him.

'Kay, how are you?' He bent and kissed her lightly on her cheek. She gave him an embarrassed smile. She guessed that he too had hidden the true extent of their argument from her mother. Her mother's face had relaxed as she chatted to Will, fussing over pouring tea and passing him cakes. He was amusing her with tales of his work in the hospital. Occasionally he looked at Kay but they spoke to each other with the politeness of distant relatives.

He looked a little tired and his laugh was not as exuberant but otherwise he seemed the same old Will. Kay was aware that she was saying nothing. She felt awkward and left out. It had taken her quite a lot of effort to talk to her mother about her relationship with her father and she had felt they were beginning to build up a mutual trust. Then Will had arrived and spoilt it.

She watched him and thought how boyish he was. She felt impatient with him. Then, as he laughed with her mother, she felt a wave of jealousy. Once it would have been the two of them laughing together about her parents. Now, here was her mother, and Will oblivious to her discomfort. She reflected ironically that these two people, one whom she had never quite got on with and the other who had been like a brother and was now almost a stranger, were her real family. Perhaps Addy was right and you never did get on with family.

'Well, darlings, I must go otherwise I'll miss my train. It's been lovely.'

'I'll come with you and see you on to the train.' Kay leapt up.

'No, that's sweet but the waiter has ordered a taxi for me.' Mrs Trevelyan bent down and kissed Kay warmly. For a second Kay squeezed her hand.

'I'll call you tonight, and thanks, Mum, for a nice tea.' So she was to be left alone with Will.

'Well, Kay, how are you? It's been a long time.' His voice was unenthusiastic.

'I'm fine, fine.'

She couldn't meet his eyes. So much had happened to her since she last saw him that she did not know where to start telling him anything and she did not even know that she wanted to tell him about her new life. He was still talking to her as if she were a vague acquaintance, in the same guarded, well-mannered tone he had used when her mother had been with them.

'Well, we do seem to have lost contact,' he said lamely.

'Yes.'

He looked as indifferent as if he'd just asked for another cup of tea.

'In fact, I meant to write to you after grandfather died. But it seemed ridiculous to write . . . '

'Ridiculous?'

'Well, you know, writing to tell you how sorry I was. Formal and pompous . . . ' He smiled nervously. Kay knew what he had left unsaid – formal and pompous when we have been so close. He was trying to share some of the blame.

'Will, it's nice to see you again, you know.'

'Is it?' He sounded genuinely surprised. 'Yes, you're right, it is, but I'm afraid I really ought to be getting back, I've so much work to do. Perhaps when I'm less busy we should meet.'

They walked across the marble floor, Kay's boots clicking on the surface. His suggestion that they meet sounded more like public school good manners to Kay than a real invitation.

'Where are you heading for?' he asked.

'Waterloo. I'm going to walk over the bridge.'

'I'll walk with you if you like.'

'Sure, if you want to.'

It was early evening and the air was cold. The sky was wispy blue, clear but hazy. The light was fading and a few lamps began to come on. They walked in silence, crossing the Strand towards the bridge. It was Kay's favourite bridge and she always felt a sense of wonder when she crossed it, the sweep of the Thames, the cold water bobbing. On one side, the City and the magnificent dome of St Paul's; on the other, the Houses of Parliament and the bridge with its wide, black-tarmaced carriageways sweeping towards the South Bank and the neon flashes of the National Theatre's announcement hoarding.

Will was silent and seemed, like her, to be taking in the panorama. They walked side by side negotiating the growing stream of commuters.

221

'You probably don't know, Kay, but I'm going to go back to India next week. I feel a bit awful leaving Granny. I don't think she's taken it in yet. But it's only for a few months.'

She's your grandmother, not your mother, thought Kay. You can't be that worried. She's my responsibility, my worry now. 'I'm sure she'll miss her favourite grandson terribly,' she snapped.

'I see your temper hasn't improved.' He grinned boyishly.

'What's so amusing? You sound like father.'

'Me, like grandfather? That's a bit hard, isn't it?'

She had stopped and was leaning over the bridge parapet. Will could not see her face.

'Do you think we should talk about the dead like this?'

'I'm sorry, Kay, I didn't mean . . .'

'No, no, I didn't mean it like that. I was teasing.' She smiled at him and put a hand on his arm. 'Do you know, I can't believe this is happening. We're standing on Waterloo Bridge and we're behaving like we used to as kids. Do you remember, when we first met, we couldn't stand each other and you were terribly polite and took everything I said literally.'

'Thanks for the fond memories! When we were kids we'd probably have discussed at great length jumping from this bridge, whether we'd drown, how long it would take to hit the water.' He peered at the surface churning and foaming against the support pillars. 'Shall we try it?' He turned to her. 'Don't look so horrified. Now I'm joking. I'm really very happy with my life, a dip in the Thames doesn't have that much appeal.'

'No, it doesn't look very inviting. Anyway, our bathing adventures don't always work out, do they?'

She realized what she'd said as soon as the words were out of her mouth.

'I mean . . . you know what I mean.' Suddenly she burst into giggles. 'Isn't it ridiculous talking about that as

222

though it was such a big deal. I mean it was years and years ago . . . '

'Like playing nurses and doctors, you mean?'

'Yes, that's exactly what I mean. Is that what you think too?'

'Yes, yes I do.'

'But what did we get so worked up about at Oxford? What about our row, you know, that day in the Victoria Arms?'

'How could I forget? But it was Oxford, wasn't it? You know what I mean?'

'I do actually. I really do.'

Kay felt ecstatic with relief. She had thought Will was being so cold because he still hated her. Instead, he had been nervous and suddenly they were getting on again. She wanted to give him an enormous hug. They were standing side by side looking downstream. She said, 'The drama, the heightened passions, the sheer, unashamed, self-indulgence . . . that was Oxford. You know that day we argued, I really thought you were being ridiculous. You got up my nose and I hated you for what you said, partly because it was true, I suppose. I suppose you thought I was being pretty ridiculous too.'

'Certainly I did. I couldn't get over how unaware you seemed to be. It was all a bit childish really. Do you know, for a whole year I thought you were the most selfish person I'd ever met. All because you fell in love with my best friend. I was jealous.' He smiled apologetically.

'Oh, Will.' Kay threw her arms round him. People stared as they passed. She disentangled herself. 'You know, if we'd only written to each other we could have sorted it out. I kept thinking it was up to you and I suppose you thought it was up to me.'

'Well, it was really. I mean, I did try but you weren't having any of it. You just didn't want to know.'

'But you ought to know that people from screwed-up families have problems, especially if you're going to be a doctor. "They fuck you up, your Mum and Dad," to quote Philip Larkin, and my dad certainly did. You were my replacement family, the elder brother I never had.'

'So that's what I was. I never appreciated your affection ran to quite such heights of adulation.'

'It didn't!' Kay giggled. 'Though I must say you made a charming nephew.'

'And you were a delightful aunt.'

They began to walk arm in arm.

'It is absurd, don't you think? The folly of youth . . . we should try again to be the perfect nephew and aunt!'

'You make it sound like we're approaching dotage.'

'No, but understanding your past is a very maturing experience, don't you think?' Kay mocked.

'Oh, sure . . . Anyway, enough about the past, how about the present, your brilliant career, love life and all that . . . ?'

They chatted easily. Will told her about his forthcoming trip and the girlfriend he was going with. Kay told him about her job, Addy and the flat. She steered clear of the subject of her love life. There wasn't a lot to say about that. It was almost like old times, and when she said goodbye Kay felt a wave of affection and regret for the time they had wasted. She looked forward to seeing him when he returned from India.

As she walked down the Regent's Park Road and turned into Chalcot Square, Kay felt very happy. A group of children were kicking a ball in the square, and a small girl and boy were having a quarrel about whose turn it was. Kay glanced affectionately at them.

'Hi, I'm back,' she shouted as she put her key in the door.

'I heard. You put one hell of a lot of energy into running up the stairs. Jesus, Kay, I wish I had some energy right now.' Addy was sprawled on the Chesterfield, her long legs propped at right angles against the wall.

'You don't look very comfortable.'

'I'm not.'

'Well, why don't you do something about it?'

'Do something? Wish I could do something, only it sounds too energetic.'

'Well, if you will stay out until four o'clock every morning, what do you expect? Can I get you a drink? I've really had a good day . . . I took the afternoon off work and saw mother and Will, my nephew. We went for tea at the Waldorf. I got on well with Mum and Will too. In fact, I feel so good I might come to the Palace with you tonight to celebrate.'

'Sure, if you want to.'

'Well, thanks for the enthusiasm.'

Addy had been trying to persuade Kay to go with her for ages but now she sounded completely indifferent.

'Sorry, only I feel like a zombie . . . I look like a zombie, Jesus, I *am* a zombie . . . not the cocktail either. That goes places fast and I couldn't go anywhere slowly right now.'

'Why, what's happened?'

'Oh, the usual . . . I stayed out last night and didn't get much sleep. I might as well have been asleep come to think of it . . . Anyway, today I was feeling lousy, really lousy. They wanted me for a full shot, bra and knickers, the lot. What a day to pick, I mean usually it's bum and legs and lack of sleep doesn't affect their bloom, does it? A brown paper bag would have looked better than my face, I tell you. The photographer did nothing but whine and tut-tut between nicotine-stained teeth. Yuk! He insisted I needed more make-up and then whinged away about how I should smile and remember I was in heaven . . . We were doing an ad for Seventh Heaven underwear, you see. I felt like saying, Look, ashtray face, how the hell can I relax and smile when my face feels like a death mask, and don't call me darling once again. So my mouth kind of smiled but my face swore at him. In the end he had a fit, went berserk, did the full "How could I waste his precious time?" scene. I thought it was hysterical, only I couldn't laugh either, in case my make-up cracked. We've got to do it all over again tomorrow!'

Kay made sympathetic noises but she couldn't take Addy completely seriously. She got like this every now and again and the next minute life would once again be wonderful.

'At least the people you work with sound interesting, Kay. I mean, half the problem with my lot is they think they're interesting only they don't know they're a complete waste of space. I know it's difficult to appreciate you're wasting space when it's you that's wasting it, but . . .'

'For someone who's tired you talk a lot.'

Addy shrugged her shoulders. 'You know me, only rigor mortis will stop my mouth. Right now I could do with a bit of rigor mortis, it might be kind of restful. Anyway, where's that drink?'

Kay mixed the drinks and determined not to let Addy spoil her mood.

'So, tell me, how's Mrs T? Did you give her my love?'

'She OK really. She's very brave when you think about it. We got on so well today, Addy. I felt we were really talking to each other. It was nice and . . .'

'Well, I always told you your mother wasn't such a bad old bird,' Addy interrupted.

Kay was becoming increasingly irritated with Addy's 'told you so' comments.

'Who else did you see? Oh, Will. This is the guy you were at Oxford with, right, and then lost touch with. So he's all right too, is he?'

'Yes, only it was a little more complicated than that.'

'It always is with families, I tell you.'

'We were very close at one time. I grew up with him and he was just like a brother except that wasn't the way he saw it.'

'What? You mean he didn't want to play happy families? Tell me, there's nothing I don't know about family fuck-ups.'

'We were inseparable but when we grew up I suppose he

226

matured at a different pace. He was more sexually aware than me and . . . '

' . . . and, don't tell me, he fancied you. Now that is a problem I haven't experienced, incest. But that was years ago, wasn't it? And what the hell, anyway. I mean, you've got to get over these things, haven't you.'

'It wasn't incest.' Kay was trying to control the anger in her voice. Here she was, trying to explain what had happened between her and Will, something she had never been able to tell anybody before, and Addy was being positively trite. She wanted to say, if it's all so easy why are you so bitter about your family, why haven't you got over it as you keep on saying, as though it were as simple as that?

'Listen, Kay, don't give the Will thing another thought. I'm sure it'll be OK now. Can I bag first bath? If I can lift my legs, that is.'

It *is* OK now, thought Kay, but only because we both did give it another thought. She couldn't expect Addy to understand everything. Only sometimes when Addy behaved like this she couldn't see how Addy understood anything.

When Addy had told Kay they were all weirdos at the Palace, Kay had wondered what she meant. Addy was the first person to love dressing up in the most outrageous outfits but the clientele at the Palace were, at first, a little too much even for her.

The Palace was really the Camden Palace but for some reason Addy referred to it as the Palais. From the outside it looked just like a sober theatre standing on the corner of a busy high street, yet it was one of the trendiest nightclubs in Europe. Inside, the layout was that of a theatre, with spacious balconies and stalls. The stage and floor in front of it were now the dance floor. A dazzling, gyrating bank of lights flashed images above the heads of the dancers. Two gigantic, papier mâché figures hung upside down on the trapezes, leering at the clientele like figures in a Beryl Cook painting.

'Well, what do you think?' Addy leant over the art deco bar, her bare legs glistening in the green light. Kay was sipping beer from a long glass. In the light the liquid looked like a weird and wonderful concoction.

'It's certainly different, I'll give you that. Actually, I quite like it. I wonder what all these people do in the daylight.'

'Oh, most of them are boring accountants.' Addy moved off to serve drinks. As ever she remained unruffled amid the press of people waiting to order.

'It's got to change.' She was back.

'What has?'

'Clientele costume. You see, the in-schmucks wear very recherché dinner suits, tuxedos, the lot. But something else must come soon. In fact, my friend standing at the end of the bar is an indication of where it's all at.'

She nodded her head in the direction of a very tall man leaning elegantly on his elbow against the bar.

'Who's he?'

'That is Orestes.'

Kay looked at him. She was sure she recognized his face. She stared. Quite openly, he was so intent on gazing at Addy. There was something about the set of his unflickering eyes and jaw . . . It was the man from the Connaught who had stared at her the first night she had been there with Richard Hawthorn.

'But isn't he breaking the rules? You're not supposed to stare,' Kay hissed.

'He's different, a really weird weirdo. Anyway, he's quite obviously besotted with me.' Addy raised her eyebrows and was gone.

Orestes had been leaning in exactly the same position watching Addy's every move for the last two hours. Kay observed him. She knew now why she thought she recognized him the first time she had seen him in the Connaught. If he had had blond hair he could almost have been a male version of Addy. He had prominent cheekbones and huge, bright eyes. He had a long, willowy body and tight, slim hips. He was dressed in a matador's costume, clinging satin leggings and a bright sash wrapped around his waist. A long cloak flowed down his back and a matador hat hung from a cord at the back of his neck. His eyes simmered. He spoke to no one.

'He's been like this for weeks. I'd almost be pissed off, but he's quite sweet really, in a sultry kind of way. I guess he thinks he's found a kindred spirit. Nice legs too.' Addy poured a foaming lager into a glass. She winked at Orestes but he gazed on, unmoved.

As it got later the bar thinned out and Addy lolled on the counter smoking. At one point she slipped from behind the bar to collect glasses. Before she left, she walked down to the corner where Orestes was standing, took something out of her pocket and placed it on the bar in front of him.

'It's a photo of me. I took a lot of mug shots. When I go anywhere I give one to Orestes.' Addy pulled a self-parodying face. 'I think it's what's called love.'

The three of them were laughing uncontrollably. They were lying on silk and velvet scatter cushions on a centrally heated marble floor. The room had a high ceiling and marble walls. There were a few paintings. Solemn, almost holy, Renaissance faces stared from the ornate gilt frames. Orestes had obviously spent too long alone in their company.

Addy lit a cigarette, leant across and put one in Orestes' mouth. He pouted his lips in thanks, the cigarette magically remaining on his lower lip. A bottle of vintage claret stood half-empty on the floor. Orestes still had not spoken, they had been very surprised to hear him laugh. It was the first noise to pass from his lips.

He had walked across to them as they were getting ready to leave the Palace and indicated with a graceful nod of his head that they should follow him. Kay had hesitated but Addy was eager. 'Come on, it's an adventure. We haven't had one since New York.'

In a side street a silver Rolls was parked. A fat woman was slumped over the wheel. Her huge shoulders and midriff struggled not to burst out of the rather incongruous evening tails which clung to her body. She was snoring loudly. Orestes put out a long finger and gave her a vicious prod. She awoke with a start.

As they drove across town, Delilah explained in a deep voice that she was Mr Orestes' chauffeuse. He wasn't the most conversational of people and she liked a bit of a chinwag now and again. She chattered to her passengers in the back seat, not giving either Addy or Kay a chance to reply but bombarding them with a torrent of words. Orestes was the ideal person to be driven around by Delilah. Silence was the best response.

Who was Orestes? What was he? Addy and Kay spent endless hours discussing this enigma. Delilah had failed to enlighten them when she drove them home in the early hours of the morning. She had merely said, 'Mr Orestes is a very rich man, lots of money.'

After that night he did not return to the Palace and Addy told Kay she missed his broody-eyed stare.

'I really liked that guy, Kay. Don't you think we got on well in our kind of way? I mean, he never stopped talking but . . . Seriously, he was bloody good-looking and the best thing is I didn't try it on with him. Sometimes I wish I had, he might have fallen madly in love with me!'

'He's different, I'll give you that.'

'You mean weird, don't you? Well, he is kind of unattainable. Mind you, perhaps if I go for the unattainable men and they really aren't, I won't be disappointed for once!'

'Well, at least you never pine after anyone – you know, unrequited love. You always get the men you want, even if you don't want them when you have them.'

'Guess it's true . . . Just goes to show it's not worth it! Why are you sounding so wistful, anyway? You're not in love with someone who's unattainable too? Kay, tell me, who is it?

'Of course I'm not. Don't be silly.'

'Kay, you're going pink. You're lying . . . Come on, come on, who is it? It had better not be serious because I'll be insanely jealous. You're bound to get him and, knowing you, it's bound to work.'

'Not in this case. Besides, I'm sure it's only a passing infatuation. I've had so few I probably don't recognize it for what it is.'

'I know who it is! You can't be serious. You can't do this to yourself. You have got to get over this, now!'

'Who? What are you talking about?'

'It's old diamond features . . . Paul Ritz. I should have guessed. The way a certain reverence creeps into your voice whenever you mention him. But, Kay, apart from the fact the man's clearly so up himself he hasn't got time to look at anyone else, he's every intelligent woman's pin-up. Be a bit more exclusive, at least.'

'You can't get much more exclusive than him. You ought to see some of the women he's seen with . . . Oh well. Anyway, why do you hate him so pathologically?'

'Oh, I never like my girlfriends' men. One, they're never good enough for them and two, I guess sometimes I feel jealous. Everybody's better at relationships than me and if they're having a relationship then I'm left out! See, it's all very basic.'

'But, Addy, he's not *my* man. We're not having a relationship. I speak to him once a day on the phone, not even that now he's incommunicado in Nicaragua. I sometimes feel more like a switchboard than a potential mistress. We have a very professional relationship.'

'Is that why you start to blush whenever you talk about him?'

'So, I find him very attractive. That's all, and I find it

231

difficult sometimes to know how to deal with him. Anyway, I'm only another female minion to him. Richard's assistant who happens to have a pretty face . . . I'd really like to get over it, as you would say.'

'Oh, I wouldn't be so sure you don't stand a chance. God, Kay, you could have almost any man you wanted.'

'Could I?'

'You bet. If you want El Ritzio you could have him. Take my word for it. Only don't give it a try. Anyway, what would you do with him once you'd got him?'

'Well . . . I can think of a few things.'

The very next day he rang her at the office.

'Kay, love, it's Paul.'

'Paul?'

'Paul Ritz?'

'Oh, you're back! How was Nicaragua? How are you?'

'I'm very well, thank you, and how are you? You sound harassed. Tell Richard to give you the afternoon off.'

'Richard's not in the office actually. He's not back until Monday.'

'Aah, I see. Well, if he could ring me first thing. Anyway, how are things with you?'

'Fine. Did you want to leave a message?'

'No, thanks. I don't suppose there's any way of getting hold of Richard, is there?'

'Not really, unless you want to telex Japan.'

'No, no, I'll wait.'

'OK, then. Goodbye.'

'Bye, love.'

Kay slammed down the phone. It hadn't been a good day so far and that was the last straw. Why didn't he want to speak to her? Why didn't he want to trust her with a message?

'I don't think Richard should have left you all this work when you're still so new.' Anna put down a cup of coffee in front of Kay. 'You look panic-stricken.'

232

'I'm fine, Anna, thank you.'

Panic-stricken was hardly the word. Kay was bored. Richard was on a trip to Japan and not much was going on in the office. When Richard was around he seemed to create work and inspire action, but when he wasn't there Kay found she didn't yet know enough to initiate her own work. It was her job to keep things ticking over, taking messages, responding to letters with a brief note that Richard would deal with when he returned, and reading unsolicited manuscripts.

She liked the reading but this week a particularly dull lot of work had come in and it was difficult to get absorbed when the phone kept ringing and Sharon and Anna had a half hour break per hour of chatting. Sharon was about to get married and there were endless discussions about her list, her dress, her bridesmaid dresses and the honeymoon. Anna was having a sordid fling with a married man whom she had met when he had come round to mend her television. She spent her lunch hours buying what she considered sexy underwear and in the afternoon she would display her purchases to Sharon and natter about what she should cook the dreadful man for dinner.

Kay lit up her tenth cigarette of the day and saw Anna adjust the purple plastic air freshener on her desk.

'Anna, if you don't want me to smoke, just say so.'

'Oh no, don't worry. I'm getting used to it.'

'Well, if she wouldn't fight then she would have to put up with it. Anna was the ultimate doormat and, although she hated herself for it, Kay was beginning to trample on her just like everyone else did. Her phone buzzed.

'Yes, Kay Trevelyan.'

'Oh dear, you don't sound in a very good mood.' Ritz's voice again.

'I'm quite all right, thank you. What can I do for you?'

'Well, I was just wondering whether I dare ask you for supper. I'm having a very small dinner party tonight and

233

I wondered, if it's not too short notice, if you'd like to come along?'

'Yes! I mean, yes in principle. Hold on a minute while I get my diary.'

Kay put down the receiver and took a deep breath. She and Addy had been planning to see a film tonight and Kay knew she wouldn't be overjoyed at the idea of being usurped by Paul Ritz. But you couldn't rely on Addy anyway. Knowing her, she would probably have forgotten.

'Hi, that looks fine. About what time?'

'Eight o'clock.'

'I'll look forward to it.'

'So will I. Ciao.'

'New boyfriend?' Sharon's ears did not miss much.

'Just a friend.'

When she got home that evening, Addy was standing in front of her mirror, glass in hand, dressed only in her underwear. 'Hello! Good evening and welcome. Have a drink. You look like you need one.'

'Are you pissed?'

'Not really but I intend to be. Do you like my new haircut?' Soft, permed curls sat on the crown of her head and the sides of her hair had been swept back and pulled into the tiniest of braids, tied with a pink, silk ribbon.

'It looks amazing. Where did you get it done? You didn't tell me you were going to have a haircut.'

'I didn't know until this morning. You remember I told you I'd applied for that hair offer in *Today's Girl*. Well, I got selected. I had to go along to Sassoon's, yes, Vidal Sassoon, no less. Nothing but the best. And after a lot of poncing around, this is what they decided to do. I then had a full make-up session and my photey taken. The "before and after" look. You may even see me on the front cover of the April issue. So, drink with me to celebrate. What will it be? Tequila Sunrise or Margarita? Tequila is my drink for the week.'

'Oh, go on then. I'll have a weak Tequila Sunrise. By the way, I'm not going to be able to go to the film tonight. I'm really sorry but something has come up.'

'Oh, don't worry, I'll amuse myself. We can slaver over Jack Nicholson another time. So who's the lucky man?'

'You'll only laugh if I tell you.'

'That Eytie hotelier – heh, you did it. Well done! Well, it had to be, I suppose. I don't hate him that much. I just think arrogant men need taking down a peg or two. And you're not going to fall in love with him, because then I really will be jealous. I don't exactly despise him . . .'

'But you would if you gave him a thought?'

'Sparkling form you're on. That's *my* best line and you're not allowed to steal it. No, really, it's just that I have an antipathy to small men. They're usually such egotists, like Napoleon. Anyway, he looks a bit anal to me.'

'What? How can you say he's anal?'

'I don't know . . . female intuition . . . he's too handsome, too meticulously dressed, know what I mean? Bet he's a lousy fuck.'

'Well, for once in your life you won't find out!'

'Temper, temper. Why are you in such a snit?'

'I'm not in a bloody snit. You're just making me more nervous than I already am. It's ages since I've done this, remember? Anyway, I don't know why I'm getting so worked up. It's only a dinner party. Hardly a tête-à-tête. Oh God, I don't feel like going.'

'Of course you're going. You can't refuse an invitation to the Ritz. So what will you wear?'

After a rushed debate they chose a gold and black checked taffeta dress with a black velvet bodice that Addy had stolen from a boutique in Camden Lock, only to find, when she got it home, that it was too short. It seemed very dressy to Kay, but Addy insisted that glamour was in order. Nevertheless, Kay pressed the doorbell of Ritz's flat at eight-fifteen that evening tremulously.

The doorman in the foyer of the building had given her a

knowing look when she asked for Mr Ritz and had called her 'madam', rather unnecessarily, all the way to the lift. The building stank of wealth, from the thick pile carpet to the chandeliers.

'Ah, Cinderella? Or is it Snow White? Come in, you look glorious.'

'Thank you.' Damn Addy for that dress! Ritz was wearing jeans and a smock. Designer jeans and a very expensive heavy cotton smock, but casual all the same. She was overdressed.

'Have a seat.' He indicated a number of chrome and white leather armchairs. The room was furnished entirely in white and the walls were dove grey. Several spotlights on slender black stands lit the corners. There were no pictures and no plants. The room looked like one of the showpieces that Kay had seen at Liberty's when there was an exhibition of modern Italian furniture. It was immaculate, chic, and she had to admit it, anal.

'A drink?'

'I'd love a glass of white wine. Am I early?'

'Early? No, approximately fifteen minutes late.' He looked at his Rolex and then back at her. 'A lady's prerogative. I did say it would be a very small party.'

'Just two in fact?'

'My favourite number.'

He walked through double doors into the next room and Kay could hear his Gucci loafers sliding slightly on the parquet floor. Addy said you could always tell a rich man by his shoes. Paul Ritz was rich, handsome, perfectly charming and a tease. She had been a fool to accept his invitation so readily. That afternoon she had suspected that he had planned a small party and some woman had dropped out, so he had invited Kay at the last moment to fill the gap. Now she could see he had invited her on a whim. Again, she had the feeling that he was playing games with her and she felt compromised. The hall porter was obviously used to Mr Ritz's little soirées. She was not. Certainly she had no

236

objection to being alone with him. It had been the subject of several dreams she had had lately, but if he was just playing games she didn't know how to deal with it.

'How's Britain's prettiest literary agent then?' He came back with a bucket of ice, a bottle of Alsatian Riesling and a glass of whisky.

'I don't know him.'

'Of course, I meant how are you?' Ritz drew a small glass coffee table between their chairs and poured her wine.

'I'm very well.'

'Still like work? Achieving your ambitions?'

'Up to a point.' She took a sip of the wine and felt it immediately in her arms and legs. Most people said that wine goes to your head, but Kay always felt it in her limbs first.

'What about *your* work? How was Nicaragua? Did you manage to collect the material you wanted? There's not much evidence of it here. In fact, this doesn't look like a journalist's room. No scribbled notes, no typewriter, no mess.' She was nervous and talking far too quickly.

'Hmmm, well of course this isn't the only room in my well-appointed apartment. No phone in here. This is where I rest and entertain. No one sees my office. Do you like this room?' Ritz was steering the conversation, dictating the terms.

'It's a bit Spartan, but yes, I suppose I do. It's not very lived in though, is it?'

'No. More wine?' He looked at his watch.

'No, thank you, that's enough. I don't like drinking too much.'

'How interesting. I shall have to make it my duty to get you tipsy. I can't see it though. Snow White slightly squiffy . . .'

' . . . At the mercy of Prince Charming!'

'Yes, well . . . When you've finished the bottle, where do you want to go? To eat, I mean.'

'Oh, anywhere. I didn't imagine we'd be going out. I

mean . . . ' What did she mean? Kay wondered why she was sounding so silly.

'Oh, I rarely cook. I'm not here enough. I'm not much good at cooking either. The only home cooking I like is Gina's and she's in Paris.'

He was a man of few but well-chosen words. Kay was curious. She longed to know who Gina was, but she would rather die than ask him. He filled her glass again and disappeared for a few moments. She tried to make herself relax. He returned having changed his smock for a red cotton shirt and a foulard silk tie. He offered her his hand as she staggered a little rising from the low chair.

'Come on, Snow White. You can't lose your glass slipper just yet, otherwise I'll turn into a pumpkin.'

'You're mixing your fairy stories,' she retorted haughtily, regaining her balance.

The restaurant was a small, select French bistro. Kay had the feeling Ritz used it often. A table had been reserved and she wondered how long ago. Had he called when he was changing or had he organized the evening long before she had arrived?

'Well, if you're not going to tell me about Nicaragua, what shall we talk about?' she decided to take her nervousness in hand and confront him.

'Why don't you tell me about yourself?' he asked.

'What on earth do you want to know?'

'Everything and nothing, I suppose.'

He found himself gazing at her and, though he was concentrating on what she was saying, for split seconds he could only watch her mouth move and remember what it was like to kiss her. She was quite unlike his usual companions. He was amused that she was trying to seem totally unimpressed with him. He admired that resilience. She was determined not to let him charm her, conscious of his reputation and proud.

They ate asparagus and lemon sole, followed by a

238

mousse au chocolat. He found it mesmerizing to listen to her talking breathlessly about her life, her trip to New York and her work now. He realized that she was the youngest person he had talked to in a long time and her aspirations and descriptions of places and people were refreshing, perceptive and unselfconscious. She was sharp but not dulled with cynicism. On occasion he wanted to rebuke her for her naiveté, her love of literature and 'art', and her optimism. But when he tried she would raise her eyebrows and look at him, encouraging him to argue, and everything he had wanted to say would disappear from his head.

A flake of chocolate clung to her lower lip as the dishes were swept away and, on impulse, he reached across the table and dabbed it away with his napkin. She flinched, but smiled. There was something about that smile. It was disarming and made him feel guilty for touching her. It was one of the reasons, Ritz supposed, he had wanted to see her again.

She paused and looked at him enquiringly. Was she aware how coquettish she looked? Ritz did not think so.

'Would you like a liqueur?'

'No thank you, really not. I've had far too much to drink already.'

'Coffee?'

'I'd love some.'

He summoned the waiter and asked for the bill. 'I make the best espresso in London – if you'd like to come back.'

The way she looked at him made him feel a complete heel. He wondered why he had said it. Habit, he supposed. Whenever he spoke this evening he seemed to use the same old clichés she expected him to. She had asked him over dessert why he had invited her to dinner and he had made some glib response, but now he was beginning to ask himself what his motives were. He had not been quite able to get the image of her in that black dress out of his head since the party. When he had discovered that afternoon that Richard was away he had impulsively invited her round. He knew Richard would never be unprofessional enough to have serious designs on someone who worked for him, but he knew also that he would be slightly jealous of them meeting. There had always been a cloud of rivalry hanging over their friendship. He would have liked to explain it to her but could not.

He knew that she expected him to suggest that they went to bed together, and he was sure she would refuse if he did, but the temptation was difficult to fight as she watched him grinding coffee and setting out two cups on his kitchen table. But, strangely, he longed for some kind of intimacy.

'Come here, love.'

'What?' She was jumpy now they were in his house again, away from neutral territory.

'I'd like to show you my office.'

'I thought you said *no one* saw your office.'

'What a memory! Well, you're so special . . . '

'I bet you say that to all the girls.'

'Well, if you're not interested . . . '

'You know I am.' She nudged his arm playfully. 'But I hope this isn't going to be the Ritz alternative to etchings . . . ?' The drink had really set in. She was pushing her luck.

'Dare you find out?' He winked at her.

She hesitated and returned his look coyly. 'Yes.'

They walked through the darkened dining room to another set of double doors and he unlocked them. It was a room that looked small because of the floor-to-ceiling rosewood bookcases crammed with magazines and dusty box files. On the floor was a Persian carpet scattered with papers and notes. Long gold velvet curtains were drawn against the street lights of Portman Square, but the most striking feature was the five stained-glass lampshades that flooded multicoloured light over the desk and the old oak filing cabinets.

'It's beautiful! The lampshades are wonderful. I thought you only saw them in Hollywood movies, hanging over billiard tables in 1920s mansions. Where did you get them?'

'I'm glad you like them.' He found it pleasing that she expressed pleasure so easily.

'They're beautiful. I love the one with fruit.' It was a hemisphere of bottle-green slats of glass, fringed with stained-glass vines and cherries.

'I've collected them. In the sixties you could get them quite cheaply at auctions. Art deco wasn't old enough to be in vogue yet then. I used to save all my money and buy them. People thought I was mad. Now they're really hard to come by. I've got several around the place. If you like them so much you should have one.'

'Oh, I'd love one, but no, really, they look so good here *en masse*. But thank you. Tell me how you work,' she said, walking round the room. 'What's this?' She pointed to a pile of books and scraps of paper on the floor by the desk.

'The new book, in embryo.'

'Well, you've kept me dangling on a string for so long . . . Now I want to hear all about it.' She looked at him through wide eyes. She liked being in this room. She shuddered slightly as he stroked her hair for a second and then withdrew his hand.

'Do you really want to know?' He hesitated for a moment. 'OK, I've been wanting to tell someone. My trip to Nicaragua was extremely successful – I now have a book.'

'Did you ever doubt that you would?'

'To be honest, I did. You know in outline what the book's about. Until recently that was all I knew too. I hadn't come up with anything solid. But then my assiduous searching paid off. I came across a name, a name that rang a bell and then I knew I had the key. Fate is a strange lady, Kay, but as it turned out, this wasn't anything to do with fate.'

He told her of his first trip to Nicaragua and how he had met Elizabeth Carleton by chance. How she had planted the idea for the book in his mind. Then two weeks ago he

241

had been going through the personnel list of Culham laboratory for 1959 and seen the name Peter Carleton. Immediately he had thought there might be a connection. He had pieced together Peter Carleton's history. Peter Carleton was a reputedly brilliant physicist who had communist sympathies. He was working on a top security project involving nuclear fusion. Then, in the summer of 1960, Peter Carleton went on holiday to Crete and supposedly drowned. His clothes were found on the beach and his body never discovered.

'But if he is dead, what possible use is he in your book?' Kay interrupted.

'Exactly – *if* he's dead. I spoke to several of his contemporaries, one of them a colleague who had been working with him on the same project. He had always suspected that Carleton was not dead but had gone over. He spoke of a woman, a girlfriend of Carleton's, who was on holiday with him when he supposedly drowned. Her name was Elizabeth. I did some digging around and discovered that she had been arrested for heroin smuggling and was sentenced to prison for six years. She served her time but then there was no record of her after that. Except that one Elizabeth Carleton had given me the idea for the book.' He looked at her triumphantly.

Kay was stunned by his story. This was the way Paul Ritz had earned his reputation as the best investigative journalist.

'And did she help him defect?'

'Yes.'

'So this Peter Carleton is in Russia today?'

'I intend to find that out. She has heard nothing of him since Crete.'

'How fascinating – you've unearthed a major scandal.'

'So it seems. But I'm just as fascinated by her story. She was the victim of a perhaps more worrying cover-up. You see, the British secret service knew Carleton had defected too late to stop him and they knew she knew. They had to

242

shut her up. As you know, that time was a turbulent one for the Establishment. The last thing they needed was another scandal. So she was framed. She had not smuggled drugs. She was guilty of nothing except idealism and helping her lover become a traitor. She had wanted to follow him to the Soviet Union. She was young, only nineteen or twenty, and she told the secret service everything when they interrogated her. She was naive and she paid for it. My book will also be about her, her part in his escape, her dreams, how it changed her life, how she became an outcast. The human angle, if you like – corny as it sounds, it's good. The story of a brilliant young woman, beautiful too, punished by the Establishment, rejected by her family and friends and forced to live at the ends of the earth and all because of a moment of youthful idealism.'

'It's a marvellous story, but is there any way of checking that it is true?'

'Of course, I'll get the facts corroborated but I believe her absolutely.'

'But why did she confess all this to you?'

'Because, Kay, confession is a very basic human need. I think that when she saw that I knew, she saw too an escape from her past. She could not live with a secret like that forever. Maybe that's why she subconsciously gave me the idea for the book in the first place.'

'She sounds like an extraordinary woman.'

'She is.' Paul Ritz had become deadly serious and Kay felt he was no longer interested in talking to her but was lost in his own thoughts.

Ritz looked down at her, seated by his feet like a disciple and awed by his story. He thought how young she was, so untouched by the cruelties life could impose. He wanted to hug her to himself.

'It's not a very happy bedtime story, is it?' Ritz broke the silence.

'Bedtime?' Kay felt herself blush.

243

'Yes, it's way past my bedtime. I think I'd better order you a taxi.'

Kay hated the way he could sit discussing something really important and interesting and then change in a second to being patronizing and teasing as everyone said he was.

'I'm perfectly capable of picking up a taxi myself, thank you,' she said haughtily. 'Is it really that late?'

'It is nearly twelve o'clock and you wouldn't want to see me change into a white mouse, would you?'

Or a rat, thought Kay.

'I'm sure we'll be in touch. I've enjoyed myself. You're a good listener and rather refreshing company.'

'It must be my youthful idealism.' Kay smiled at him.

'How about lunch next week? Have you been to La Pomme d'Amour? No? Oh, but it's just the place for you. It's a sort of conservatory. You'll look like a hothouse flower surrounded with all that foliage.'

He bent slightly to kiss her. Kay closed her eyes and inclined her head. He kissed her forehead and when she opened her eyes he was laughing at her expression. 'Not yet, sweetheart,' he said.

Why 'not yet?' She walked down Baker Street feeling embarrassed. She hated herself for giving her own feelings away so obviously – and she hated him for being so arrogant as to assume . . . But she knew he had wanted to kiss her properly. He would not make comments about hothouse flowers if he did not find her attractive. What was he playing at?

Paul Ritz wandered back into his study, poured himself a large whisky and sat down once again in his green leather armchair. He could still detect a faint waft of her perfume in the air. It was light and flowery, the smell of a garden after a summer shower. When he had bent to kiss her he had noticed her skin was soft like a child's. When he was

244

with her he sometimes felt he was with a child. She was so delicate. But she was a woman too. A woman who inspired more than the usual twinges of lust.

And yet that smile of hers haunted him. It made him check his instincts. Somehow he couldn't bring himself to start an affair. She was too precious to be hurt and he always managed to hurt. But he was tempted. She was strong too – perhaps, in truth, he was afraid of her. Perhaps he would be the one who would be discarded. Ritz picked up the phone and dialled.

'Allo?'

'Gina, *cara*, it's Paul.'

'Paolo! You're back. I was worried. How was Nicaragua? Did you find out about your woman?'

'So many questions, my sweet. Yes, I found out. I have much work to do. Listen, can I come and stay? I have to check out some contacts in Paris.'

'Of course. You are always welcome. Why Paris – I thought your research was in England?'

'It is, mostly, but there is some work I can do in Paris. I need to get away.'

'But you are only just back. Paolo, what are you running from?'

'I'm not running.' Ritz paused.

'It's a woman. I knew it! Who is she?'

'There is a young lady . . . leave me be, Gina, don't ask any questions. I'm just doing the decent thing. She's very young – far too young for me.'

'In that case, by all means come here. Don't break a young girl's heart, Paolo.'

'Gina, don't be so melodramatic. I have no intention of breaking anyone's heart.'

Kay lay on the Chesterfield staring blankly at the novel in her hands. She sighed and her eyes focused on the stripy deck chairs. They were beginning to irritate her. She looked away and then back again. Why had she ever agreed to let Addy put them in the living room? She threw the book on the floor and rolled on to her back. She was in a bad mood. The deck chairs got on her nerves and the record playing on the turntable jarred. If she got up to turn it off she would not be able to stand the silence, but there was nothing else that she wanted to hear. She did nothing.

It was only ten o'clock on a Monday evening and she felt tired. She knew she couldn't really be tired, merely apathetic. She had come in from a gruelling day at work to find the fridge empty. There wasn't even a drop of milk for a cup of coffee and the shops were shut. It was Addy's turn to take the rubbish out, but once again she had not remembered. It stank.

She hadn't seen Addy for what seemed like ages. She never seemed to come back to the flat these days, at least not until Kay was fast asleep when she would bang the front door loudly and run the bath noisily. She had come in to find a note hastily scribbled from Addy saying 'Having FUN and more FUN – hope you are. A.'

No, I'm bloody not, she thought, and for the first time she realized how much she minded. There was Addy leading her usual wild life and there was she feeling miserable. She felt a stab of jealousy and it shocked her. Jealousy was a feeling Kay had never really experienced towards Addy. Now and again she wished she had Addy's sex life and love affairs, if you could call them that, but to feel Addy was having a better time than her and resent it, was new.

As she lay gloomily staring into space she began to think that perhaps it wasn't Addy she was annoyed with but herself. She was trying to find a scapegoat. Everything had been going so well. Work was exciting. She was learning a lot and meeting new people. But suddenly life had lost its spark. It was positively bleak.

She had felt more let down than she should have done when Paul Ritz had flown off to Paris without mentioning their lunch date and since then speaking to him had become

246

a nightmare. Whenever he called, Kay felt embarrassed and uncomfortable. She could not think what to say and she detected a note of coolness in the way he talked to her.

But still when the telephone rang her heart leapt in case it was him, and when it was she always put down the receiver feeling utterly downcast. He no longer flirted with her. She tried to reason with herself that that was the best way after all. He was a client, their relationship should be purely professional. If she were going to be a leading literary agent, as she now wanted, she would have to deal with authors far more difficult than Paul Ritz. But somehow he had destroyed her peace of mind. He made her feel clumsy and young. At times she wished she had never met him.

Well, damn Paul Ritz. She tried to bring some resolve to her thoughts. She had her own life and she was going to enjoy it. She should invite some friends around, have a dinner party. That was a brilliant idea. She would cultivate her own social life, look up old friends, learn a few lessons from Addy.

Simon Leach stretched back in an armchair, his face hard and contemplative. He was wearing a tweed suit brightened only by a blue and white spotted bow tie.

Kay had bumped into him in Patisserie Valerie in Soho. She had not seen him since Oxford. He had been sitting at a table reading a copy of the *Financial Times*. The casual décor, Polish waitresses, crisp brown flaky pastries, cream cakes and rich sponge chocolate gateaux provided an incongruous background for their meeting – it mixed the perfectly ordinary with excess and self-indulgence.

Even as he greeted her, Kay knew this was not the Simon Leach she had known at Oxford. He was working in the BBC on *Panorama*. He had a future ahead of him. No one knew this better than he. He was totally absorbed in this new world he had carved ruthlessly for himself. Ambition had dulled him. His camp, free-hitting witticisms had disappeared. But with her new resolve to broaden her sphere, Kay had issued an invitation to her dinner party.

He had been the first to arrive and as she poured a glass of Kir he had said, 'I hear Oxford's prettiest heterosexual couple are no longer. What a pity, Kay. Though I have to say I never did think you and Bob were quite right for each other, except in purely aesthetic terms. He lacked a certain intellectual finesse, don't you think, and if you can't acquire that after the best education in the world, well . . .'

He watched through half-closed eyes for Kay's reaction. She smiled gracefully and was about to reply when he said, 'I also hear through the grapevine young Bob is trying his hand at becoming a novelist, locked himself away in some country cottage in fairest Devon, bashing away at the old typewriter. Well, they say we've all got a novel in us somewhere . . .'

'When you produce yours I'd be delighted to read it.' Kay forced a smile. She would not show Simon Leach she had lost any of her Oxford gaiety or wit. That would be seen to be a failure.

'I'll take you up on that offer someday. I only hope you'll be kinder to me than you were to some of the authors you reviewed for *Isis*. I never understood how such a delightful mind could produce such cruel insight, so telling, so telling.'

'I must say, looking back, I think a lot of what I wrote was pretentious rubbish but if it gave you pleasure . . .'

Then Addy emerged from her bedroom in a short black leather miniskirt and a fake leopard-skin bikini top. 'Hi, no, don't tell me, Robin Day,' she said as he held out his hand limply for her to shake.

He had blanched. That was the sort of comment he was used to making. He detested women who upstaged him. It served him right, thought Kay. He was behaving like a middle-aged, self-opinionated, has-been. Even his face had lost its incisive mannerisms. He had acquired a double chin.

Richard Hawthorn arrived, a bottle of Bollinger in hand, and instantly Kay could see he was fascinated by Addy, as always the centre of attention. Simon Leach seemed determined to compete with her. They exchanged cool glances like two boxers in a ring sizing up the competition.

'So, Addy, what do you do to amuse yourself?' he asked.

'Amuse myself? Oh, I don't, I get other people to do that.'

'Oh dear me no, I meant what do you do, you know, to bring in the pennies.'

'I model. Knickers,' Addy replied icily.

'I see . . . well. Interesting. Excuse my perverted sense of humour but I suppose someone has to start at the bottom . . .'

'No, only asses.'

Richard Hawthorn was loving it. Kay wondered if he was making mental notes to taunt her with at work. The rest of the evening passed with a great deal of bonhomie and compliments for Kay's cooking. Simon Leach and Addy seemed to agree to tolerate each other for the duration of the evening and after a few glasses of champagne they even weakly laughed at each other's quips.

When Addy decided they should play charades, Richard loudly added his support. In the end, only the two of them played. Kay sat helpless with laughter as they mimed the most perverse scenes. Simon Leach muttered disparaging comments, his chin buried in his bow tie. Kay was enjoying seeing her boss behaving like a young boy at prep school after lights out.

After a while they ran out of energy and Addy collapsed on to the sofa beside Richard. Kay talked to Simon Leach and was beginning to think he wasn't quite so dreadful after all when he was relaxed. They were all by now quite drunk. Simon was in the middle of a long monologue on the evils of television as a medium when Kay heard

249

Richard say to Addy: 'You know, young lady, you really ought to do something more than flaunt limbs at cameras, delightful as I'm sure they are.'

'There's doing and doing, don't you think?' Addy leant back provocatively. 'Besides, I'm about to really do something, if you call being a model in Paris for a fashion house really doing something. I guess I must think it is otherwise I wouldn't be about to do it. Though that's not strictly speaking true. I spend half my life doing things I don't give a damn about. But the great thing about this is I'll be able to earn stacks of money to compensate.'

For a moment Kay thought Addy was going to describe one of her usual fantasies.

'And what, my dear, do you intend to do?' Richard asked.

'Oh, I've been offered a brilliant contract and I'll be in Paris. I've always wanted to go to Paris and now I'll do it in style. If ever you're over there you must visit me.'

Kay lost the drift of what Simon was saying as she strained to listen. What was Addy on about?

'It's for Beauts, the top London modelling agency. It's a real lucky break. You see, I was mad enough to apply for one of those magazine "before and after" affairs. They take you to a top salon and you're coiffured and beautified by a top hairdresser and make-up expert. That's where I got my beautiful curls from.' Addy pointed emphatically at her blonde crown. 'My face, hairstyle and all, believe it or not, made the front cover. Some talent spotter spotted it, mistook it for talent and offered little old me a contract for Electra Fashions. Apparently my fresh, English complexion, and gamine-like beauty, whatever that is, are all the rage. So I'm off to gay Paris to be a clothes horse.'

Kay could not believe her ears. But Addy seemed perfectly serious.

'Well, congratulations, my dear.' Richard was impressed. 'I think we should keep our eye on your soaring career. There may even be a book in you yet. *The Model*

Life, The Model Model's Way to Beauty and Health, and if you don't have time to write I'm sure young Kay here could ghost it for you. You see, your fame and fortune are just beginning, if you do me the honour of letting me be your agent.'

'You bet. Here's to us.' Addy drained her glass and beamed triumphantly. Kay was beside herself with fury. She wanted to flash Richard a withering look but was desperately trying to pretend she had heard nothing.

When Richard and Simon had gone, Kay stood at the window staring down into the square. It was deadly quiet and the wind blew tree shadows across the pavement. Tears pricked her eyes.

'Look, kiddo, let's leave this horrible mess until tomorrow. It's the weekend and I'll help you clean up. Thanks for a lovely evening, Kay. It was great. That Leach guy is worse than . . . but Richard's a dream. I like him. You're lucky to have him to work for. But then you're lucky in lots of ways, I guess.'

'What do you mean?' Kay growled. She was seething with rage and did not dare turn round.

'Oh, you know, you've got it all sussed. You may not think so at the moment but I'm telling you, you have. I mean me . . . I appear to be having a ball but underneath . . .'

'You're being very philosophical tonight.'

'Kay, whatever's the matter? You sound really pissed off. It was a good party, really.'

'I don't give a damn about the fucking party!' Kay turned round. Her face was flushed with anger and tears were beginning to seep down her cheeks.

'Kay, what the hell?'

'What the hell? What the hell? You tell Richard, my boss and a total stranger, that by the way you're off to Paris, you've got some amazing job. Just like that in the middle of my dinner party. And then, then to crown it all, he suggests I write your fucking awful book about beauty or some such crap. And you ask me what's wrong? You're meant to be the closest friend I have in the world. I've put up with enough from you and you don't even tell me you're going. I thought only family was supposed to fuck you over, to use your expression, not friends, and not you, Addy.'

Addy stared open mouthed at Kay and for a moment an expression of real fear crossed her face. She said nothing and put her hands to her head, resting her elbows on the table.

'It's the final straw. You're a real bitch,' Kay screamed hysterically. 'Why don't you go right now, if you're so keen to go? You've used me, I was mad, I should have known. I always lose my friends in the end. They either con me or they die.' She ran out of the room and flung herself on her bed, howling and kicking. Eventually, when she found she could not breathe between sobs, she stopped and lay quietly weeping.

Addy stood in the doorway. Her face was blotchy from tears. 'Oh leave me alone.' Kay spat the words.

'Please don't say that.' Addy started to cry. 'I'm sorry . . . you're absolutely right . . . absolutely. I've behaved like an absolute jerk. I really mean it. I meant to tell you about Paris. Of course, you were the first person I wanted to tell. Only I didn't get the chance and it just slipped out. I guess I was trying to impress old Hawthorn. I am truly sorry, really. You've got to believe that.'

'I don't know when I believe you any more.' Kay's nose started to run and she sniffed.

'Jesus, Kay, how can you say that?' Addy handed her a tissue. 'I mean, that's ridiculous. I suppose it's my fault again. Why should you believe me? I behave like a pig at times. Only thing is, I can't bear it if you don't believe me. Look, I'm sorry if I've taken you for granted these last few weeks. I knew you were feeling low only I didn't know what to say to help. I mean, men, you know they really hurt. There's nothing anyone can say. Me? I'm the last person to advise you on them.'

252

'It's not that . . . well, not just that . . . I don't want you to go.'

'Oh, Kay . . . ' Addy put her arms round her and they sat rocking from side to side.

Eventually Addy said, 'Look, I know it's really bad. You've been a great friend. You are a great friend. I've loved my time with you, it's like home. It *is* my home now, only you know me, I've got itchy feet. I can't stay around in the same place. I know sometimes it looks as if I'm running away from things, but this time it might be different. It came up and I had to take it. The wonderful thing is you don't know the best yet. You will never in a month of Sundays guess who owns Electra Fashions. Go on . . . guess . . . oh, OK, I'll tell you – Orestes! Yes, Orestes, our silent friend. So Paris could be a great place to be.'

'Good, I'm really glad for you.'

'Oh, Kay, don't be like that. I can't bear it. We've never argued like this and nobody's ever cared what I did before. I don't know how to cope with it. Look, I'm not leaving you. I couldn't. I've got it all planned. You're going to come and visit me, every weekend, if you like. Or I'll visit you. I want to keep most of my things here, if that's OK, because it does feel like home. Look, if you look any sadder I'll start crying again and then we'll be really embarrassed.'

'You're right. I'm overreacting. I'm sorry. I don't know what's the matter with me these days. I just feel everyone's going off and leaving me.'

'Oh, Kay.' Addy held out her arms and gave Kay another hug. 'It'll work out, I promise you. Really, you're not the fuck-up I am.'

'I don't think you're a fuck-up at all. Look at me sobbing my eyes out. It's pathetic.'

'Well, we're both as pathetic as each other then.'

Kay grinned at her and blew her nose. 'Sorry. I feel better now. It's great about your contract. It took me by surprise, that's all. I'd love to come and visit you in Paris and, of course, you can leave your things here. On one condition only. You've got to buy an enormous apartment in Paris and give me a room in exchange!'

'Sure. No problem. You know who you can visit in Paris, don't you?'

'Who?'

'Oh, come on, surely you don't need a prompt now. You know, the man I love to hate, Paul of the Ritz.'

'Oh, him. I don't think so. It's crazy falling for a man like that. I've made up my mind to forget him.'

'But you can't, right?'

'Of course I can. If I really try.'

'Only you don't want to . . . '

'No, I mean, yes . . . shit, I don't know what I mean. It's not easy to forget him seeing as I spend half my professional career dealing with him. Oh, listen to me, talking about him again.'

'Honey, if it helps you get the jerk out of your system, talk, talk, talk.' Kay grinned and yawned. 'Look, Kay, you get into bed and I'll bring you the ultimate hangover cure.'

'But I haven't got a hangover yet.'

'Best to make a preemptive strike. I have the perfect concoction in mind.'

'Forget it! I know your concoctions, Addy George. I'll probably be sick!'

'That's the idea – get it out before it gets you!'

254

COMING TO TERMS

NICARAGUA

Damn Paul Ritz, it was all his fault. He had made her feel displaced. The years had gone by and she had slipped into a calm routine, involving herself in the lives of everyone who lived in the village and its surrounds. Their illnesses, their fears, their joys, their births and their deaths, she had known them all. Even the revolution had left them relatively undisturbed. When she made the occasional trip to Managua, she saw what was happening only too clearly and feared for her life and her adopted country. She had created a new life and forced herself to forget the past. But since Paul Ritz had come, she remembered it often and clearly.

'Elizabeth?'

She turned round with a start. 'Oh, it's you.' She smiled. 'Why don't you join me out here for a drink?'

Cesar bowed his head. 'You were thinking about something and I made you jump. Everything is all right?'

She said yes. Cesar walked towards the kitchen door. He moved lightly on his feet, padding silently across the wooden boards. His back was long and muscular and it gave her pleasure to stare at it. When he came back she was looking into the distance at the sinking sun, her head resting on her hand. Without looking round she asked, 'How was your day? Give me a kiss.'

He bent and kissed the top of her head, and as he straightened up she caught his hand and turned to look at him.

'Yes?' He was surprised.

'No, nothing. Cesar, you have beautiful eyes.'

'Elizabeth, that is not talk for now.' He let go of her hand. 'It's not like you. Are you sure you are OK? You are a strange woman, Elizabeta, sometimes I think I will never understand you, never.'

'Then, that makes two of us.' She clapped her hands together and laughed.

'You look like a child when you do that. A young girl.'

'Yes, I was always told that I would never grow old because of my natural innocence. It would defy my wrinkles. Ha! But sometimes now I feel well and truly like an old lady.'

'Why?'

But she couldn't tell him. Paul Ritz had distanced her from her closest friend. Cesar knew something of her past. The pieces she had elected to tell him. And those ten years with Cesar had made him her present, the happy times with him had almost persuaded her that the rest of her world had ceased to exist. Ritz's visit had reminded her that it continued in her absence. She would never be independent of it. Since Ritz had gone she had thought often about them all still going on with their lives. Sometimes she yearned to look at them but remain invisible herself, and that yearning was becoming an obsession.

Cesar was gnawing a piece of bread and occasionally slurping at the bottle of *chicha* that stood on the ground between them. It struck her how easy his manners were, almost uncouth. But manners were a trivial, bourgeois invention. They should be the last thing on her mind, but for a moment she felt they mattered terribly. She leant across and touched his hand.

'Well?' he asked.

She couldn't find anything to say. They didn't often have long conversations. Nearly always their silences were by mutual consent. It wasn't that they had nothing of importance to say to each other, only that neither felt the need to make small talk. They were completely at ease. Long ago when they had first met, after the first few months of intense curiosity, Elizabeth had found the silences difficult. She had wanted to talk, to discuss, to get thoughts out of

258

her system. But she had grown to enjoy the silent companionship. It was a pleasure she had been tutored in by Cesar. But now she was uneasy. He seemed to sense her mood and began to tell her a funny story he had just remembered to fill the silence. She giggled and began to laugh out loud. Her shoulders shook.

'But it is not so funny! Have I missed something?' She shook her head but couldn't stop laughing. 'What is it? I haven't heard you giggle like this for a long time?'

She stopped as suddenly as she had started. 'No, it's nothing. I suddenly felt that if I didn't laugh I would cry. Don't you feel that sometimes?'

'No.' They both laughed.

'No, it's just . . . it's just . . . I think that journalist who came here – you know, had more effect on me than I thought he would. He has linked me with my past again, and somehow I am not content any more . . . '

'You are saying you want to leave me?'

'No, oh no. But I don't think I will ever be the same. But I can't explain. I don't even think I understand it exactly myself. What shall I do?'

'Tell me.' He held both her hands, his eyes demanding honesty.

'I feel I have been pretending. I *have* been pretending. All this time I have been here and been so happy I have left my past unresolved, and now it has found me and I can't just tell it to go away. I have started to question myself, I feel I need to justify myself . . . '

'But Elizabeth, the journalist left a long time ago. He won't trouble you again. You said so yourself. And you have told me many times before. You did not do anything so wrong. Don't cry. I love you.' Then his strong arms were around her. She clung to him. She loved him. But even he who knew her so well did not know it all. How could he? She had never told him the most important thing of all. For once she took no comfort from his presence.

* * *

Later that night, when Cesar had gone to bed, Elizabeth remained sitting in candlelight at the bare wooden table where she had drunk and exchanged confidences with Ritz. Large tears rolled down her face on to the writing paper in front of her as she began to write the letter she knew she must write to Paul Ritz.

He was the only person who could give her the ability to see what was going on in the rest of her life, without being seen. He was the only person who might be able to exorcize her regrets and give her the real peace she craved. She managed to smile at the irony of finally telling the whole story to a journalist. To someone she hardly knew but somehow trusted.

She covered two sheets of paper with her sprawling handwriting, surprising herself at how easy it was to write it all out at last, to confess to someone who was not involved.

PARIS

The wind whipped across the square. For May it was very cold. This couldn't be Paris in the springtime, more like Paris in November. Even the lights from the Latin Quarter across the river looked cold and yellow.

Kay dug her hands deeper into her pockets and paced up and down. Her long coat flapped against her black leather boots. It was her favourite coat, a deep petrol blue, with wide shoulders and a full skirt. She had borrowed one of Addy's hats. A dark blue velvet cap which perched on the back of her head sporting an elegant feather. It was a cheeky hat, but chic at the same time. 'What is this?' Addy had shrieked. 'Make up your mind. Do you want to be a cool blue dame with no-messing shoulders, or a pageboy? Are you having some kind of identity crisis?' Kay was ambivalent about the evening. She did not know what would happen, or what she wanted to happen. The forecourt of Notre Dame was not a place to be in moments of indecision. The Gothic towers hung like fate above her head.

'I think I prefer English Gothic myself. But the lady, Our Lady, is not without a certain charm.'

She spun round. She could always picture Paul Ritz when she thought about him, but every time she saw him it was like a first time.

'That's a rather anthropomorphic way to talk about one of the world's greatest cathedrals, but I take your point. How are you?' She was not sure how to greet him and in her embarrassment she found herself holding out her hand.

'*Che gelida manina*, my dear. Your tiny hand is frozen. I hope you haven't been waiting too long.'

'Oh no, I only just got here. Are you a cathedral buff as well as an opera buff then?'

261

'Hardly. I think Notre Dame is overrated. Now if you want to see a fairy palace cathedral go to Saint Denis Basilique. Well worth a trip. You meet some interesting characters in churches.'

'You mean "How I met lecherous Lola in Chartres Cathedral" or "The Franciscan monk who begged me to renounce all ways of the flesh before salvation slipped from my grasp"?'

'I'm quite shocked. For someone who was lecturing me on the evils of referring to Notre Dame as a lady with great charm, you're being remarkably irreverent yourself. But I suppose the godless younger generation can speak the unspoken.'

'Oh, I rather thought it was your generation who were godless. Remember the swinging sixties, free love, licence and marijuana?'

'How could I forget? Whereas, of course, yours is the generation sobered by unemployment, back to short back and sides and "Yes, sir, No, sir, a quick snort of coke, sir, but only if no one's looking!" '

'Well, unfortunately we don't have your advantages to keep us on our toes. No rallying freedom causes, no great wars like Vietnam to show us what life is really all about.'

'Quite. You are, as you say, a cosseted generation. There is a price to pay for everything.' He was deadly serious. She had overstepped the boundaries of pleasant banter.

'I'm sorry if I was flippant.'

'Yes, it was flippant.'

'Well, why don't you educate me so I'll know better next time?'

He glanced sideways at her because she could not hide the mocking tone in her voice. 'I wouldn't be so crude.'

'Vietnam. Richard said something about you being there. Is that true? He said you'd been a mercenary.'

He laughed. 'You're a gullible audience and Richard Hawthorn should be a writer. He has a way with facts. Yes,

262

I was in Vietnam. I happened to be in the right place at the right time, if you'll excuse the turn of phrase. But he's mixing up his antiheroes. I've never been a mercenary in my life.'

'What about Vietnam?'

'I was a stringer. An accident of circumstance, I can assure you. I made a lousy war correspondent. Luckily I was only used until the professionals arrived. Look, love, shall we have a pax from now on and try to be more civil to each other? Come on, how about a smile?'

She resented the way he steered the conversation to where he wanted it to go. It was almost as if he were saying that as her elder he knew better. 'But I'd love to hear about Vietnam,' she insisted.

'What about over a bottle of Chateau Mouton Rothschild 1962? How very cosy!'

This time he had succeeded in making her feel ashamed and she blushed. As if sensing her discomfort, he took her arm and slipped it through his and they walked on in silence. 'So tell me,' he said, 'How long are you in Paris, a long weekend?'

'Yes, Addy's working for Electra Fashions. Her career seems to be blossoming. I get a bit sick of seeing her face in glossy photographs, I must admit. But anyway she's very happy. She's got an amazing apartment on the Boulevard St Germain.'

'You know Paris quite well?'

'Well, quite. I came out to visit a friend when I was at Oxford.' She was disappointed when he did not ask who she had been to see in Paris.

'How would you like to see my favourite square? We could have a drink and then go on to eat. Would that please mademoiselle?'

'Sounds lovely. I hope you didn't mind me calling you out of the blue and imposing a night out on you. No doubt you're very busy.'

'Not at all. It was a very pleasant surprise. I was glad of

the distraction. Besides, I love it when beautiful young ladies invite me out.'

'You make it sound like I'm a babe in arms and you're some decrepit old cradle-snatcher.'

'Well, let's face it, love, I'm practically old enough to be your father.'

'Don't exaggerate.' She had surprised him by the sharpness of her tone but she was not going to retract. He was being so formal this evening. Kay was not sure if it was that that was irritating her or the fact that every time he complimented her it sounded like an easy cliché he used for every attractive female he met. 'So where are we going?'

'Place des Vosges. You'll like it.'

They sat by the window in a small café near one corner of the square. In the light from the old, iron streetlamps the trees in the square looked stark. The branches were just beginning to bristle with leaf buds.

'It's wonderful.'

'I knew you'd like it. It's the oldest square in Paris. Those buildings over there, the ones with the symmetrical facades, are what's left of the original palace. Victor Hugo lived somewhere near here.'

They ordered drinks and Kay had a glass of red wine which was cool and delicious. Paul Ritz ordered whisky.

'How can you drink whisky before eating?' she asked. 'I think you have some very suspect habits.'

He laughed. 'My cosmopolitan background, you know. It's the only drink you can trust worldwide. Sometimes the whisky is purer than the water.'

'I didn't realize you had a drink problem.'

'I don't. I'm sure there are lots of things you don't realize about me.'

'How deeply mysterious! The enigma of Paul Ritz! But then I've always thought that was an image. Not the real you.'

'I'm flattered that you spare me the time for an odd

264

thought. Hasn't your lovely head got more pleasant thoughts to fill it?'

Kay was lost for a comeback. He was sitting directly opposite her and their elbows almost touched. Every time she looked him full in the eyes she was aware of his face in all its detail. She wanted to say, 'No, I haven't, you're beautiful.' Between the waves of desire, she felt irritated with him. He was good at teasing. Their banter was lighthearted yet intimate. It was also a verbal barricade. Kay felt sure Paul Ritz used his wit to keep her firmly at a distance. She wanted to break his defences down. But she felt sure he was not going to let her. 'Why did you choose to meet outside Notre Dame?' she asked.

'Whatever makes you ask that?'

'Oh, I don't know. But you were very insistent . . . '

'I never insist on anything with a lady. But don't you think Our Lady a romantic place to meet?'

'Our Lady? You keep saying that. Are you a Catholic?'

'My parents were devout Catholics. That accounts for a lot. You're not religious are you? I thought not.'

'You said that as though I'm a heathen, too frivolous for things of the spirit.'

'Not at all. My God, love, don't be so defensive. I wasn't making a personal criticism, you know.'

'Sounded like it.'

He caught her wrist. 'Hey, calm down, young lady. Let me get you another drink.'

'Can I ask you something? Can you stop calling me "young lady" and making oblique references to my lack of experience in comparison to your vast wealth of years and *savoir-faire*?'

'Well, well . . . ' He let go of her wrist.

She could feel the wine warm in her blood. 'I think you do it subconsciously so that you can avoid being serious about anything.'

'That's above my head, I'm afraid, Ms Shrink.'

'Shall I explain? You tease and play the older man so that

265

you can avoid anyone peering behind your social mask. You don't like people getting close.'

'Well, what a swingeing analysis. Rather along the lines of that article you once wrote. I see your perceptions haven't changed. But aren't you making an assumption? That this is a mask, as you call it. What if it's the real me? And as for my not wanting to be serious about anything, if that's what you really mean, I spend my working day being very serious. If you mean I don't want to be serious about anyone, that is a different matter.'

'I suppose I shouldn't be so personal. I can see you don't like it.'

'Be as personal as you like. I think it's very charming.'

'I'm glad you find me charming. I find you patronizing.' She straightened her back and glared at him.

'Listen, I thought we had a pax. We could try and be civil, or at least I'll try harder not to arouse your ire. You can be daunting when you frown in that inimitable way you have. Sorry, did I say something funny?'

'No, I just thought you were about to say, "But darling, you look so beautiful when you're angry." '

Ritz looked abashed. 'If it had been some other lady, I think I might.' He grinned. 'I think, Kay, you're turning out to be part of my further education.'

They had talked from the moment they had been seated in the imposing surrounds of Julien's. The waiters danced a solemn but unobtrusive attendance. The *Poulet Veronique* had been delicious and the ambience perfection. For once, Kay had done all the listening, her head resting on her hand. They were seated in a secluded corner surrounded by tall green plants. The restaurant was full and above the quiet clinking of plates, sophisticated conversations floated on the air. The wine waiter seemed to know Ritz and recommended a wine 'specially for mademoiselle'. Ritz exchanged a few sentences with him and patted him on the back like an old friend.

'Why were you speaking Italian?'

'Sergio is Italian, and so was my father.'

'Oh, I remember you telling me. And your mother was Irish. But how did an Irishwoman come to marry an Italian? What an extraordinary combination.'

'They were. But it seemed to work very well. A marriage made in heaven. Or so it seemed. I didn't know my parents very well at all, particularly not my father. Of course, I adored my mother. They're both dead now.'

'My father's dead too. I didn't get on with my parents at all, especially my father. We used to have furious rows, especially over politics. Father was a big figure in the City.' There was a tremor in her voice. She was trying to make light of something that, Ritz noticed, made her eyes look very sad.

'You called him "Father" then. That's very formal. Strangely enough, despite being a hot-tempered, emotional Italian, my father insisted I called him "sir". He had his pretensions. It seems we do have something in common – father problems!'

She didn't reply and was silent for a moment. Ritz thought how wrong he had been to think her untouched by life's cruelties. He reached to pour her another glass of wine and the candlelight glinted on his ring.

'What a beautiful ring that is. Has it an intriguing history?' She delicately touched the small twisting silver band on his little finger.

'It belonged to someone.' Why had she picked that? It was Susan's ring. It had arrived in an empty envelope the day after she killed herself. The unlucky charm he had worn since then.

'Someone very special? Someone you were madly and passionately in love with? A woman?' Kay giggled.

They were uncannily delving deep into each other's past. He almost wished she would draw him out, but he fought back the temptation to let her.

'What incredible logic. You have a devastating mind, Kay. *L'addition s'il vous plaît.*' His accent was impeccable.

'Well, Kay, thank you for a lovely evening. I feel ten years younger despite the strain of combating your incisive wit. We must do this again sometime.'

'I've enjoyed it too. Thank you.' The room was beginning to turn in a warm, hazy swirl. He had insisted she had a whole bottle of wine to herself. The bottle of Puligny Montrachet 1969 stood practically empty on the table. 'I'm going to keep the cork.' She spoke like a child, gleeful after a treat.

'It hasn't been that memorable, surely?'

'It's Paris, and yes it has been a memorable evening.' She was too drunk to care what she sounded like. She was riding the crest of a wave. *In vino veritas*. Any minute now and surely there would be some great revelation. Life felt good. She did not even care that she might be about to disgrace herself.

As she put down her empty glass she knew desperately that she wanted to go to bed with Paul Ritz. There was nothing, absolutely nothing on earth, that could persuade her otherwise. She leant further across the table, one hand resting lightly on her cheek. She had to seize the moment, take fate into her own hands. What if she just casually said, 'I don't want this evening to end. Let's spend the night together.'

'You were about to say?' He was looking at her.

'I don't want . . . nothing. I've forgotten. I've had too much to drink. I've enjoyed this evening so much. I don't want to go away without asking you about your book.'

'Oh, is that all? I thought you were on the verge of some great revelation. How very disappointing. The writing is coming along nicely.'

They waited for the bill. Kay fingered the rim of her wine glass. It was too late. She had blown it. They would say goodbye and go their own ways and Paul Ritz would continue to blow in and out of her life, teasing and flirting and tantalizing her.

'Do you still make the best espresso in town?' she asked.

'Only in London.'

'Oh.'

'How rude of me, of course, you must have a coffee.'

'No, no, don't bother to call the waiter back. It's too much fuss, honestly. I can survive without coffee, even your best espresso.'

'I would offer to do the honours and produce the best espresso in Paris only the flat is out of bounds this evening. Gina is entertaining a friend and I have strict instructions.'

'Oh, I see. Well, never mind. It's been perfect and I shouldn't expect another thing.' Gina. She had forgotten all about her. What was going on there?

'Oh, you must never let go of your expectations, Kay. Hang on to them for grim life. Rising to the challenge is what makes life interesting.'

Well, he had obviously decided that she was not a challenge that would make life interesting.

'I'm sorry to have to let you down over coffee but I can't interrupt my sister's intimate dinner party.'

'Gina is your sister?'

'Yes, of course. She kindly tolerates my chaos when I'm in Paris.' He looked her full in the eyes and she thought he was about to say, why, whoever did you think Gina was? She would have hated him if he had.

'You must meet her sometime. I think you'd approve of each other. Anyway, let's think where we can get you a wonderful caffeine experience, if not here.'

'Do you know what I'd really like to do?'

'No, do tell me.' He was laughing at her.

'I'd like to go to a very select hotel and have coffee in some place oozing with Parisian history.'

'Well, grey eyes, you're in luck. I know just the place.'

Her skin was soft and hot. He could feel her ribs and the vertebrae in her spine. He ran his fingers from her underarms to her pelvis and traced the outline of her stomach. Their bodies were separated by her arching back

269

and there was space only between their shoulders and stomachs. He could feel the air in that space undulating as she rocked gently from side to side. He wanted her body to join his completely, but that cushion of moving air excited him. One of her hands supported her, one gripped the back of his neck. She moved randomly as if she could sense exactly what he was feeling. She made him glide in and out of her leisurely and then thrust fast, slowing, quickening, moving. His body gasped for relief but pleaded for it to continue. He opened his eyes. Her skin was glowing, her hair hung vertically over him and brushed his forehead. Her eyes were closed but she was smiling. A smile more relaxed and seraphic than ever.

He reached up his hands and pulled her, collapsing, on to his chest. Their flesh smacked together. His hands messed her hair. He felt her dry tongue licking his eyelids and burying itself in his mouth. Her fingers dug into his back and pulled him on top of her. Half her body was on the bed, her feet spread wide on the floor. He withdrew completely for a second. She leapt involuntarily at his shoulders and dragged him back into her, and when he came inside her he could feel her muscles shuddering with him. When he raised his head and looked at her, she was still shuddering, oblivious to him, her arms spread like a crucifix and her fingers clasping and unclasping the air.

'You are so beautiful.' He kissed each breast and brushed her lips, but she didn't hear him.

'Where did that come from?' She was sprayed with a faint mist of bubbles as a champagne cork popped. She opened one eye. The rosy light seemed unaccountably bright.

'Compliments of the Ritz. Why do you call me Ritz?'

'Do I? When?'

'All the time. Just now.'

'Well, it suits you,' Kay mused. 'It's more glamorous than Paul. Anyway, you shouldn't quote what I said just now.'

'Of course not. Pillow talk. I beg your pardon. Still, you did keep on saying Ritz.' He handed her a glass of champagne and she sat up. 'To us.' He clinked her glass and sipped.

'I thought you only drank whisky.'

'I save champagne for really very special occasions.'

She looked at him over the top of her glass. Even naked he looked as composed as ever. His hair was slightly ruffled and his lips were redder than usual, his chest was more sculptured and stronger than she had envisaged. She adored him. Perhaps that was why she had been so uninhibited with him. She couldn't tell what was going on in his mind even now, but it didn't seem to matter. All she had known when they had been sitting in the lounge downstairs was that she wanted him. That evening they had been on the verge of becoming friends or lovers and for one moment she had wanted to become his lover for one night more than his friend for life. How she had enjoyed seeing him speechless! For the first time in her life she had really pounced. She giggled when she thought about it now, and he leant forward and kissed her, then wrapped his arms around her body and held her. 'What are you laughing about?'

'What are you thinking about?' He had smiled over his coffee.

'I was wondering how I could ask you to go to bed with me without compromising myself.' She had delivered the words in her most businesslike voice. He had looked nervous, almost worried and said nothing. It was as if he was expecting her to say 'joke' and laugh at him.

'Well, this is a hotel, is it not?' she said. 'I expect they have bedrooms.' She had taken his hand and led him to the reception desk. She had snatched the key from the porter and it was only in the lift that her nerve had begun to fade. But he had squeezed her hand and trailed his thumb down her wrist and her doubts had disappeared.

The room was small, with two windows on to the

rooftops. It was almost entirely occupied with an old-fashioned brass bedstead. At first, they had hung out of separate windows, saying nothing, as if they had made the journey only to admire the view. The noise of traffic and music drifted up with the smell of food and charcoal. Then he said, 'Come and look. I can see Notre Dame from here.' And she had gone to his window and looked, as if she couldn't see it from her window, and she had felt his hand on the small of her back. And she had turned towards him and raised her head and kissed him.

Now she was kissing him again and he fell back into the pillows, letting the champagne glass slip slowly on to the floor. They both stopped for a moment, waiting to hear it break, but it rolled away on the rug to the skirting board and they laughed, watching it, then cuddled. He ran his tongue between her breasts and down her stomach in one stroke from neck to pubis. She guided his head with her hands and gasped. Then she drew her body down so that his tongue traced the same wet line up her body to her mouth. She pushed down with her feet to open herself to him. It was blissful to have his weight resting on her and she whispered that she wanted it to go on forever. The first time, she had been the initiator, now he was. They both seemed to know each other's needs and desires.

When she awoke, he was still sprawled across her and his skin was pale in the dawn light. It was cold and she hung over the bed to reach the blankets that had been kicked to the floor. The room that had looked so rosy and romantic the night before was shabby in daylight. The bedstead was tarnished and wallpaper peeled away from the corners of the ceiling. She looked at him sleeping and snuggled closer to him. She fingered him and prodded him gently, wanting him to become aware of her again. She licked one of his ears very softly. He twitched and frowned but still didn't wake up.

She had always thought that waking up with someone

272

was more intimate than going to bed with him. Bob had always woken up before her and leapt out of bed making coffee, clattering cups and chiding her for sleeping. Now, she didn't want to chide Paul Ritz. She wanted to watch over him and touch his skin and listen to him breathing.

She lay for an hour, holding him and gently dozing until he awoke.

'Good morning, my beauty.' He rubbed his eyes like a little boy and kissed her forehead.

'Hi.'

'What do you plan to do with your day today?'

'Oh, I don't know. I suppose I'll go and watch Addy posing.'

'Hmm. She sounds like a terrifying harpy.'

'She isn't really. You ought to meet her. Only she doesn't approve of you, but that's because she's just got a thing about small men . . . ooops!'

'Thanks a lot. Well, I've just got this thing for small women.' He kissed her again. 'Shall we have a bath together?'

The water was lukewarm and the enamel on the bath was chipped. They soaped each other and familiarized themselves with each other's bodies, shivering and joking at the seedy surroundings. He traced his signature on her back and she blew bubbles at him. Her hand crept slowly towards the top of his leg and she could feel his toes caressing the back of her neck. He sighed. 'This is nice. Do you really have to go and watch Addy's session today?'

'What else did you have in mind?'

'Well, some croissants and coffee. Then I could buy you some roses. Isn't that what lovers on weekends in Paris are supposed to do? Then we could return to the flat. I could pick up my mail. If Gina's there I can introduce you two and if she's not I'm sure we can think of a way to spend the afternoon . . . '

'Sounds perfect . . . ' Kay shifted and let the water envelop her body. 'Oh, by the way, talking of your mail,

273

did you get that letter I sent on the other day?'

'No, what letter? Who was it from?'

'Don't know. I didn't open it, but I suppose it was from that Elizabeth character. It was postmarked Nicaragua. I'm surprised you haven't received it because I sent it express. I thought it might be important . . . '

'When did you forward it?' Ritz interrupted impatiently. He sat up abruptly.

'Oh, a couple of days back. Just before I came out here.'

'Jesus Christ! Why didn't you tell me before, Kay?' He was out of the bath and picking up his clothes.

'I'd completely forgotten, I'm sorry.'

'Oh, I'm sorry, darling, I didn't mean to shout, but I've got to go and see if it has arrived. It might be crucial.'

They parted in the street, exchanging the briefest of hugs. She watched him running down the street after a cab.

She sat looking into a steaming cup of milky coffee. She was elated but empty. She had been frightened of sleeping with anyone since Bob. Afraid she wouldn't know what to do. But she hadn't been frightened of Ritz. It had been passionate, liberating, addictive. And like no other experience she had ever had. She could still feel every inch of his body and hers. She was aware of a smile creeping across her lips and tried to suppress it, imagining that the men in the café watching her must know what she was thinking about. In a rush of excitement she knew she was in love with him. But now he had gone. It was the way he had called her 'darling' and rushed off, as if she were some nameless one-night stand. He had gone without asking her telephone number in Paris. Why his sudden change of mood? A letter couldn't be so important. It might not have even arrived yet. He had obviously made the excuse to get rid of her. How could she have been so naive? She had let herself become just another good lay he could chalk up on his list.

274

When she told Addy all about it later that day, and insisted that she didn't care whether she saw Paul Ritz again in her life, Addy roared with laughter. 'You'll have to do better than that, honey. Just look at your face, glowing with all those secret thoughts. You're smitten. And if he is twice the man I think he is, I bet he will be too.'

Kay wanted so much to believe that, but she left Paris without hearing from him.

LONDON

Dear Paul,

I hope so much this reaches you. I expect you're thinking that it is strange for me to be wanting so desperately to get back in touch with you. Here I am sitting at the table where we sat, in the hot, hot night, drinking and listening to the rumbling of the forest and of my conscience. Sounds melodramatic, doesn't it? But there we are, Paul, that's what I have become in my old age. This is a cry for help. Only you can help and you must. If you hadn't come here, I would have maintained my isolation. But you broke that spell. It wouldn't have been so shattering if we hadn't already known each other, but remembering Oxford and Susan and all those things has made me realize what a small and fragile world this is. And then when you came back, with my secrets in your briefcase, I knew I couldn't hope to escape for ever. The strange thing is that I don't think I want to any more. I hope I don't need to say that what I am about to tell you is confidential. I don't want it used in your book . . .

Ritz folded the letter carefully and put it in his pocket. He had read it so many times now, he almost knew it by heart. He needed some air, a walk in the park, something to clear his thoughts. The cold grey living room of his London flat, which he had always found so relaxing, was making him claustrophobic with its clinical pallor. He had flown straight back, away from Gina's questions. He had needed space to think. But he didn't seem able to find it even here.

. . . I didn't tell you everything. I think you sensed that. I told you everything you needed to know about Peter

Carleton, but not about me. You know about the drugs case, the framing, my innocence (in both senses of the word!) and my prison sentence . . .

Yes, he had sensed she was holding something back. He had suspected she was concealing something. It had disturbed him. Her presence had remained with him and now she was asking him to be part of her life.

Ritz walked briskly down Baker Street.

. . . What you don't know is that I was pregnant. They discovered it in the prison medical. They tried to make me have an abortion, but I wouldn't. Carleton and I always planned to have a child, later, when we would be together and be able to bring it up in the sort of society we wanted. I was so pleased when they told me. I thought they *must* let me go now. They didn't. The child was like a part of Carleton still being there and I dreamed that he would find out and arrange to have me jumped from prison. Perceptions get cloudy when you're shut away. I have never known whether he even tried to help me come to him. Sometimes I think he hasn't thought of me once, since we said goodbye. I can't even remember his face now. But then, that unborn child was a symbol of our union.

I still had years to serve when she was born. My fantasies of being rescued had gone and I had given up hope. My parents offered to take the baby. I only had a glimpse of her. They took the child on condition that I never saw her again. It sounds so callous now, but I understood it then. Everything that had happened had made me think of myself as an unfit human being. And as far as my parents were concerned, I was a convicted drug smuggler. If I had told them the truth they would have thought I was raving. If they had believed me it would have been worse for them. There would have been no question of forgiveness to a traitor. Not in my family.

When I got out I went to Sevenoaks where they lived, and spied on the child. She was playing in the garden. I hid there and watched her, like a criminal on the run. I had intended to take her away, to kidnap my own daughter. But when I saw her running down the lawn in her little Harrods dress, I just couldn't. I knew I could never provide her with security and clothes and a big garden. I was a broken and desperate woman, but at least I wasn't desperate enough to deny her some sort of decent life. I DIDN'T ABANDON MY CHILD. Don't ever think I did. But I've never been sure I was right. How could I be? What do you think, Paul Ritz? Was I wrong . . . ?

Yes, yes she *was* wrong. Ritz watched the fingers of late-afternoon sun linger on the copper dome of the mosque in Regent's Park.

. . . She would be twenty-three now. I miss her. I don't want to destroy her life now. But I have to know how she is. What is she like? Whether she knows about me. You, if anyone, can find out. It's your job, investigator! I'm asking you to spy on my daughter, Paul, just as I did twenty years ago.

I don't know her first name. But my parents are called Trevelyan. My father, Oswald Trevelyan, may still be alive. He shouldn't be too hard to find. I can't pay you high rates. But you will always have my gratitude and affection as payment. If that means anything to you. FIND MY DAUGHTER. LET ME KNOW IF SHE IS HAPPY. GIVE ME BACK MY PEACE OF MIND. Elizabeth.

Elizabeth. If you knew, what would you want me to do? The question had wracked his mind for two weeks. He felt somehow fraudulent. He had used none of his investigative powers in deducing that Kay was her daughter. At first, he was unable to believe the ironies and coincidences that fate had meted out. He had phoned the Sevenoaks number anonymously and asked the right questions of Mrs Trevelyan to confirm without incurring her suspicion. But all the time he knew. He did not need to check.

He cursed himself for intruding. His book had ploughed up fields of the past that should have been left fallow. He felt now that he must have known at some subconscious level all along. How could he not? That smile. That disarming, charming, beautiful, mysterious smile. Like mother, like daughter. It was so obvious.

Ritz found himself in the north side of the park, heading towards Primrose Hill. Perhaps he was hoping to bump into her accidentally. He ached to see her again. Had the circumstances been different, he thought she would have been the person he most wanted to tell. He wanted to hear her fresh black-and-white outlook, her mocking of life's ironies. She would have helped him collect his thoughts. But to tell her would be to throw her life into confusion. Not to tell her would be a betrayal. What right did he have to know when she didn't? He wanted to see her, but he didn't know if he were strong enough for the closeness that had been imposed on him.

And there was Elizabeth, waiting so far away for his reply. Not to tell her would be to betray too. He wondered what she would want him to do now.

This wasn't supposed to happen. He wasn't supposed to care. But Elizabeth's letter had forced him to accept that he had changed. He cared very much. Kay. Kay. Kay. The tough Kay who would never forgive him for knowing. The proud Kay who would shout at him for leaving her in Paris. The vulnerable Kay who hated him now for staying silent for two weeks.

It was beginning to drizzle, and he hailed a taxi back to his bleak flat. For once in his life, Paul Ritz was unable to make a decision.

*   *   *

279

The phone made her jump. These days the flat seemed so quiet.

'Kay?'

'Addy.' Oh, why was it Addy? She was disappointed and her voice was flat. 'What's new?'

'Lots and I mean *lots*. I've got things to tell you, honey, you just wouldn't believe. Just wait.'

'Oh, come on, Addy, give me a clue.' Addy's guessing games always managed to cheer Kay up.

'OK, then, Orestes.'

'What about him? Oh Addy, you can't be serious. You and Orestes? How long has this been going on? Since I left. That's two weeks. Congratulations, it's a long time for you. Are you in love?'

'Well, the earth moves. Yes, really. I've moved in with him. He adores me. Keeps asking me to marry him. What more can I say? But anyway, enough of that, how are you? Been seeing anyone?'

'No, London's dead without you around. Listen, are you going to marry him?'

'Only if you'll give me away. No, seriously, it's all too much. Tell me something to calm me down. What are you doing? Been having a wonderful time with that little Eytie, *qui s'appelle Ritz*? Don't you think my French is coming along?'

'*Formidable*! Sorry to disappoint you though but on that front *rien de tout*. I haven't heard a word since Paris. For all I know, he could be rotting in a Parisian gutter.'

'I hope he is. What a bastard.'

'I'm so pissed off with him, Addy.'

'I'm real sorry, honey. You know I really did think . . .'

'That leopards change their spots? Not this particular breed. Oh well, you live and learn. Like you say "get over it". It's not easy though.'

'I know, I know. Listen, Kay, I've got to go now. Orestes is taking me out to buy me an enormous diamond.

But I'll ring you tonight. Let's have a real long chat on his phone bill. Will you be there?'

Of course she'd be there. It was Saturday evening but she hadn't made any plans. These last few weeks since Paris, she hadn't gone out at all. She had sunk into work, in the office and at home, reading and doing ironing that didn't need to be done. The flat was spotless. She could hardly think of any excuses herself to stay in. But she did stay, and sat and realized that Addy's *bon mot* 'a watched phone never rings' was absurdly true. She turned on the radio to full volume and lit her last cigarette. She'd have to go out and get some more. She was really smoking too much these days, but what the hell.

She had just closed the front door when the telephone rang. Damn the latch, why didn't the key fit easily?

'Hello.'

'Kay, love, it's Paul . . . Kay, are you there?'

'Yes.'

'Are you all right?'

'Never better, thank you. What can I do for you?'

'Oh, Kay, don't be like that . . . '

'Like what? How would you like me to be? Look, I'm just in the middle of doing something, actually.'

'I do apologize. Can it wait? Can I send a cab for you?'

'What, now? I don't know . . . why?'

'It's very important, love.'

'Well I don't know. I'm very busy.'

'Kay, sweetheart. It *is* important. Trust me.'

Trust him! She stared into the mirror. She looked a mess. There were bags under her eyes. Trust *him*! But like a fool she was brushing her hair and reaching for her jacket. Well, this was the last time.

'Darling.' He was standing in his living room, perfectly casually dressed in a rough grey silk shirt and donkey cords.

'Don't call me that.' She averted her eyes and when he tried to kiss her she stepped backwards. 'Well?'

'Well, I've got a lot of explaining to do.' He looked nervous. 'Kay, don't look at me like that. This is not going to be easy. Look, I'm sorry, let me take your jacket.'

'I'm not staying long actually.'

'I think you might change your mind when you hear what I have to say.'

In the cool, airy, white room, she felt sick and claustrophobic. As she watched him walk into the kitchen to make coffee, she wanted to follow him and demand an explanation. She wanted to shake him and tell him how much she despised him for what he had done to her. But she remained motionless, rigid on the soft leather couch. She heard the clink of cups as if in a dream.

'Kay.'

'Yes.'

'Before I say what I have to, I just want you to know that I didn't want it to be like this. I didn't want to have this responsibility.'

'No, I can imagine responsibility isn't something you like at all.'

'That, my love, is very unfair.' Silence as she picked up the cup and took a sip. It was too hot to drink. 'I bought you some perfume. I hope you like it. I'll get it.' She took the gift-wrapped package and put it beside her on the sofa, unopened. He was sitting in the chair farthest away from her.

'OK. Let's get this business cleared up before we talk about other things.' He got up and began to pace the room. 'This story begins with my book . . .'

'You mean you've brought me here to talk about your bloody book?'

' . . . and ends with you.'

'It had better be a happy ending.'

'That, love, depends on a lot of things. No, don't interrupt, I've got a lot to get through. You remember that letter you sent on to me? It wasn't easy, you know, just to rush off . . .'

282

'Oh, spare me this. I watched you. It looked extremely easy.'

'Hold on. Let's not argue that point now. Let me speak and don't look like that. Just listen to me . . .'

'I don't seem to have a choice.' Kay sighed resignedly.

' . . . it was from Elizabeth in Nicaragua.'

'So what?'

'For Christ's sake, Kay, shut up!' He had shouted at her for the first time and she was so shaken she obeyed him.

' . . . I don't remember how much I told you. When she was a young, rather brilliant young woman, she was involved with CND and met a young scientist called Peter Carleton when they were trying to establish a splinter group called Scientists Ban the Bomb. I told you about his defection and her arrest for alleged drug smuggling. When the secret services interrogated her, she thought they would let her go if she came clean. She was naive and that was her undoing. She let them frame her for the drugs charge. Poor girl. She served four of the six years. Her family completely disowned her. She couldn't see a way of telling them that she was innocent, because they would have thought her more guilty if she had told them the truth. They were staunch Conservatives, with a diplomat in the family. Knowingly aiding a traitor would have been equally unforgivable for them.'

'I can understand that.' Despite her anger with him, Kay was interested in Elizabeth's story.

'I hoped you would. She's a wonderful woman, Kay, and very brave. I admired her when I met her. Her story touched me. But I felt then there was something she had left out. Now, I don't know what to do.'

'Why?'

'She has written to me, admitting that she did not tell me everything. You see, she was pregnant when she was arrested. She found out at the prison examination. They tried to make her get rid of it, but even they couldn't make her do that. She wanted to have the baby. It was a symbol of her union with Carleton. And her parents weren't quite the ogres she thought they were. In this, at least, they stood by her. The baby was born in prison and they adopted it. But only on condition that she never tried to contact them or the baby again.'

'Well, that's understandable if they thought she was a drug addict and the father was dead.'

'I'm glad you said that. You see, oh God, this is the worst thing I've ever had to do. I feel I've deceived you telling you all this first. But I had to explain . . . '

'What are you getting so emotional about? What are you trying to say? I don't understand why you're telling *me* all this . . . '

'Because that baby is you, Kay. Elizabeth Carleton is your mother.'

'What? Is this some sort of joke? Because if it is I think it is a very sick one.'

'No, I'm sorry. I had to be blunt. Read this letter. Read it. I don't expect you to believe me, but believe it.'

'This is just stupid. I'm leaving. I think you've gone mad.' She got up and walked towards the door.

'No, don't go.' He put a hand on her shoulder. She hesitated.

'I just don't understand what you're doing. How dare you make me a pawn in your little bit of scandal? Don't you realize the implications of what you're saying? You're trying to make me believe that I'm not who I think I am. But it won't work, you see, I know who my mother is. I'll ring her. She'll tell you.'

'You can't, love, she's in Nicaragua.'

'Oh, don't be so ridiculous. You really are taking this a bit far. She's in Sevenoaks. Where's your phone?' She looked at him. The look on his face frightened her. She realized he was convinced he was right.

'Kay, listen to me. Sit down. Read this letter. Think. Ask me all the questions you want to. Trust me.'

'Trust you? Why? You don't care about me. But if you're so insistent, I'll read it, but I think you're absolutely perverse. Haven't you got a life of your own without fabricating other people's? Haven't you mucked me about enough? Why are you treating me like this?' She burst into tears.

Watching her despair, Ritz found himself choked too. 'Kay, I don't want to leave you, but you've got to read that letter and accept what it says. You know where coffee and drink are. You know, you're wrong. I do care very much about you.'

She didn't know how long it took her to dare to read the two pieces of flimsy paper. In her heart she knew that what Ritz had said could be the explanation for so many things. It was all there. In black and white. Her whole life was a lie. She had been able to appreciate the motives of the characters in the drama Ritz had described, but when she found she knew the actors and the play had been her life, she resented them all. And she hated having been deceived for so long. She felt she could rely on no one now except . . . She found herself ringing Paris.

'Addy? Addy, just listen and don't say anything. I can't bear it. I've had really strange news. It's like being in a dream and I can't wake myself up . . . '

She spoke for a long time, sorting it out in her own mind, as much as telling her friend. For once in her life, Addy didn't interrupt.

' . . . and so my mother is my grandmother. My sister is my aunt. Will is my cousin. Both my fathers are dead. Perhaps. God, what shall I do?' She crumpled into tears.

But Addy's voice was firm and decisive. 'Are you serious? You have got to go see your mother, of course. Leave it to me. I'll arrange the tickets. I'll even come with you if you want. We're family too, remember? Kay, it will be all right. It'll be good. It's *good* news, Kay. Don't worry. I hope Paul's looking after you there.'

'Paul?'

'Yeah, you know. Ritz.'

'I don't even know where he is. I said some terrible things to him.'

'He'll be back. But take my advice. Don't let him go again.'

'I thought you hated him.'

'Yeah, well, a person can change her mind, right? Jesus, Kay, I've just thought of something. Those fortune cookies we had were so right. THERE ARE TWO SIDES TO EVERY STORY and SOMETIMES YOUR HEART MUST RULE YOUR HEAD. Remember?'

'Kay, sorry to interrupt. I didn't mean to make you jump. I bought these for you.' He was standing awkwardly by the study door with a huge bunch of orange lilies.

'Paul, I don't know what to say. I'm sorry I took it out on you. Thank you for telling me.'

'I'm sorry I had to.' He sat down on the floor.

'I suppose I had better go now. I've got to pack. I've decided to go to Nicaragua. I think my real mother and I should meet at last. Is it late?'

'Late, but not too late, I hope. I want to say something to you, if you can bear to hear any more. You look exhausted. But I want to say it now.'

'Go ahead.'

'I didn't mean to get obsessed with your life. I didn't mean to get obsessed with you. There are some things in my life that I have done and later regretted. But I know that this won't turn out to be one of them . . .'

'I suppose I am a most unfortunate plaything for you to have stumbled on . . .'

'Dammit, can't you get it into your beautiful head that I'm not playing with words, or with you. What I'm trying to say, if you'll only let me finish, is that I am, against my better judgement, in love with you . . . Kay, do you realize what I've just said?'

'Yes.' She got up, walked across the room and put her arms around him.

286

'You are my daughter. I feel I could tell that even if I didn't know.' Elizabeth stretched across the table and took Kay's hand. 'We don't have to earn each other's love. It's just there. You were frightened I wouldn't like you, but I was frightened too. I never dared imagine what it would be like to meet my child. I would never let myself think of you, not as a growing woman who would sit opposite me and talk, almost like a youthful mirror image of myself. Now I can't believe that I haven't been responsible for what you are like.'

'But in a way you have. Neither of us would be the people we are without each other. Our lives are just as much about what didn't happen as what did. Finding you has made it all make sense.'

'We both owe a great deal to Paul Ritz. What will happen between you two?'

'I don't know. I am totally in love with him. But I realize I have a lot of growing up to do.'

'Who is ever grown up? Look at these wrinkles, and I am still a girl inside! Perhaps we don't ever grow up. We just come to terms.'

Fontana Paperbacks: Fiction

Fontana is a leading paperback publisher of both non-fiction, popular and academic, and fiction. Below are some recent fiction titles.

- ☐ COMING TO TERMS Imogen Winn £2.25
- ☐ TAPPING THE SOURCE Kem Nunn £1.95
- ☐ METZGER'S DOG Thomas Perry £2.50
- ☐ THE SKYLARK'S SONG Audrey Howard £1.95
- ☐ THE MYSTERY OF THE BLUE TRAIN Agatha Christie £1.75
- ☐ A SPLENDID DEFIANCE Stella Riley £1.95
- ☐ ALMOST PARADISE Susan Isaacs £2.95
- ☐ NIGHT OF ERROR Desmond Bagley £1.95
- ☐ SABRA Nigel Slater £1.75
- ☐ THE FALLEN ANGELS Susannah Kells £2.50
- ☐ THE RAGING OF THE SEA Charles Gidley £2.95
- ☐ CRESCENT CITY Belva Plain £2.75
- ☐ THE KILLING ANNIVERSARY Ian St James £2.95
- ☐ LEMONADE SPRINGS Denise Jefferies £1.95
- ☐ THE BONE COLLECTORS Brian Callison £1.95

You can buy Fontana paperbacks at your local bookshop or newsagent. Or you can order them from Fontana Paperbacks, Cash Sales Department, Box 29, Douglas, Isle of Man. Please send a cheque, postal or money order (not currency) worth the purchase price plus 15p per book for postage (maximum postage is £3.00 for orders within the UK).

NAME (Block letters) _____

ADDRESS _____

_____

While every effort is made to keep prices low, it is sometimes necessary to increase them at short notice. Fontana Paperbacks reserve the right to show new retail prices on covers which may differ from those previously advertised in the text or elsewhere.